Becoming Ruthless

by

Rita H Rowe

Yes, this one is for John too.

Prologue

This was it. She knew it had to end someday; in fact, it lasted much longer than she thought it would. She glanced down at her pink-and-white heels, shimmering lace so intricately woven around white beads, and wondered who had chosen them for her. She put out her foot and took a step onto the white stone floor that looked cold and foreboding, paused, and looked up. In front of her, already halfway down the aisle, she could see the back of Karen, her pink balloon sleeves flouncing about her as she nodded and smiled at guests, who were nodding and smiling back politely.

Her head spun and the back of her neck felt moist. She wondered whether a bead of sweat would run down the side of her neck and put a blemish on her white satin bodice. A scarlet letter would be better suited for the likes of her. She looked at her bosom now, half expecting it to be embroidered there, but little diamantes that sat along the edges of her dress glinted back at her, laughing, mocking, challenging.

She looked up again, trying to ignore the warning signs her body was giving her. But seeing the faces as they turned towards her in a sick anticipation, she felt faint. They waited for her, all of them, ready to attack, ready to condemn her for her sins. She blinked hard, hoping that when she opened her eyes, they would not be there, that she would be somewhere far away, wishing it was not too late. But here she was, about to walk in the middle of the throngs who sat in their pews ready for the harlot to be wed.

She took a deep breath and tried to drown out the ringing in her ears by focusing on the loud music that boomed out of the organ—the Wedding March. She wished she had been more active in choosing the song, perhaps one that made her move along more quickly, speeding up this farce.

The faces smiled at her now, encouraging people who were joyous for her and for her happiness. They knew nothing, she told herself, as her heart banged wildly in her chest; they knew nothing of her sins. She sneered inwardly at the irony: *her* sins, when it was more like *their* sins that had made her who she was. She took a step back as a memory of her first love, the man who had first taken her down this path, this very same aisle, came flashing through her mind. He was here too, the one who started it all.

A nudge on her elbow woke her up from her reverie and she lifted her head, finding the eyes of her father, his brow knotted. He was leaning towards her and was saying something, but she couldn't understand what, she just saw his lips move. She nodded and looked to the front of the church, to her future. She raised her chin and moved forward. It was too late. She had to go through with it.

With each step, her heart beat a little faster and she could feel her belly turn; the smell of the white orchids that hung brightly on the edge of every pew was overpowering. She caught sight of Paul, sitting there, a sad, but encouraging smile framing his face, and she wanted to stop, to run to him, to grab his hand and escape this ridiculous charade. The sound of the organ still echoed through the domed ceiling, thundering in her brain, and she wished it would stop. 'All dressed in white.' Those words had hammered at her head from the moment she donned her gown and again she wondered if she had actually chosen this costume that felt as heavy as a suit of armour dragging her under water.

Her feet obeyed her command and moved slowly forward. She turned her face to the front, to the altar where Derek stood, just half an aisle away now. She waited for the smile, the look of adoration, the one she knew she needed to help her along, but it wasn't there. In its place, a look of contempt, of anger, those eyes usually bright, inviting, now narrowed. She wondered if her paranoia made him look that way; she had never seen that expression on his face before, but as she continued to stare, he began to walk towards her. It wasn't a walk, it was a sharp stride, and she stopped, still halfway down the aisle.

He knew.

Now her fear was real and everything around her, the faces, the music, the flowers, became blurred. She slipped her arm out of her father's grip and retreated slowly, seeing nothing but Derek, whose lips sat in a sneer. He was gaining on her.

She was nearly at the doors, which were about to be closed by two pious ushers who had their hands on their chests and bowed as they moved the doors together slowly. She turned and bolted, pushing the little men aside, one of them falling flat on his buttocks. She didn't stop, she just ran, clutching together her heavy gown, completely oblivious to the shock and murmurs of the guests. She rushed through the foyer, where other ushers stood idly waiting for the service to end, before they could hand out rose petals to the guests, through the carpark, where the chauffeur of her hired Jaguar leaned on the car, his eyes on his phone and a cigarette hanging from his lips, through the gates, where cars breezed past lazily. Her veil caught on a twig and she tugged at it, leaving it waving at her from its perch, her tiara still attached to it.

She stopped for a moment to catch her breath, and then began to run again. Still on the footpath, she could hear the sounds of birds and smell the scent of Melbourne in winter dripping from the eucalyptus trees. She didn't stop now, heaving her ballooned dress above her knees and wishing her lacy heels weren't so high and tightly strapped up around her ankles; she could have discarded them too. She didn't look back, she was afraid of what she might see, so she kept her eyes firmly ahead on the familiar streets of her childhood, not knowing where she was running to and not caring. She was free and a fresh burst of relief now pounded at her heart.

She opened her mouth to laugh, her eyes directly on the path ahead. Even so, she barely had time to see the car that mounted the kerb, hurtling right towards her.

PART 1
LOSING RUTH

Chapter 1

2005

Oliver was her first real love. Skinny and nervous, but with a smile so shy it melted her heart, Oliver was the perfect first of many firsts.

'Hello, Ruth,' he mumbled into his chequered shirt collar, after he walked uncertainly towards her at Karen's nineteenth birthday party, his head slightly bent, his eyes lowered, his hands in his pockets.

Ruth would not have looked twice at him, he was not her type at all, except that she could feel his nervousness, way across the grassy yard that was twinkling with little lights that bordered the eaves on the patio. He had been standing by himself, watching drunken teenagers making fools of themselves on the makeshift dance floor, a slight frown on his pale face. She wanted to put him at ease as he gazed at her, at first with trepidation and then a little more boldly once he saw he had her attention.

When she first looked up at Oliver, out of pure curiosity and perhaps more than a little boredom, the intensity of his blue eyes dazzled her and she turned away, somewhat alarmed at her attraction to him. Jeff, one of the boys from school whom Karen felt she had to invite—why she couldn't understand, as school had been done and dusted a year before—had been trying to paw at her all evening. Ruth had no interest in talking to him, especially when she knew what he was and had always been after. He had now moved to the front of the house to have a cigarette, as there was no smoking allowed in the house, even in the backyard, and Ruth was relieved. She had been trying to get rid of him all night and was considering leaving, before he moved off. She just hadn't wanted to abandon her best friend and Karen had beseeched her to stay a little longer when she mentioned begging off earlier.

Ruth wasn't thinking about leaving anymore. She looked back at Oliver and smiled; her own dazzling smile worked well, she knew, if past experiences were anything to go by. She had seen Oliver at Karen's house before. He was a friend of Karen's older brother, Martin, but as Karen was six years younger than her brother, and because the siblings never got along, Ruth only saw Oliver in passing, never taking much notice of the shy boy who looked away every time she glanced his way. If she had thought about it at all, she would have dismissed his glances as those of a man who found her youth irritating.

But here he was, talking to her, and she could feel a tingle in her belly. 'Hi,' he said again.

'Hi, back.' Ruth parted her lips to reveal her perfectly straight teeth. She prided herself on never needing braces and used her smile to good effect; she practised enough in the mirror as a gangly teenager, before she grew into herself. She did, however, now wish that she had made more of an effort with her outfit. The green cardigan that was covering ample breasts had been thrown on in a huff, after her mother chided her for dressing like a tramp. It made the usually glossy highlights in her hair look like a shade of old olives. She had kept it on all evening as it had become a little chilly in the mid-February evening, resentfully thanking her mother, but she had pulled it tightly together at the front after Jeff had spent more time looking below her chin than at her face. She wanted to slide it off now to reveal the red lacy corset blouse that Karen had bought her for her own nineteenth just three weeks before, but she couldn't. That would be too obvious.

'Do you need a drink?' he asked, encouraged by her inviting response, and placed his elbow on the wooden frame of the window that Ruth had placed herself next to. The backyard was not paved or decked and Ruth had already found her stiletto heels covered with mud and grass that she had sunk straight into when she arrived. Since then, she had hovered near the doorway, where a small path to the backdoor was paved with concrete.

'I'm fine,' she replied, lifting the full glass of Coke she held in her hand. She tried not to giggle, though she desperately wanted to, and not just at his inane conversation starter; she could feel her stomach flutter.

Oliver clearly didn't know what to say next and Ruth was tempted to gulp down the drink so she could give him something to do, just so he wouldn't look so awkward. But she didn't, instead looking past him to Karen, who was bobbing her blonde head up and down in a manic dance. Ruth laughed now. This was so unlike Karen; the Vodka Cruisers that Ruth brought her were already making their way out of her pores.

'Nice party,' Oliver offered, following Ruth's gaze towards Karen, who was now bending over backwards in a limbo, except without a stick. She looked quite comical and Ruth would have laughed again, but she wanted Oliver to look back at her.

'Yes, it is,' she returned, then leaned in towards him, widening her brown eyes that were lined with a catlike swipe. 'But is it, really?' She wrinkled her nose.

Oliver chuckled. 'Hmmm …' He was emboldened now. 'Want to get out of here?'

'That's a line!' Ruth laughed. 'But yeah, I do.'

Oliver reached out his hand and Ruth took it. She would deal with Karen, who probably wouldn't notice if she left anyway, tomorrow.

It may not have been the whirlwind romance that Ruth envisioned, but it wasn't long before she was in love. Oliver kissed her for the first time that night, made love to her two weeks later and they were engaged within two months.

Ruth was, by nature, impulsive to a degree and she knew it.

She had had her share of boyfriends in high school and even became serious with Marty, a jock of a boy, who prided himself on being the star of the local soccer team. School sports were not elite enough for him, he had boasted, and chose to sit on the edge of the oval, sucking on Ruth's ear, only stopping to comment on the blunders of the players on the field who weren't as talented as himself and who were forced to participate in school teams because they couldn't get into the 'real teams'. Ruth was enamoured with Marty and she chose to see his pride as something that he would grow out of. It was a habit of hers to make excuses for the mistakes of other people, a habit she developed from her mother, a pious and soft-hearted woman. She gave herself to Marty three months after he asked her to go steady with him. She realised too late that this was his goal. She was known at school for having parents who were quite conservative, especially a mother who quoted the Bible without cause, and only later did she realise that she was seen as a challenge, a feather in their cap if she let a boy get past first base.

Five months after their courtship began, Ruth had still not introduced Marty to her parents, and he was getting quite shirty, having already taken her to meet his own, who seemed as prideful as him.

'Why don't you do it already?' remarked Karen, Ruth's best friend for as long as she could remember, who sometimes seemed as conservative as her parents. 'It looks like he's going to hang around for a while. Maybe he's the one.' Karen leaned her head back, her large glares shielding her eyes from the rays of the sun.

They were sitting on Ruth's porch, trying to study for their final exams, but enjoying the unexpected sunshine that had been non-existent for the last few days. It had been a dreary start to summer.

'I don't know,' said Ruth, chewing on the end of her pen. She was uneasy about Marty. Lately he had been disinterested and appeared to be avoiding her. When she called him, he always seemed to be about to go out with his friends, or about to head off to soccer practice, and yesterday, he said he needed to study for his exams. She would have laughed if she hadn't known what it meant. Ruth had never been one to chase boys, but she felt like she was already a little in love with him, and she found herself having panic attacks at the thought of him dumping her. 'It's still early days.'

'Five months is not early days,' declared Karen, pulling her glasses up to scrutinise Ruth.

Ruth usually told Karen everything, about how she felt, about what was going on in her life, but she didn't know what to say now; she felt a little embarrassed at her predicament. 'It's a busy time anyway …'

'Hey, you two.'

Ruth and Karen looked up to see Erica crossing the street towards them. She lived right across the road from Ruth and popped in quite often, so much so, that Ruth's parents thought they were closer than they were, often inviting her to stay for dinner. Karen groaned under her breath, but Ruth gave her a quick warning look.

Erica was the opposite of Karen. A tomboy, she gave the boys more than she probably should have. She didn't begin that way, starting out as a shy girl in seventh grade, but when her breasts finally developed and her braces were removed, Erica began to get attention, which she took complete advantage of. More than once, she had been suspended for inappropriate behaviour, having been found in various positions and states of undress by teachers. Not that she cared—Erica revelled in being the bad girl, the girl whom everyone wanted to be and wanted to hate. Ruth had a soft spot for Erica. She knew she didn't have many girlfriends and in their maths class, they always sat together, while Ruth listened to one of Erica's tales of her adventures on the weekend. She found Erica entertaining and she was, in fact, quite funny. Ruth just wished Erica could keep her legs closed long enough to retrieve her reputation. But she was not close enough to Erica to share her thoughts on her behaviour.

'Hi, Erica,' Ruth called out. 'Just finishing up for English.'

'Mind if I join?' She already had books with her.

'Sure,' said Ruth and pulled out a folding chair that leaned against the wall.

Erica planted her ample bottom in the chair and stretched her long legs up onto the table. Instead of opening her books, she leaned her head back and closed her eyes, taking a deep breath of the warm air. Again Karen made a face but Ruth ignored it.

'I feel like going to the beach today,' said Erica, undoing the button on her top to let the sun tan her chest. 'Hey, how's Marty? I saw him at Jasie's yesterday.'

This time it was Ruth who made a face. This was not what she wanted to hear. There wasn't going to be a lot of studying done today.

It wasn't until her exams were over and Ruth waited for Marty at the beach, where a bunch of students had gone to party, that she realised it was over. Marty had not come, had made up some excuse about going for a drive with the boys, and she wondered where he had really gone. She still wanted to go out with the others, celebrate the end of school with her friends, and she was glad she did. The evening was beautiful; a fire burned in the sand and the kids were behaving as people who had just finished school did. Even the waves were warm and inviting, and as Ruth dipped her feet in the water with Karen, she saw Erica heading their way. She knew by the look on her face, the one that displayed jubilance with a touch of remorse, that she was going to be the bearer of bad news.

Ruth hadn't spoken to Erica since that day. She chose to ignore Marty's yellow Lancer each time she saw it parked across the road, while she also ignored the pain in her heart, which eventually went away around the same time that Marty's car disappeared.

Chapter 2

'This is madness,' said Roberta, Ruth's mother, who was so shocked she had to sit down, still keeping her fingers on her temples. 'Are you pregnant? Have you … let him, you know?'

Ruth wanted to laugh at her mother who couldn't even bring herself to say the words, but instead, she put out her left hand, hoping that she could bedazzle her mother with the rock that Oliver had presented to her the evening before. Sure, it was modest, but on Oliver's salary as an intern in an accounting firm, it was more than he could afford and she was proud of it.

Roberta sniffed at the ring. 'At least he's not pretentious.'

'Ma, he's good and kind and …' She stared into the distance, her eyes glazed. 'Oh Ma, I'm so in love with him.'

Ruth decided that it would be best to break the news to her mother by herself, so when her father had gone out on bowling night, she helped Roberta clear the dishwasher and sat down at the dining table, twiddling her thumbs.

'Ruthy, you're only nineteen.' Roberta gathered her daughter's hands in hers. 'There will be time for love, time for everything that comes with it.'

'But I found someone who makes me happy,' Ruth pleaded. 'Don't you want me to be happy, like you and Pa?' She thought flattery would help her cause.

'That takes work,' Roberta said. But she saw the earnest look in her daughter's eyes and softened. She rolled her eyes and sighed. 'Just promise me you will finish uni before you get married.'

'That's more than a year away,' Ruth protested.

'But then at least you will be sure about how you feel. And you can make sure that you are both on the same path, the right path.'

Ruth knew the 'right path' her mother meant. She wanted to ensure that Oliver was a good Christian boy and that her grandkids would be too. Ruth also knew that Oliver's parents felt the same and it would be hard for Oliver to convince them too.

As if reading her mind, Roberta asked, 'Have you met his parents? Do they know?'

Ruth knew that her mother would be irritated if she wasn't the first to know, so she went with it. 'I've met them. They seem nice.' Ruth didn't want to elaborate.

Oliver's mother didn't want her son to marry so soon either, especially to a girl who looked as Ruth did. His mother was more prudish than hers; she didn't miss the raised eyebrows of the old crow, who looked like she had come out of an old horror movie, when she first met her three weeks earlier. She had opened the door and very deliberately looked Ruth up and down, and Ruth could see that she very clearly didn't like what she saw. Ruth wished for a moment that she was duller, her long, blonde locks less luscious, her lips less plump and less red. She was glad that she had wrapped herself in that green cardigan again.

It had been a peculiar meeting. Oliver's father had his head buried in an old encyclopedia and didn't even notice when his son brought Ruth through the door. He was an ageing man, but with a kindly smile that he sent Ruth's way when he finally tore his eyes away from his book, and begrudgingly got up to acknowledge his son's new sweetheart. After shaking her hand like a dead fish, he went back to his desk.

'Bart,' Oliver's mother barked to him. 'She's here to have tea with us.'

'It's okay,' said Ruth. 'I can't stay long. I just wanted so badly to meet you both.' She flashed her teeth broadly, hoping her smile would thaw the ice that was rapidly forming between them.

The eyebrows went up again and Oliver's mother just wandered away without another word. Ruth had not seen them since, but knew she would have to do so, especially now that she was engaged to their son. She was dreading it, dreading going into that dark house, so unlike her own, with its dark-blue wallpaper, and dark-grey carpet. Ruth didn't stay long enough to see the pictures on the walls, black-and-white photographs that would have made Oliver's parents a little more interesting.

Now Ruth and Oliver were here to let them know of their impending marriage and that didn't go down very well either, with his mother getting out of her armchair to place a kiss on her son's head and a pat on Ruth's shoulder. She wandered away again. His father left his desk and hugged them both briefly, before returning to his books.

Ruth was baffled by their conduct.

'It's not you,' said Oliver when Ruth asked if she had offended them in some way. 'They have old-fashioned ideas.'

'And I'm too new-fashioned for them?'

'It's not just that,' he said, hesitating. And then Oliver explained that his mother had wanted her son to marry his childhood sweetheart, quite literally the girl next door.

Her name was Suzanne and she appeared to Ruth as dowdy and as stuck-up as his mother. Ruth had met Suzanne several times by now as she seemed to be in every local establishment she and Oliver visited. She was at the café, sipping on iced tea with her straight back and pinkie hanging off the edge of the teacup, when they stopped in for a donut run. She was at the supermarket when they stopped to get groceries as Oliver wanted desperately to show her he could cook. She was at the park, walking her little fluffy pooch on a long pink leash when they rode their bikes past, and Oliver, of course, had to stop and say hello.

Ruth found Suzanne pleasant enough, but she didn't miss the same raised eyebrows as his mother when they asked her if she would like to attend the wedding. Ruth put her feelings down to jealousy, but she didn't really like the way Suzanne put her hand on Oliver's arm when she laughed shrilly at a joke that he had made, which Ruth felt wasn't all that funny.

But now Ruth had to contend with her own parents. Her mother had been first and she knew she had to do it by herself. Her father was the hard part.

'Well, have you told his parents yet?'

'We'll tell them soon.' Ruth bit her tongue at the lie and quickly went on. 'But Dad, will he be okay with it?'

Roberta seemed pleased that she was needed, that she was called upon to calm any waters that may become wavy. 'Well, if you promise to wait a bit, we can break it to him together. Ease him in, you know,' she said with a wink.

Ruth was her father's little girl, the clear favourite over Patty, her elder sister, who was as straight-laced as her mother. Ruth was the outgoing one, the tomboy, who revelled in her father's affection, giving him reason to forget his disappointment at not having a boy. When Patty married, almost straight out of high school, no one lifted an eyebrow. It was just the way it was supposed to be.

Patty was born to be a wife, a mother, and at twenty-three, already had three little girls, and was now trying for a fourth, a boy, that would make her husband, Mark, happy. Patty also wanted to please her father, whose attention she craved, and she resented Ruth for stealing it from her, the result of which was a barely tolerable relationship between the two sisters. Patty couldn't understand how their father could be so enamoured with Ruth's harebrained ideas and non-committal attitude to life when she, serious and hard-working Patty, was providing him with grandchildren, a continuation of his legacy.

Ruth, on the other hand, was relishing her youth, enjoyed being a little flighty and felt that the time would come for her to take life more seriously. Marriage didn't have to be one of those things that made her an old sop like her sister, and her mother, although clearly having some reservations, seemed to understand.

'Thanks, Ma.' Ruth beamed, relieved that it had been easier than she had initially thought. She reached over and hugged her mother tight. 'We'll talk about waiting.'

Less than three months later, Ruth's father, a frown on his face, walked his daughter down the aisle. Gary was less than impressed with Oliver; he thought him shady and too shy and retiring for the likes of his high-spirited daughter.

'He will bore you,' he warned after he met Oliver for the first time, but seeing the dejected look on Ruth's face, he quickly changed his tack. 'Just promise you'll not become a boring, worn-out little wife.'

Ruth knew what the rest of his sentence would sound like—*like your sister*—but she just smiled and hugged him. 'Never; I'm my dad's daughter, you can't beat the spirit out of me!'

Chapter 3

Yet not even a year into marriage, she was just that. Bored. Oliver managed to beat the spunk and spark out of her; not with his fists, but with his attitude and his controlling nature. Ruth loved him with all her heart but he was domineering, in that ever so subtle way that he did everything else.

At the beginning before they had wed, it was like Ruth was floating in a dream, the hype of the upcoming nuptials keeping their love at a peak. Paid for by their parents, there wasn't any stress attached to the wedding, except the decision between tulle and lace. Karen was her maid of honour, which peeved her sister, who was already in a bad mood about not getting pregnant again. But Ruth, who had never felt the need to answer to anyone before, dismissed the nasty remarks voiced by Patty about any aspect of the wedding.

Oliver left the preparations to Ruth, who tried not to let it take over her life, balancing it with the stress of her studies. But Ruth loved to be busy; she always felt the need to keep moving and used the stress as a motivator. She needed to let Roberta know that she could handle it all, that she was ready for married life. So for the five months between their meeting and the wedding, Ruth's days were rushed and fatigued. But late in the evenings, after recapping her day to Oliver and his to her, they would sneak away to Lover's Lane, a dusty shore on Chap's River, half an hour away from their suburban homes, and make love in the back of Oliver's Chevy, his pride and joy. The big black car was so unlike him and when she had first seen it, Ruth was taken aback. She, of course, was smitten with the thing, and wished her own little coupe had more zoom. But for someone like Oliver to own such a machine—Oliver, who was quiet and reserved—it just didn't seem like him. When she mentioned it, he seemed miffed.

'Why do you say that?' he asked when she remarked the car wasn't something she thought he would own.

'Oh, I just thought that you would drive something like a Toyota or something a little more, you know, you.' She bit her tongue, knowing how that sounded once it came out of her mouth. Oliver's frown appeared and disappeared as quickly and she knew she had irritated him. She hoped she hadn't been too offensive with her careless remark.

'I like my cars with guts, just like my women,' he replied.

Ruth liked that. It meant he knew who she was and loved that about her.

'Are you excited?' she asked one evening after they lay in each other's arms in the spacious back seat of the Chevy.

'I was,' Oliver snickered. 'Couldn't you tell?'

Ruth playfully slapped his arm that was slung around her

neck. 'It's less than a week away.'

'Everything's ready,' he said casually. 'I just can't wait to do this in a real bed.'

'Is that all you think of?' Ruth turned to him. 'But is it really too soon? Should we have waited a bit longer to get married?'

'A bit late for those …' He sat up. 'Second thoughts?' A look of concern crossed his face.

'No, of course not.' Ruth smiled and rested her head on his chest.

She did have some reservations, but knew it was natural, especially after such a short period of dating. It was probably too soon. A longer courtship such as her mother had suggested would have been the smart thing to do, but Ruth had never been the waiting type. When she knew she wanted something, there was no waiting. 'Impulsivity', that's what her mother had called it. It was too late to think about that now anyway. She was sure she wanted to spend the rest of her life with this man.

Oliver leaned back on the seat and closed his eyes and Ruth wondered how he was so relaxed, so calm. He took everything in his stride and she envied his composure. They were really chalk and cheese, but she beamed at their compatibility.

'Opposites attract,' she said softly.

'We sure do,' said Oliver and planted a kiss on her forehead.

Now, a little over a year later, she was restless. Her arts degree was complete and Ruth still didn't know what exactly she wanted to do with her life. She thought that while she made up her mind, it was time to get into full-time work and she certainly had no intention of having children at a young age as her sister had.

She applied for a job at a bank in the city and got the job on the spot. She understood her appearance and confidence had secured it and felt some guilt when she figured she was not as qualified as some of the other applicants, those of who chatted with her while waiting for their interviews. She could feel some of them envy her presentation and her easy manner as she made conversation about the weather and other run-of-the-mill things with them. Most of them were shy and scared, which made them look questionable, especially to work at a job that required constant communication with the public as a bank teller would. When she left the interview, Ruth avoided looking at the other applicants that still waited to be interviewed, knowing she had just taken what could have been theirs. She put it out of her mind as soon as her feet hit the footpath.

She couldn't see then how this would become a habit for her, how her deliberate dismissal of a person's feelings in order to alleviate her own guilt would turn her into something she would come to despise.

Oliver was ecstatic about her new employment. He quizzed her on all aspects of her job, as it related to his own interests, but Ruth was not as enthusiastic. To her, it was just a job: one that brought in a regular pay cheque that was put away as savings for their new home that Oliver sought in a country town that Ruth had no intention of moving to. His dream was to live in a quiet area, with plenty of land and no neighbours close enough to intrude on their life. Ruth thought she would keep her feelings about the idea to herself for a while, and hoped that by living so close to the centre of Melbourne, he would change his mind and come to enjoy the things that she did—the bright lights, the noise, the crowds, the shopping … what Oliver referred to as 'shallow' living. He scoffed at the idea that people enjoyed such things, that it fulfilled them, and Ruth wondered if he thought of her in the same way.

'Am I not deep?' she questioned her father on one occasion, after Oliver rolled his eyes when she suggested a walk down Bourke Street Mall, just to window shop.

'You're twenty. How deep can you be at twenty?' Gary laughed.

'Don't make fun,' she pouted. 'I feel like a child with him sometimes.' She looked at her father in accusation. 'Maybe you didn't give us enough trouble when we were children.'

Gary wrinkled his eyes in confusion. 'What do you mean?'

'Well, from what I see of people, from what I read, from movies and even from Karen, there has to be something traumatic in your life to make you grow, you know, to mature.'

Gary guffawed. 'That's the most ridiculous thing I've ever heard.'

'But it makes sense,' she pressed. 'If you have a nice childhood, good parents …' She raised her eyebrows to him while he smiled and looked mighty chuffed. 'How do you grow?'

'Sorry we couldn't help you with that.' Gary laughed.

'I just don't want to be thought of as air-headed or shallow all my life.'

'If you're happy, does it matter?'

'I don't know.' Ruth really didn't know. She hadn't had much to worry about in her short life: no grief, except the death of her grandparents when she was too young to remember, loving parents who gave their daughters everything they needed. She was a popular student, not excelling too much in her studies to be threatening but working hard enough to get into the design course she applied for.

'Don't overthink it,' said Gary, planting a kiss on his daughter's head to signal the end of a conversation he thought a bit absurd. 'For what it's worth, if it keeps you from heartache, I hope you will remain shallow your whole life.'

For now she had won the living situation, their new home rented to them from a friend of her mother at half the price something like that usually went for. The flat near the city, as poky as it seemed, was convenient and even Oliver couldn't find fault with it, particularly the amount of time it took him to commute to and from work. For Ruth it was perfect, especially with the sights and sounds so close they could be seen and heard. She sometimes looked out of the window at the passers-by, dressed to the hilt, preparing for a night on the town. She could hear their excited banter and wished that she could just pop out and go along with them. But that's all she could do—wish. Oliver never wanted to go out and complained that after a long day at his own job, now as an entry level clerk at an accounting firm, he had had enough of the busyness of the day and wanted to remain at home, in front of the television, his feet up on the wooden table, a glass of brandy in his hand. Ruth sometimes looked at him and marvelled at his imitation of an old man, and one evening when she stepped into the lounge room after her evening shower, she got a shock; he was beginning to resemble his father! He was just twenty-six.

He was older than her, she was quite aware of that, but by only six years, yet he spoke to her like a wizened old person, always soft and slow, with deliberation. He complained about journeying too far when she'd suggest they go for a drive instead of visiting the city; he preferred to stay at home, working on his collection of postcards or watching the television. Even the drive of twenty minutes that it took to get to their parents' house seemed to tire him out.

Ruth was used to the bright lights of Melbourne. Before she began seeing Oliver, she revelled in the buzz of the city, travelling by train with Karen or other friends to the museum or to the movies, and many an evening they would hop on a bus that would take them to a nightclub. When she first met Oliver, Ruth expected that he would want to join her on her city trips, hoping he would love the sounds, the sights and even the smell as she did. It was a sad realisation, during their first months together, when she grasped that he had no intention of doing the same, as much as she tried to entice him. But Ruth was so smitten that she didn't care at that time, hoping that being so close to it all, he would feel its vibe and be drawn to it. Her father's words returned to her mind more and more—he'll bore you—but she just wanted to spend every minute with Oliver, so she pushed any nagging doubts out of her mind; he would come around. They were going to be married and live happily ever after, just like her parents, she never doubted it for a moment; they would have to meet somewhere in the middle. It would just take some time.

Now his initial charm was beginning to wear thin and she realised they had much less in common than she originally thought. That was no reason for her to stop loving him though, and she sought ways in which they could spend time together doing things that she enjoyed as well. She tried often.

'Let's go out!' she'd declare and would immediately see the irritation rise in him. He didn't need to say it, she could see his shoulders rise and a small crease appear under his eyes.

'I'm tired, aren't you?' He wouldn't even look at her to acknowledge her suggestion.

'Yes, I guess, but listen to it …' She paused to take in the sound of the trams and buses as they whooshed past their flat on Drysdale Street.

'All I can hear is trouble,' he'd replied. He flicked a channel on the remote. 'It's Friday, there's usually a good movie on.'

The conversation would vary, Ruth trying different tactics each time, but the outcome remained the same. That would be the end of it and Ruth would climb on the sofa next to him and wait until he flicked through all the channels, stopping at the same one he began with. She'd grab a blanket and a bowl of chips and settle down on the sofa next to him, envying the people so close out there enjoying themselves, while she fumed and tried to laugh along while Oliver guffawed at a movie he had probably watched a hundred times.

Karen came over often, especially on weekends, having a place to hang out without lurking parents, and Ruth would try to keep her over for as long as she could, even though she knew that Oliver was not fond of her friends. He usually retired to the back porch, showing his disdain for her company.

'Air-headed,' he had said once about Karen, and Ruth had sat silently, words of anger flying through her mind, but staying quiet for the sake of peace.

'He's still getting to know me and my life. I have to bend a little too,' she would tell herself, even knowing that she was losing something of herself in the process.

For his part, Oliver kept his own to himself, going to Rivera, their hometown, where he would catch up with his old friend, Karen's brother, Martin. He never made any friends at work, calling them silly and dim-witted, and said he didn't have time for extra pastimes in his life that were meaningless. He would occasionally visit his parents and Ruth was happy to let him go by himself.

Whenever they visited them together, usually on a Sunday after calling in on her own parents' place, she could feel the stark difference in atmosphere from one home to the other. While hers was warm and inviting, with her mother insisting they sit down and share a meal she'd made, Oliver's home was cold, quite literally, and his parents sat with them awkwardly as if they were waiting for the two of them to leave. So when he got the sudden urge to see them, sometimes during the week, Ruth was quite happy for him to go on his own, relieved it would save her from visiting them on the weekend.

It was when he was on one of these visits, a Friday night, that Karen called Ruth and asked if she was free, as Oliver was at her house visiting Martin.

'Oh, I thought he was at his parents' house.'

'Well, he just popped in. Let's go out for a drink.' Karen's voice was excited. 'It's been so damn long.'

'I know, but I haven't asked Oliver.' She realised how it sounded. 'Um, I need to let him know … so he knows where I am,' Ruth said, trying not to sound like a controlled wife, but Ruth didn't care what she sounded like right now; she really wanted to go out with her friends. She rubbed at her feet, which were sore after a long day at work, but she could bear the pain a little longer, just to have some fun, just to feel normal and young again.

Karen paused. 'Well, I can tell him, he's right here.' She called out to Oliver as Ruth sat with the phone tight against her ear, waiting to hear what he'd say, and more to the point, *how* he'd say it.

She heard the hesitation in his voice when he said with forced nonchalance, 'Sure, if she's free.' For some reason, it maddened Ruth and she gritted her teeth once more.

'Yay,' squealed Karen. 'Be ready in twenty. I'm leaving now.'

Ruth put the music on loud and set about getting ready, singing through her make-up routine, but a lump of lead seemed to be stuck in the pit of her stomach. She knew that although Oliver had agreed, he would not have been happy about it. She wondered when things were going to change and *if* they ever would.

The evening with Karen was wonderful, just two friends chatting about their lives, and she felt like a load had lifted, that she could be herself and talk of things that didn't make her feel like a child. It had only been a few months since they had been married, but Ruth realised that evening how stifled and controlled she had become, whether or not Oliver meant to make her feel that way.

'I want to stay out late tonight,' she said, looking at the evening sky that glowed purple above the skyscrapers. She breathed in the fumes of the late evening traffic and closed her eyes and sighed. It was just after ten p.m. and they were walking back to Ruth's place where Karen had left her car.

'It's been a while since we've gone out together,' said Karen, her arm slung in Ruth's. 'I miss you.'

'Me too,' Ruth replied with a quiver in her voice.

'Is everything okay?' Karen asked suddenly.

'Yes, of course.' Ruth cleared her throat and attempted a laugh.

'I mean with Oliver,' Karen said and then quickly continued. 'I mean, I don't want to pry, but ...'

'Yes, of course!' Ruth replied, more upbeat than she felt.

The sounds of ACDC came roaring out of a bar they were walking past and Karen pulled at Ruth's arm. 'One more drink?'

Ruth grinned. 'Yes, I think so.'

She wanted to talk about it all to Karen, about how she had been feeling, but felt like she was being traitorous to Oliver, so she tried to have fun without thinking about him. Karen, still single and waiting for the right one, gave her much to think and laugh about, telling her of her adventures with other mutual friends of theirs, which made Ruth slightly envious of the life that she had so casually discarded.

Ruth went home that night with trepidation, wondering how Oliver would react to her going out, but also with some hope. She had to be able to control her own life, to do what she enjoyed doing, or else her father would have been right: Oliver would have succeeded in sucking the life out of her. She was already beginning to dislike the person she was becoming—unhappy, complaining and above all, weak.

So, when she crept in at close to midnight, knowing Oliver would be well asleep, she had resolved to being the vivacious person she once was. She was going to make him meet her in the middle, not just continue to move to his side, where she might eventually become a clone of his mother, a thought that made her shudder. Crawling into the bed next to Oliver, Ruth felt a tinge of resentment towards him, but as he gently snored, she moved closer and rested her head on his bare back. Everything was going to be okay.

The next morning, Ruth sat at the dining table nursing a very strong black coffee, trying to ignore her aching head. She had far too much to drink and the throb at her temples was palpable. She was not thinking about doing anything today and was relieved that Oliver hadn't made any plans, not that he ever did.

She heard the shower turn off and Oliver emerged, his hair wet, his face in a smile. He kissed her head and sat down opposite her. Ruth was ready for the inquisition and she groaned inwardly.

'What would you like to do today?' he asked.

Ruth almost choked on her coffee. 'Uh, yes, how about a movie? Or even, let's just go to the market!' She may have been hungover, but Ruth was not going to let a chance like this get past her.

His eyes creased. 'Oh, I was thinking about taking a drive to Geelong. Maybe stopping in to see the parents on the way back.'

'Oh, I thought you meant somewhere fun.' She regretted her choice of words even before they came out of her mouth. 'I mean, I thought you meant going into the city.'

'It's so loud.' He grimaced. 'I thought a nice drive, maybe a picnic?'

'Yeah, okay,' Ruth said, trying to sound a little excited. 'I thought you were in town yesterday. Why didn't you drive by your parents' place then?'

'I, um … I just thought we could go together, that's all.'

While Ruth got some sandwiches ready, she speculated about

his lack of curiosity about her evening with Karen. She thought he would be all over it and wondered why he hadn't asked. Throwing an aspirin down her throat, she promised herself she was going to have a good time on their picnic.

The day was gorgeous for November and the fresh breeze that drifted into and out of the windows of the Chevy gave Ruth a feeling of contentment. She inhaled the scent of the receding spring and knew she was sabotaging her happiness by having unkind thoughts about her husband, who she knew adored her.

'Oh, by the way, I had a good time with Karen last night. It's been ages since we caught up like that.' Ruth took his hand while they drove along the freeway where for once there wasn't a lot of traffic.

'Hmmm, never was fond of her.' Oliver screwed up his nose. 'Just a little bit whiny and childish.'

'Of course she was.' Ruth laughed, trying not to take offence on behalf of her very best friend. 'She's always been Martin's annoying little sister to you.'

Oliver didn't seem to connect it with that. 'No, I just think she was not, you know, a good sort.'

'What do you mean?' Ruth wished she hadn't said anything. She was having such a nice time listening to the mellow music that matched the mood she was in. Now she felt that irritation again, a pull in her chest, ready to defend against anything Oliver said.

'Just, Karen is very flighty, too free-spirited.'

'Well, what do you call me then?' Ruth let go of his hand and crossed her arms against her chest.

'You just needed to grow up a bit.' He smiled, a condescending grin.

'And I have?' Ruth was already beginning to feel the fire glowing under her light-green cotton top.

'Yes, I think so.' Oliver didn't seem to sense her change in mood or her sarcasm. 'You were a bit spirited too.' Again, that matter-of-fact tone, almost paternal, except, thought Ruth, this was her husband, not her father.

'And you want to break my spirit?' She could feel herself becoming more wound up, but she didn't want to let this go. It was time she put a stop to him treating her like a child.

'No, no, not at all,' he replied. 'But I think that there's always a time when one has to grow up.'

'So you married me to turn me into something you wanted me to be?' Ruth knew she was turning this into a fight, but she couldn't stop herself. She'd rather know what he really thought.

'Don't twist this,' Oliver said, again calmly.

'What's to twist?' Ruth wanted to argue now; she could feel her old feisty self come back to her and she was damned if she was going to be his quiet little wife anymore. She was not her sister.

'Are you trying to have a fight?'

'I don't know what this is. We've never had a fight before.' Ruth stopped, realising that they had never had a real argument. As different as they were, they always seemed to agree on things, but now she also realised that it wasn't agreeance, it was avoidance, the resistance to resistance. And that was certainly not going to make either of them happy.

The rest of the day was pleasant enough, with Oliver seeming to have forgotten about their conversation in the car. They sat on the warm sand, lunched on sandwiches and Coke, and Ruth even dived into the water alone, Oliver not interested in going with her. She did notice, however, that when she chatted with fellow bathers along the shoreline, Oliver was watching intently. She removed herself from the group and came back to him, playfully splaying her hair about, splashing water on him.

'Ruthy! My book is wet,' Oliver admonished, shaking *The Great Gatsby*, a book she had seen him read over and over again.

'We are at the beach, there's water. What do you expect?' she teased and lay down next to him. She raised her face to the sun, feeling its rays already begin to warm her body.

'Cover yourself a little,' he demanded.

Ruth shielded her eyes as she looked up at him, suddenly seeing a face full of menace. It changed almost imperceptibly, a small frown replacing it. His eyes moved to her bikini top which she now looked down at too. He hadn't said anything about it before, the emerald-green strip that covered what it was supposed to.

'If you hadn't noticed, we are at the beach,' she repeated. 'Look around, everyone is wearing the same, some less.'

'Well, they're not my wife.' That word had always given Ruth a warm feeling in her stomach—*wife*. It didn't now. Now it was a word of possession and control and Ruth fought against the words that were begging to escape her mouth.

'Well, husband, do things to me that husbands do with their wives,' she said instead, putting her hand on his thigh. She knew she had to change the mood, again resisting an argument.

Oliver smiled at that. 'Well, when we get home, I will do everything you want me to do,' he said and leaning over her, grabbed the towel and lay it across her body.

It occurred to her then that at least they had that in common, something that was very important in a marriage. Ruth had not been with another man so very intimately before, Marty not coming close to what she had with Oliver, and Oliver heightened every one of her senses when he made love to her. He was completely another person—wild, exciting and generous. But it seemed to be the only time she saw that side of him. It was enough to know that he could be unadulterated and Ruth thought that perhaps she needed to nudge at his inhibitions in more than one way.

For now, she leaned her hat over her eyes, silently fuming.

They stopped at her parents' house on the way home, where Roberta already had a stew on the boil. Ruth was hungry now and Oliver sniffed appreciatively at the aroma that accosted them as they entered the house. Gary greeted his daughter with a warm hug and his son-in-law with a firm handshake and Ruth felt the familiarity of home.

They all sat down to dinner, talking about the news of Patty's pregnancy.

'It's so exciting,' Ruth said. 'I hope they finally get that boy!'

'Yes, I hope so,' Roberta replied. 'I've been praying for that. It will take the pressure off. Too many children for her to deal with. It's not good for her body.'

'Is something wrong, Ma?'

'No, I don't think so, but she is so tired all the time already. I'm just worried for her.'

'Well, with all those children, what do you expect?' Gary chimed in. 'She's always been a little sickly, I think she should stop now.' A frown appeared on his face.

'But children are a blessing too,' said Roberta. 'As many as God wants to give us.'

'Yes, I agree.' All eyes turned to Oliver. 'We will be having as many as we are blessed with. And the sooner the better, I think.' He reached out to Ruth and squeezed her hand.

Ruth turned to him, wide-eyed. They had talked about children, of course, but it was a distant goal in their life plan. Ruth had barely begun her twenties. She wanted to have a career, although she wasn't sure of what that was yet, she wanted to live a little first, but it was clear motherhood was not yet calling as it did so easily to other women, women like her sister. Children would be part of her life one day, but certainly not now. She looked away and then gave Gary a warning glance. Her father was observing her, concern in his eyes, and she knew he was thinking the same thing she was.

Ruth gave a quick laugh and changed the subject. 'So, have

you seen Patty lately?'

As they were on their way out, Gary called to Ruth. 'I have something to show you, I almost forgot.' He smiled at Oliver and ushered Ruth to her old bedroom.

'What is it, Pa?' she said, looking around as Gary closed the door. The room had not changed since she had left her little haven, but why would it? It served well as a guest bedroom and it also seemed to suggest that there would always be somewhere to come to if she ever felt the need.

'Are you okay?' Gary asked.

Ruth shrugged.

'I know what your mother would say, but as for me, you can come home whenever you want.'

'Oh Pa, it's nothing like that.' Ruth smiled wanly and sat on the edge of her old bed. 'Just some teething problems, you know. Getting to know each other properly. Children are a part of the discussion, I guess, but we haven't really talked about it properly.'

'By the sound of it, this is important. I don't want to interfere, but it just seemed … well, a little inharmonious in there.'

Ruth smiled. Just like her father to use a word like that, to make it sound decent.

'Really, Dad,' she said as she stood up. 'We're fine.' She looked at his troubled eyes. 'Really.'

It wasn't fine, she knew that, but she was determined to make it that way. So she brushed aside her own frustrations and for the next six months, Ruth became the wife she knew Oliver wanted her to be. She came home from work every day, watched television with him, tried to avoid the discussion on children and, though she wanted to go out and do things that other twenty-somethings were doing, she had made the choice to marry Oliver, the man she loved very much.

Ruth tried to understand that Oliver worked late and when he got home, he was tired, and being on her feet all day at the bank, Ruth felt the same. But their weekends were much the same as their weekdays, and they visited their parents every fortnight on a Saturday, Ruth counting the days until she could see them.

Ruth made friends at work. It was impossible for her not to; everyone was friendly and she was the same, but she never invited them back to her place or went out with them for drinks after work, as much as she wanted to and as much as she was asked. She spoke to Karen once a week and saw her on occasion when she came to visit, which was usually the times Oliver went to her house to see Martin. Ruth wished she could get to know his best friend a little more, perhaps have at least someone they could socialise with, but Martin never seemed to warm to Ruth and Oliver never encouraged her to do the same. It was as if he were trying to keep her all to himself.

Then one day, late in March, when the weather was still warm, Oliver suggested Ruth have a girls' night out with Karen.

'You haven't seen her for a while,' he said. 'Besides, I thought it might be nice for me to catch up with Martin too. I haven't even met his girlfriend yet.'

Ruth was surprised but jumped at the chance and they organised a Saturday evening when she could see her friend. They had dinner at Pellegrini's, the old-school place on Bourke Street, and Ruth was able to catch up on everything she couldn't when she was on the phone with Karen. They laughed about their silly behaviour at high school, groaned at their choice in boys and even talked about Erica, who had recently phoned Ruth to apologise for her treachery.

'She even used that word,' Ruth said, thinking about how the phone nearly dropped from her ear when she heard Erica's voice on the other end.

'Why did she call you?'

Ruth shrugged. 'She said something about how I was such a good friend to her, the only one she had in high school. She was making amends for her bad choices, blah, blah, blah …'

Karen laughed at that. 'You're too soft,' she said, shaking her head. 'Just don't be taken in so easily again.'

'She was young, I guess, and she had her share of problems …'

'You knew her better than I did. Just be careful though, you know.'

'I've forgiven and forgotten, Karen, and honestly, I'm grateful to Erica for taking that narcissistic boy off my hands.' Ruth laughed, but a ping of hurt still touched her heart. 'Let's talk about something else …'

It was a wonderful evening, and even though Ruth spoke

with Karen on the phone, it just wasn't the same, with Oliver always in listening distance, probably hanging on every word that was said. She measured her words carefully, wondering why she did and irritated that it was necessary. She had nothing to hide, yet she felt that she couldn't be herself, realising that Oliver would probably think her childish if she were to be so.

'Are you okay?' Karen asked as they sipped on their coffees before heading back home. Ruth was subdued, wishing this evening didn't have to end so soon.

'Yes, what do you mean?' Ruth was taken aback by the unexpected question. They had been reminiscing about their childhood just a moment before and this came out of the blue.

'I don't know. I don't want to interfere, but I've barely seen you in the last year.' She smiled sadly. 'And I miss you.'

Ruth reached out her hand to Karen. 'I know, just been so busy with life. My job, as boring as it is, drains me and ...'

'Is it just your job?' Karen had always been upfront with Ruth.

Ruth felt a stirring of something; she was already getting her back up, knowing where Karen was headed. As much as she would have liked to have someone to talk to about how she felt, she decided to defuse it again. 'I'm fine, Karen; I'm still just getting used to being a wife.'

Karen squeezed her hand. 'Well, I'm always here for you. I know I don't need to tell you that, but just in case ...'

Chapter 4

Ruth watched the rain slap at the window and looked at the giant clock on the mantel, a wedding gift from her aunt. Someone said that it was a bad omen to get a clock as a wedding present and now Ruth wondered if it were true. Oliver was out again and she rested her head on the back of the sofa, listening to the drops as they hit and then slithered down the pane, the smell of the pasta she had cooked receding, as was the day.

He had been working late almost every day and Ruth was becoming exasperated, dutifully sitting alone at home. She didn't want to upset him by going out while he worked, so she usually prepared dinner and read or watched television while she patiently waited. When he got home, they would eat, watch more TV, maybe make love if Oliver wasn't too tired; lately, as he was trying to climb the corporate ladder, he was taking as much overtime as his firm offered him. At least he called to let her know and on occasion, Ruth accepted offers to have after-work drinks with her colleagues. She was sure not to tell Oliver about it, there was no point in upsetting him. Besides, there would be endless questions about it, albeit in that calm manner, his mouth in a straight line the whole time, while she felt a guilt for what, she didn't know. She was starting to dislike his calmness, as much as she knew it was generally a good characteristic for someone to have and which she hoped to one day master herself.

It was nearly seven and dinner was growing cold, when the sound of her phone jerked her out of her reverie.

'You need to come here,' Karen said breathlessly before Ruth had the chance to greet her.

'What's wrong?' Ruth clutched the phone tight. 'Are you okay? What happened?' Ruth envisioned a number of scenarios in her head, all involving something terrible … a house fire, an accident … 'Are you hurt?'

'No, no, I'm fine.' Karen sounded frustrated with Ruth's questions.

'Then what?'

'Just come … I need you.'

'I'm just waiting for …'

'Ruth!' Karen was almost screaming. 'Just get down here, please.'

'On my way.' Ruth hung up, threw on her boots and dashed out the door.

On the way to the car, she realised she had forgotten her coat, but the panic in Karen's voice stopped her from turning back. She was glad it was past peak hour and the drive was easy. What could be so wrong? Karen had been having trouble with her new boyfriend, Rob, but that was usually something Karen didn't have to drag Ruth across town to tell her. She hoped she'd be able to get back home before Oliver found her gone and checked herself. Something could be horribly wrong and here she was, thinking about herself.

A thought crossed her mind. Maybe something happened to Karen's parents, and then a shudder ran down her spine. Maybe it was her own parents! No, she realised that Karen would have come over to her place instead. She turned up the music to drown out the terrifying possibilities and tried to sing along to Whitney Houston, but only a croak came out. Nevertheless, the music was successful in distracting her, at least a little bit.

Her car almost skidded into the back of Karen's as she sped into the driveway, where her friend, a cigarette in hand, was waiting for her on the doorstep. Karen stubbed out the cigarette under her shoe and bolted to the passenger side of Ruth's car.

'Just drive,' she said.

'Karen! What is it? What's going on?'

'Ruth, you need to see this, trust me.'

'Just tell me …'

'You won't believe me, just drive. Grove Crescent.'

Ruth squinted her eyes as she peered through the windscreen, her wipers dashing about trying to clear the glass of the pelting rain, her brain in a rut. She couldn't fathom what the problem was, and now gave up trying in an effort to get to wherever Karen was taking her without skidding off the road. As they neared Grove Crescent, a cul-de-sac that housed a number of little flats, Karen motioned for her to slow down. Ruth eased the car to a crawl and scanned the road. Her throat caught. Parked at the edge of the kerb just ahead was Oliver's Chevy.

'What ...?'

'Yes, it's his car.' Karen put her hand on Ruth's arm.

'Well, what's it doing here?' Ruth put the car into park just behind it.

'It's been here almost every evening for the past two weeks.'

'Where is "here"?' Ruth looked about the street, which was quiet, almost eerie in the cold winter night.

'Okay, don't get mad at me, but I maybe did some snooping before I was sure,' Karen muttered, her head low.

Ruth raised her eyebrows. 'Okay, so just tell me.'

'That's Suzanne's apartment.' She pointed to a yellow door that stood between a number of other little apartments, also with yellow doors. It looked like an image from *The Stepford Wives*.

'Suzanne?' Ruth furrowed her brows now, trying to recall, and then it dawned on her. 'Suzanne!' She hadn't seen that woman since the wedding, when she fawned over Ruth's dress and threw glances of longing at Oliver.

Karen nodded and chewed on her thumbnail. 'I followed him one day after I had seen his car drive right past our house. I suspected something a while ago when I overheard her name in a conversation with Martin. Then when I saw his car a couple of times in town, I drove here and there it was. I saw him drive up again tonight and I knew I had to …' She looked at Ruth, who was trying to work something out in her head, to put some pieces together, but knew she couldn't yet, not right now. 'Ruth, I'm sorry …'

'Maybe they're just friends?' Ruth leaned back in her seat, staring at Oliver's car, knowing already it wasn't that. Karen shook her head slowly and Ruth felt a wave of panic.

'Maybe we should go,' said Karen, looking around, but Ruth was already opening the car door and Karen reached out and grabbed her arm. 'Don't, Ruth, just don't,' she pleaded.

'You brought me here!' Ruth retorted.

'But you may not like what you see.'

Ruth hesitated. 'What will I see?' She saw apprehension in Karen's eyes. 'What did you see?'

'Things I didn't want to.'

Ruth shook her arm free from Karen's grip and rushed to the door, Karen hot on her heels. As she was about to rap on the door, Karen pulled her to the side of the house.

'Ruth, please, don't. You can …' She stopped at Ruth's expression.

Ruth was looking through the lace-curtained window where she saw a half-naked Oliver spread out on a red vinyl sofa, Suzanne sprawled atop him. His eyes closed, he was stroking her long black hair and she was stroking something else. Ruth's jaw dropped, and suddenly all she could feel were the hairs on her arms rise. Absently she wondered if it was the rain.

She could feel herself being tugged at, but she stood frozen as she watched her husband, her shy, retiring husband, being pleasured by another woman. Ruth felt like she was watching a love scene being played out in one of those tacky films, a B grade movie, where the lights from the fireplace shimmered over their moving figures. Oliver now had his hands on Suzanne's face and she was laughing. Ruth stood frozen, wanting to see more, wanting the dagger that was piercing her heart to twist and turn so it would kill her.

'Let's go,' she heard Karen beseech her and she now allowed herself to be dragged back to her car, her hair bedraggled, and her heart broken in two.

She sat in silence for a moment, ignoring the pleas of Karen for Ruth to say something to her, then turned on the ignition. She drove to Karen's place in silence and waited for her to get out. Then she drove home and waited for Oliver to arrive.

Chapter 5

At least she got to keep the flat.

Those first few months were horrible; the memories of Oliver lingered as did his messages on her answering machine. She kept those messages, missing him immensely, and wondering what she had done so terribly wrong that he needed to turn to someone else. And of all people, Suzanne, who he always insisted was just like a sister to him after their brief interlude in their teens. She tortured herself, trying to remember the times when he left the house—how had he looked, was he excited to leave? Oliver's face never gave much away at any given time, but Ruth still thought that she should have known, or at least felt something.

When Oliver returned home that fateful evening, Ruth had worked herself up into a state. She was utterly distraught, but also somewhat numb. The phone kept ringing and knowing that it must have been Karen, she ignored it. She didn't know how to feel about Karen right now, having taken her to see Oliver's deceit for herself. She wondered how she would have dealt with it had she been in

Karen's position. But her thoughts of Karen didn't linger; Ruth just wanted to know what was going on … and for how long.

It was past nine when Oliver strolled through the door, a sour look on his face. He placed his briefcase on the floor and sighed. 'This better be worth it,' he said. 'They're still holding off on that bloody promotion …'

Ruth sat at the dining table, a glass of wine in her hand, which she swirled with deliberate nonchalance, as her heart thudded in her chest.

Oliver took off his overcoat and hung it neatly on the coat rack. 'I know I've earned it. I'm sick of coming home so late,' he said.

Ruth didn't reply.

'And the traffic, I can't deal with it anymore. Once I get it …'

Ruth continued to stare, waiting for Oliver to look at her.

'… then maybe I could get home on time,' he said, and Ruth blanched at his bare-faced lie. He regarded her now.

Around her shoulders was draped a long, red, silk, sheer scarf, covering her naked breasts. It was one that she had bought for herself despite Oliver's objection to its overt allure. Oliver stopped and stared in surprise.

'Hey, Ruth,' he said, as if just noticing that she was there.

'Hi, there, lover,' said Ruth, licking her lips slowly.

'Nice scarf.' He cleared his throat. 'New?'

'Nope, this old thing?' She swished the scarf about, revealing glimpses of her breasts, and saw that Oliver was now swallowing hard. She could always tell when he got excited and right now she felt ill; he was almost frothing at the mouth, having just come from the arms of another woman.

'Dessert already?' he asked, moving forward, his eyes nearly falling out of his face.

Ruth stood up and let the scarf fall to the floor, revealing her fully nude body. She held up her hand to stop him from advancing and he halted, his eyes still scanning her figure. She wanted to laugh at the expression on his face; his tongue was actually beginning to hang from his mouth.

'I just wanted you to take a good look,' she said and waited, leaning on the table as she watched his eyes continue to roam over her. 'Have you?'

Oliver nodded and swallowed.

'Good, because that's the last you're going to see of it.' She picked up her coat from the back of her chair and wrapped it around her.

Walking past him, his jaw slack, she grabbed her packed suitcase that stood next to the front door along with her keys and slammed the door behind her. She was already at her car when she heard the front door open again and she fumbled with her keys, tears already spilling down her cheeks. She could hear him saying something, calling to her, but she was thankfully in her car when he got to her. His eyes were wide as he banged on the window, but with one last look, she reversed out at full speed, leaving him with a frightened look in his eyes and a bulge in his pants.

She knew it was a cop out, but the next day, she asked her father to get some of her things from her flat. When he returned, he explained that Oliver wasn't home; however, there was a note saying he was in Rivera with his parents.

'To be with … that girl,' she sobbed, as her father held her and her mother ran around trying to get her to eat something.

'Baby, I already told you he was not good enough, no balls, that man. He deserves less and let him have it.' Gary was fuming and Ruth was glad that Oliver hadn't been home. Her father would have killed him. He was not one to hold back, especially with someone who had hurt his beloved daughter.

'I still love him, Dad,' Ruth said. 'Even if …'

'Would you take him back? Right now?'

Ruth shook her head emphatically. 'No, never. I never want to be with him again, not after … that.'

'What will you do?'

'I don't know. Can I stay here for a bit?'

Gary's eyes lit up. 'You can move back in, if you want! Your room is always waiting.'

But the next day, Ruth decided that if Oliver didn't want the flat, she was happy to have it; besides, she was the one who loved living where they lived, not him. After another night of tears and disbelief, she rose the next morning with a renewed attitude. She took a deep breath and picked up the phone, calling his parents' house. His mother answered, and hearing Ruth's voice, she quickly passed the phone to Oliver.

'Hi, Ruthy.' His voice was again calm. She could hear his hesitation and she was pleased.

'I just wanted to let you know that I want the flat.' She paused, waiting for him to respond.

It was a few moments before he did. 'Do you want to talk about it?'

Ruth clutched the edge of her bed tight so as not to burst into tears. 'No, not really,' she said, trying to maintain a calm in her voice, similar to his. How she wanted him to beg for forgiveness and how she wanted to tell him she knew it was a mistake, how they could make it work, even with their differences. But he didn't tell her he was sorry; maybe it would have been the straw that broke her resolve.

'Ruthy …' His voice had an urgency to it that Ruth hadn't heard before.

'Please don't call me that. I always hated it.' She rushed on. 'Anyway, how long will you need to get your stuff out of there?'

'What about the furniture?' His calm had returned.

'Take what you want, I don't care. Is a week okay? Fine then, thanks.' She hung up and then burst into tears.

Oliver, to his credit, had moved all his things out and left most of the furniture, save for his swivel chair, which Ruth didn't like anyway. He left a note on the table. Not really a note, just a word. 'Sorry'. She smiled ruefully, crushed it and threw it in the bin immediately and sat in the armchair he'd left behind, his favourite, the dents of his body still embedded in it. She curled up into it and cried.

In the days after she moved back, he left messages on her answering machine, messages of love, of regret, and some even blaming her for not having the same goals as him, her nervous nature that went completely against his own.

'Opposites don't always attract then,' she said dully.

Oliver

He hung up the phone after speaking to the machine again, knowing full well that he had ruined it all. He wondered if it were too late and felt the faint glimmer of hope dying out. Ruth hadn't answered any of his calls or messages; she had completely ignored him. He had even tried to speak to Karen, which he was loath to do, but he just had to do something to get her back. Karen had also ignored him, going so far as to suggest her brother get better friends at the top of her voice when Oliver had come to her house.

'Oliver, is that you?' his mother's voice called and Oliver sighed, his eyes still on the phone, hoping Ruth would call back but knowing she wouldn't. She had always had a stubborn streak.

'Yes, it's me, Mother,' he called back, knowing he would have to move out of here as quickly as possible. After spending more than a year away from home, he knew he couldn't stay here indefinitely. It was already driving him insane, the coldness, the monotony, and he wondered why he had never noticed it before.

There was a knock on his bedroom door and before he could answer, his mother opened it. 'I didn't know you were home. Weren't you at work today?'

'I took the day off. I had some things to do.'

'Right, well, you can't keep taking days off. They will fire you.' She rolled her eyes and wiped her hands on her apron. 'Besides, I think you've spent enough time crying over that silly girl.'

'It's been a week, Mother,' said Oliver, irritable.

'Well, if you had listened to me in the first place …'

Oliver rose and walked to the door, waiting for his mother to move aside before walking past her.

'… you wouldn't be in this position,' she called after him.

Oliver picked up his keys and walked out the front door. He sat heavily in his Chevy and stroked the steering wheel. At least this car never let him down like everything else in his life had. He leaned his head back and drove, feeling more in control. At first, it was just around in circles, but before he knew it, he was parked outside what was now Ruth's flat, wondering what she was doing. He imagined her onto her next man, who may already be taking his place, keeping his armchair warm. He seethed with anger and jealousy, but he knew he couldn't do anything to rectify the situation. It was done.

He lit a cigarette, a new habit he had acquired from Suzanne, and thought about Ruth. He loved her so much and had so many plans for their future. He wanted to spend the rest of his life with her, even at the mocking of his mother. He smiled at that. Ruth made his mother mad. He remembered the first time she had met Ruth, the look on her face as she appraised her—utter disdain. And when he returned home after dropping Ruth off at her own house, he had gotten a sour look from his mother.

'Why would you go for that, when you had Suzie?'

His mind moved to Suzanne, a childhood romance that had lasted a few months, but she had been his first love. Love was not the word for it after he met Ruth. With Ruth, he knew what that word really meant. The need to be with her at all times, the thought of her when she wasn't around, the niggling feeling that he would never be good enough for her. If only he could have given her all the things she wanted. But he knew he couldn't. They were too different, and she made him feel like nothing without ever meaning to. It was just her nature, the way people responded to her and looked at him like he was her pastime, someone who she would eventually tire of.

He thought of himself in that way even before the night of Karen's party, when he would watch her as she flitted about her friend's house, knowing she would never give him a second look. When she'd catch his glance, he'd look away, feeling like a creep, and knew she must be teasing him when she tried to give him a smile. But that night, when he saw her look away in disgust as that boy tried to come on to her, he saw she wasn't a girl anymore, he saw the woman she had become. And when she gave him that beckoning smile, he knew he would not have another chance.

He tried to change for her, he really did. Tried to mix things up a bit by taking her out to the beach, to the mountains. But she never seemed to be happy as much as he tried. So he let her do things without him, go out with that childish friend of hers. But what was he supposed to do in the meantime? Stay home and wait for her to return one night and tell him she was done with him? That she'd found someone else, someone more interesting, someone who wanted to take her to that damned city that she loved so much?

Then one evening when he was visiting Martin, he decided to stop in at his parents' house on his way home. His mother had been calling a lot lately complaining that his father was not feeling well and he thought it best to at least show some concern. When he arrived, he found Suzanne making his mother a cup of tea. Oliver was surprised to find out that she visited them quite often and he appreciated the gesture.

'Thanks,' he said to Suzanne, as he pulled out a packet of biscuits and spread them on a tray. 'You are really sweet to do this.'

'It's fine. I like coming here,' she replied with a smile and Oliver wondered why on earth she ever would.

When he placed his mother's cup on the table beside her, she leaned over and whispered, 'I knew you chose the wrong one.'

As Oliver was leaving, Suzanne decided it was time for her to leave as well. They said goodbye to his parents and she lingered next to Oliver's car.

'I love this thing,' she said, leaning her torso on it. 'I wish you had it when we were together.' She looked up at him under her lashes, her hair splayed around her face, and Oliver felt an impulse to take those locks in his hand and draw her to him. He didn't. 'I haven't ever been in it,' she continued.

'For one, I didn't have my licence when we were together.' He laughed and then he began to understand what she meant. 'Want to?' he asked, feeling a rush of nervousness.

'Yes!' she exclaimed, then her face fell. 'I have my car with me though. Think we can drop it off at my place first?'

Oliver followed Suzanne to her flat, a sense of excitement coursing through his body. He knew this wasn't a good thing, not for his marriage, but he didn't try to resist the feeling, just let it float past his brain. Suzanne parked her car in her driveway and Oliver waited in his car, still trying to ignore the little voice that told him to drive away. Suzanne in his car? How would he explain that to Ruth? Well, she never needed to know, and he wasn't doing anything wrong by talking to his old friend, he justified.

'Hey,' said Suzanne, her face at his window; Oliver rolled it down. 'Do you mind if I just get changed? You can wait inside.'

Again, Oliver knew this was the wrong move, but he nodded and got out of the car.

****

Oliver saw the light go on in Ruth's bedroom and panicked.

If she looked out the window or came out the door, she would see him immediately and he couldn't let her do that. He turned the key in the ignition and drove away.

Chapter 6

Ruth cried a lot in those first few weeks. She listened to Oliver's messages constantly, but refused to answer the phone, waiting for whoever it was that called to begin speaking before she picked it up. And there were many calls, from her father, mother, Karen and even her sister, who kindly asked if she needed anything. But she knew that Patty only wanted to gloat; she wasn't the one with the failed marriage and she finally had one up on Ruth.

Ruth didn't need anything. She just wanted Oliver back. She missed him so much, she kept a pillow next to her all night, trying to convince herself that he was there with her. She spent the days at work in a trance and when she got home, she sat around eating take-away food or leftovers with a blanket around her, in front of the television. She sat by the phone almost all the time, willing it to ring and trying not to be tempted to use it to call him.

In late July, three months later, she had an unexpected visitor. Marielle, a friend from university, knocked on Ruth's door. It was odd because Ruth had never considered herself close to Marielle, even though they had friends in common, albeit friends she didn't see anymore. Ruth always viewed Marielle as a little snobbish, someone who didn't have time for the common folk, such as her.

'Can I come in?' Marielle stood in the cold evening, shivering, as Ruth just stared at her, wide-eyed.

She was already in her pyjamas even though it was only six in the evening, her McDonald's meal on the lounge room table, half eaten. She opened the door wider and swallowed the fries still in her mouth. She led Marielle to the lounge room and quickly began to clear up the mess that was her flat these days. She realised there was no hope, shrugged her shoulders and sighed.

'Can I get you something?' Ruth placed herself on the armchair, while Marielle sat on the edge of the small sofa, leaning her large case on the table in front of her. She wasn't sure what Marielle wanted, so didn't quite know what to say.

'No, no, thanks.' Marielle looked around her and following Marielle's gaze, Ruth's face flushed. 'I, well, I was wondering if you were busy.' She saw Ruth's blank expression and continued. 'It's just that, well, I needed a worker, a person to help me with some of the graphic design work. I remembered that you were top of our class.'

Ruth was surprised and clearly, it showed. She looked at this young woman with her fluffy jacket, her legs stylishly crossed, her back very straight and her eyes, a silvery grey, lined with thick mascara, and wondered what on earth made her think of Ruth.

'Well, are you working?'

Ruth nodded, thinking of the dreary bank job, where she trudged without enthusiasm every morning. 'I'm not fond of it.' She shrugged again and smiled.

'I'm starting up a company with a couple of others. It's called Mari,' she said with a wry smile. 'Evan from uni and another investor. It won't pay a lot, at least not at the beginning, but I already have a couple of clients.'

Marielle opened a large folder and extracted a brochure. She spread it out on the table and Ruth looked at it, trying to discern what exactly it was supposed to be advertising. She scrunched up her nose in repugnance and then chuckled in embarrassment.

Marielle laughed out loud. 'Well, yes, that's the problem. We have some good people, but none of us have the finishing touch. And I guess that's when I thought of you.'

Ruth was working for Marielle by the next week, having given her notice to the bank the next day. The excitement of something new, the busyness of the moment, became a welcome distraction for her and soon she made it through more than a few hours without the temptation to call Oliver.

The betrayal though, was another matter. She wanted to know why; what hadn't she done that pleased him and what had she done that hadn't? She tried to be the wife he wanted, so much so that she felt she'd lost a part of who she was. When her father asked her to go to a football match with him, as they used to, she felt no inclination, whereas in the past he wouldn't even have finished the question when she was already getting her jersey on.

When Karen came over and wanted to whisk her off to the new nightclub on Bourke Street, she preferred to stay at home watching a movie, wrapped in a blanket.

Ruth also found herself complaining a lot. She knew she was being annoying, but she couldn't help herself. It wasn't who she was and she knew it but she just wanted to scream sometimes. She couldn't fathom what had gone so horribly wrong.

'Maybe I should talk to him?' Ruth asked Karen as she sipped on wine which was becoming an everyday feature of her evenings.

It was a Friday evening, the last day of Ruth's bank job, and she came straight home, refusing to go to happy hour even though her colleagues at the bank insisted she should farewell her old job with a celebratory drink. Some envied her position, being able to up and go to something newer, more exciting, something that was interesting to her and matched her skill set, and Ruth wondered why she hadn't thought to leave earlier. But she turned them down and instead Karen had shown up, a bottle of wine in hand, with the intention of going out for a night on the town. Ruth had rained on her parade and with an exasperated sigh, Karen had poured the wine and had sat herself on the sofa, while Ruth snuggled into Oliver's chair.

'Maybe you should just move on,' Karen replied, her tone suggesting that she was already bored with where this was going.

Ruth sensed it immediately. 'I'm sorry if my life is irritating to you,' she said curtly.

'Ruth.' Karen sat up and leaned towards her, her expression serious. 'It's been three months. You have a new job, something exciting to do now, something that you can actually love. This should be your turning point, at least.'

Ruth teared up. 'You don't understand.'

Karen put her glass on the table. 'Okay, maybe the truth will hurt, but you need to hear it.'

Ruth looked up, wide-eyed, unsure of where this was going. Karen had been her rock through these awful months.

'Oliver has moved on. Yes, with that skank. I think we all knew that was going to happen.' She looked at Ruth for any signs of panic. Ruth stared, willing her to go on, enjoying the pain she felt with each word Karen threw at her. 'Well, they belong together. I know I sound like your dad, but he's right. That spineless weakling was not the man for you. He never was. He tried to break your spirit and from what I am witnessing right now, he damn well succeeded.'

'You thought this? All this time?'

Karen sighed. 'What do you want me to say, Ruth? You were enamoured.' She rolled her eyes. 'Why, I will never understand. He was never your type anyway.'

'But why didn't you say …'

'What was I to say when you were making wedding plans the day you met him?'

'But as my friend, I feel …'

'Oh, enough about how you frickin' feel!' Karen got off the

sofa and began to put on her shoes.

Ruth couldn't understand why her friend was angry with her. 'Karen!'

'Stop wallowing. I … we've all had enough. You've become a hermit; you became everything he wanted you to be and then he left you to go to the woman he should have been with in the first place.' Ruth felt a tear sting her cheek and Karen softened. 'I'm just saying that you've lost who you are, who you used to be. Now it's time to get that girl back before you lose even more.'

Ruth watched in silence as Karen picked up her bag from the dining table. She came over and planted a kiss on top of her head.

'I'm sorry,' she said as she headed to the door, where she turned back to Ruth. 'Do you even know about what's going on in *my* life right now?' A tear rolled down her face.

'What …' Ruth began to rise from her seat.

Karen shook her head. 'Never mind,' she said and walked out.

Ruth drank the rest of the bottle of wine, which was still quite full when Karen left. She looked at pictures of Oliver and her that were still strewn around the place. She turned on the music, listened to the crooning love songs, her heart breaking as she pored over each picture, loving and hating Oliver in equal measure.

When she woke the next morning, her breath smelled like something had died in her mouth and her eyes felt like they were glued together. The tears, the wine and her pining had certainly taken their toll. But this was not a new experience. In fact, she felt like this almost every day, and realised how one night of alcohol in the early days of their break-up had become a nasty habit.

As much as her mind and body resisted, she jumped into the shower, feeling the cold spindles of the water shake her nerves. She dressed and downed a glass of green juice her mother kept pestering her to drink. It tasted like death, but she knew she needed something to pep her up; she had a long day ahead—in fact, a few long days.

Turning on the morning music on the television to full blast, she set about cleaning her flat and ridding herself of Oliver. She knew that at some stage, she would bump into him again, considering the proximity of his parents' house to hers. But while she didn't have to, she decided it was best not to see him. She packed up all the photos, including the giant wedding print that hung in the hallway, some even still in their frames, and threw them into large garbage bags. Little things of his he'd left behind, his cufflinks and tweezers, she also threw out.

'Well, he hasn't needed them in three months, so I guess they can just go,' she justified, a little smile appearing as she dropped his favourite embossed handkerchiefs in the plastic bag. 'Shouldn't have left them here if you wanted them.'

It was noon by the time Ruth looked around her flat, admiring her handiwork. She had rearranged the place, as little as it was, and had dragged Oliver's armchair onto the sidewalk, hoping someone would want it. As it happened, it was gone by the time Ruth emerged from her flat a couple of hours later. But now she smiled, the sense of emptiness that had taken over her now slowing filling with hope.

She wished she had a bottle of wine to celebrate her new mood and was then glad the fridge was empty. Ruth left the music on and sat on the doorstep, where the sun was shining brightly, an unusually warm breeze wafting by, carrying with it the smell of honey. She inhaled deeply and looked to the skies and breathed.

Chapter 7

2008

The bed was warm and Ruth patted the side on which Paul usually slept, sniffing and trying to keep her sense of calm. She couldn't lose it again, not like the last time with Terrence. She had to be strong this time. She had to let him go, as much as it hurt. It really seemed that she had it this time, that Paul was the one. He was so perfect for her, just so …

Images of Terrence jumped to her mind. Terrence who she had fallen for, so very hard. Terrence with his wavy locks of hair so black it looked fake, his straight mouth and chiselled jaw and eyes so blue, Ruth felt she was swimming in them every time he looked at her.

Terrence had taken her by surprise, coming into her life just a few months after Oliver had departed from it. Ruth had begun her new job which had taken her mind off her husband and she even began the process of applying for a divorce, determined to set a new path for herself. But she thought she still wasn't over Oliver, when there he was, Terrence, leaning an elbow on the bar in Boards, the nightclub she and Karen had begun frequenting, his eyes boring into hers, his lips twisted in a playful smile. Karen, seeing Ruth interested in a guy for the first time in a long time, nudged her, raising her eyebrows towards him as she did, a wicked grin on her lips.

'He's cute,' she said.

Ruth felt her cheeks grow warm. 'Stop it,' she said with a mock frown. But she had already noticed the intensity of his gaze.

'Smile back,' said Karen. Then she strolled away with a wink.

It didn't take more than another glance his way for Terrence to saunter over. Ruth felt the glow in her cheeks begin to burn and clutched tightly to the glass of vodka that stood in front of her.

'Having a good time?' His voice felt like a soothing wine and Ruth sensed the warmth flush into her belly.

'I am now,' Ruth said cheekily, feeling her old self burst back into her body.

'I have the urge to kiss you,' he said, not smiling anymore, and Ruth's legs wanted to give way as he looked at her with piercing eyes.

'What's stopping you?' Ruth said, letting Terrence move towards her and take her in his arms. He grazed her lips lightly and she closed her eyes.

Ruth was smitten. This time it was quicker than the first, and it was only a week later when she wondered what she ever saw in Oliver, not that she stopped to think of much else when Terrence was around. He moved in less than a month later, bringing along his boxes and boxes of paperwork, and Ruth was glad she had rid herself of Oliver's armchair that had taken up so much space. Her little flat was cramped again and Ruth was comforted by it.

'You don't mind moving in together so quickly do you?' he asked, as Ruth pushed together the desk and the bookshelf to make room for his filing cabinet.

'Not at all.' She laughed. 'What a silly question.'

'Are you able to make a bit of space on that bookcase? I have to fit these somewhere too.' He lifted a cardboard box with manila folders sticking out of the top and placed it on the desk.

'Of course,' she said, leaning over and pecking him on his cheek.

'Maybe that can wait,' he murmured, drawing her to him and pulling her to the floor.

Terrence was a lawyer and nearly ten years older than Ruth and she wondered whether the age gap had been the attraction. He knew what he was doing and was masterful in every way, taking her to bed almost immediately, and it was hard not to fault Oliver's inexperience in comparison. Terrence was also a social being, like Ruth, charming everyone he met, including her father, who seemed almost intimidated by this man who had unbroken his daughter's heart. He wined and dined her, taking her on interstate trips on the weekends and sometimes even during the week, which Marielle allowed, as long as she took her work with her.

Business for the fledgling company was slow while it was still building a client base, and Marielle had been impressed with the standard of Ruth's work. It was already wooing potential clients in the few months she had been there and Marielle was a dream boss, attentive to her needs, but giving her plenty of room for trial and error.

Ruth's job also gave her plenty of flexibility, with the opportunity to work from home when she couldn't be on-site, which suited her relationship with Terrence just fine. Sometimes, when Terrence worked at home, Ruth called in to work, gathered her tasks for the day, and they spent the day together working on their own projects, finding time to snuggle, grab a coffee at the corner café and make love when the mood hit them.

Karen was glad that Ruth was happy, even though she had dramas of her own. Her parents had been talking divorce and even though Karen was old enough to accept it, she found it hard to believe that two people who had spent their lives together could stop loving one another.

'I think Dad is seeing someone else,' said Karen dully, not sounding completely surprised.

'Why would you say that?' Ruth was taken aback at Karen's candour.

'I don't know for sure, but I know Mum thinks so.'

Ruth's thoughts went to Oliver. Were all men lousy cheating bastards? Her father's face flashed in her mind but she dismissed the thought before it could lodge itself in her brain. 'How are you feeling about it? Should we hunt her down and rip her hair out?' Ruth knew the best way to distract Karen was to make her laugh.

'Yeah.' Karen's eyes lit up. 'Stalk her and maybe scare her?'

Ruth laughed. She was now in a good head space and was glad she could be there for her friend in her time of need as Karen had been for her, but she did worry about Karen. She had been miserable lately, her fling with Rob ending in disaster. She really thought she loved him and it would last, but the moment Karen began to envision a future with him, Rob had just left. No conversation, no call. Just a text to tell her it was over without any real reason. She didn't even reply to it, she was so stunned, but Karen was too nice and too giving and people walked all over her. Ruth wanted to scream at her sometimes, but she knew that Karen was content with herself and she could live with herself knowing she did the right thing, even if it did hurt her. She admired her friend who moped for exactly two days and then straightened her shoulders to get on with her life.

Now it was Ruth who was again happy, but she couldn't escape the feeling that Karen was not terribly fond of Terrence. It wasn't anything she said or how she acted when he was around, but she knew her friend well.

'What do you think of Terrence?' Ruth broached the topic one evening when Terrence was out with his friends, which happened quite often.

'He's made you happy.' Karen laughed. 'He's practically

your saviour!'

'Well, no. That's not fair. You are!'

Karen giggled. 'Good answer.'

'But really. You haven't seemed to … warm up to him.'

'He's fine. Handsome, smart, certainly keeps you on your toes.' Karen shrugged, looking like she didn't want to continue on this trajectory.

Ruth didn't want to let it go. 'But remember when you told me that you had some misgivings about Oliver in the beginning. You didn't tell me until it was too late.' She saw Karen start and quickly continued. 'I'm not saying it's your fault, nothing like that, but you seem to have an instinct, even through high school. I just want to know what you think.'

'Would you have done anything differently if I had said what I felt? You were in love, and what do I know anyway? Look how things turned out for me and Rob.' Karen sighed. 'As for Terrence, I don't know him too well, just be …' She paused. 'His friend Pete is nice,' she said with a wink, and grinned, her eyes lighting up.

Ruth laughed. 'Yes, I think it's about time you two stopped flirting and did something about your feelings. It's getting quite obvious, you know.' Ruth knew Karen was changing the subject but she realised she didn't want to hear anything bad about Terrence. It was too late; she was already in love.

She ignored the misgivings she herself had had lately and tried to look past the fact that Terrence had left his girlfriend for Ruth, moving from her place directly into Ruth's. She ignored the calls that came to the house, his ex-girlfriend, Layla, having discovered her phone number. At first, Ruth was flattered and chose to ignore the fact that Terrence had done to Layla what Oliver had done to her. When Layla left obscene messages, Ruth disconnected the machine, but was a little troubled when Terrence laughed about it.

'She's just obsessed,' he said. 'That's what was so annoying about Layla, that she just didn't get it, but she was a great lay … get it, lay, as in *Lay*la.' He laughed heartily at his joke and Ruth humoured him by chuckling lightly, but she wondered at his lack of concern or regret as well as his dark humour about someone he had been with for such a long time—three years, in fact—someone he must have cared about very deeply, at least at some stage. However, Ruth was determined not to sabotage her happiness. Terrence was fun-loving, liked to take her out, spoiled her with gifts and gave her space to be herself. She was finally discovering what it was like to be herself again and she was enjoying it. She called the shots on her life now—at least that's what she thought—and it was a heady feeling after the drudgery of life with Oliver.

'You are the best thing that's happened to me,' he would tell her, while he showered her with little kisses that began at her forehead and ended at her knees, which would be trembling when he got to them.

Ruth felt like the most special person in the world when he looked at her and she would sometimes stare at his beauty, taking in the curve of his cheekbones, the little goatee that was beginning to form, the lick of hair that fell over his eye as he intently studied his files. At night she lay in bed, gazing at his sleeping form, turned away from her, and she would reach out and lightly touch his back, a melancholy enveloping her. Somehow, she knew it wouldn't last.

It began with a mysterious wallet Ruth found in Terrence's car, a slick, red BMW, not more than three months after he moved in with her.

'Whose is this?' she asked, plucking it from beneath her shoe. She had stepped on it as she hopped into his car on their way to dinner.

Terrence looked over to her and took it. Without even looking into it, he flicked it into the back seat. 'Ruby's, I think. A client of mine. I had to drop her home after the meeting last night.'

'Oh.' Ruth reached for it, but Terrence grabbed her hand and squeezed it.

'Don't worry about it, I'll drop it to her tomorrow.' He leaned over and kissed her.

Ruth dismissed the incident until two days later when a woman phoned the flat.

'Is Terry home?' said the voice.

'No, he's not. Who's calling?' Ruth was used to clients calling for Terrence, but not that many, if any, called him Terry.

'It's, er … Ruby.'

'Oh, hello, Ruby,' Ruth replied. 'He's not at home, but he was going to bring you back your purse. You left it in the car.'

'My what?' The voice stopped. 'Oh, yes, of course. Sure,

thank you.' The line went dead.

Ruth stared into the receiver, wondering about the call. It was strange. Shouldn't Ruby have known that her purse was left in the car? In fact, wasn't Terrence meant to have returned it the day before? It didn't add up.

Ruth's spine twitched in worry and her ears began to tingle, as a flash of Oliver came to her mind. She shook her head, dismissing any suspicion before it took hold of her.

But there were other signs too, things she purposely dismissed. Ruth knew something wasn't quite right, but she was too afraid to lose Terrence so she kept quiet about his late nights, the scent of Lilies, a perfume she never used, and his constant state of lethargy. It seemed not long ago that he had barely walked through the door when he practically mauled her and he now barely kissed her and walked straight into the bedroom, sometimes without even having dinner, mumbling something about having to eat out with clients. And when she got there, sometimes a few minutes after he did, he was already tucked into bed and snoring.

She could see the signs but couldn't let him go. She had never felt this kind of animal attraction, this need to be near him at all times; 'obsession' was what Karen had called it. Karen, who was just beginning a relationship with Pete, Terrence's best friend, a mature and gentle young man, quite the opposite of the outgoing Terrence, was taking it slowly and was yet to understand how Ruth felt. She was on cloud nine, and Ruth thought her friend never seemed happier. Ruth didn't want to rain on Karen's parade by discussing her suspicions with her, so she kept them to herself, trying to banish the thought, feeling that she was perhaps being too paranoid after Oliver's deception.

But for Ruth, this was a love different to how she felt for Oliver. Sure, she had been attracted to Oliver, but she now thought that perhaps it was because of his calm nature, that he balanced her own immature one.

'I don't quite know how to explain it,' she said to Karen one afternoon when both friends were free, which these days didn't happen very often. 'It's so different from what I had with Oliver.'

'I thought we were done talking about him,' said Karen.

'I know, I know.' Ruth bit her lip and wondered whether Karen would talk to Pete about their conversations, but she needed to talk to someone about the crazy things going on inside her. 'But this is different. With Terrence, we were like animals, wild, uninhibited.' She thought about last night, when she had waited for him to finish his work and he hadn't come to bed. She had crept into the lounge to find him asleep on the sofa, tucked in as though it were intentional—he hadn't just dozed off. Not long ago, their lovemaking had been fierce, leaving them both panting and sated. Now he was avoiding her?

'Too much information,' said Karen.

'No,' laughed Ruth. 'I'm not getting into details, it's just that …'

'What is it, Ruth?' Karen touched her friend's hand, encouraging her on.

'Maybe it's me.'

'To me, you are the girl who called the shots.' Karen turned Ruth's gloomy face to hers. 'You were the one with all the spirit, the confident person people wished they could be. I wished I could be you.'

'I don't feel it,' said Ruth. 'I don't think I ever thought that.'

'That's what made you that way. You just were. You just did. And no one told you otherwise.'

'But I feel like this person who turns into what her man wants her to be.'

'What does Terrence want you to be?'

'I don't know. That's just it. I wish I did.'

'And you would become that person?'

'Oh Karen, I don't know anymore. I'm just so …' She paused, trying to find the right word. 'Suspicious? Mad? Crazy?'

'I don't know what to tell you, Ruth. Just don't become something you're not again.'

Ruth sighed. 'I don't know what I am anymore.'

So when Ruth began to suspect something was going on with Terrence, she at first thought that she was being unnecessarily suspicious, but she was also not going to sit quietly and just take it as she had before. She had been burned before and she wanted the truth, but she knew she wasn't ready for it. She really believed she could turn him into the person she wanted him to be, someone who was faithful, who loved only her. She battled with herself, changing her perception on the situation from day to day, depending on the mood she was in and on what Terrence had said and done. Perhaps if she let him get it out of his system, he would choose her. And she wanted to be chosen, even if the nagging doubts kept creeping in whenever he looked at her, and more, when he didn't.

Ruth couldn't understand how he didn't love her when he seemed so possessive and jealous of Ruth's friends and acquaintances. She knew he loved having her on his arm when they went out and took every chance to compliment her on how she looked, but he would hold on to her hand tightly and if any man looked her way, he would stare at them fiercely or drag Ruth home. Ruth enjoyed this protective behaviour, or at least that's what Terrence called it—'There are a lot of lousy guys out there,' he'd say and Ruth wondered whether he was one of them.

One evening, after they had had dinner and Terrence was lying back on the sofa, reading through his never-ending mountain of paperwork, Ruth was discussing the new project that Marielle and Paul, Marielle's new designer, were working on.

'… and the width just didn't fit, no matter what we did. But Paul was the saviour,' she said, explaining the format of a design. 'He is a genius, and his photography! I saw this whole catalogue of work on his computer.' She laughed. 'But he didn't want me to see it, so he closed it when he got back to his desk. I was so embarrassed. Like I was snooping! But Marielle was right to …'

'Who is this Paul?' Terrence was sitting up now.

'I told you about him. Marielle hired him at the same time as me.' She cocked her head. 'Actually, a bit after.'

'What's he like?'

'I don't know. Nice, I guess.' Ruth had not really thought about Paul. He was nice, good-looking … She saw the interest in Terrence pique, and she felt a warm glow. 'He's from Brighton, he used to be a photographer …'

'You know a lot about him,' Terrence said, frowning above his glasses.

'I guess I have to. I helped Marielle select him.'

'So you chose him?' Terrence was frowning.

'Yes, he was the best candidate for the job. His portfolio was amazing.'

'There were no women applicants?'

'There were. He was just better qualified.' Ruth was liking this game now. *If he didn't love me, he wouldn't be jealous,* she thought.

'Has he got a wife?'

'No, but I don't have a husband either. What's that got to do with anything?'

Terrence turned back to his work, his eyebrows still locked together. 'I just don't like it,' he mumbled, and Ruth felt her heart warm again.

Ruth tried not to think about their problems and she thought that it was, in fact, her problem, her suspicious mind. There may not be anything going on at all. Maybe Terrence was as happy with her as she was with him. She thought that perhaps she was again trying to sabotage something that could be really good. She was in love with Terrence and didn't want to ever think about them not being together. She hung on to his every word, waited for him to come home from work, chewing on her nails until he did, and answered every phone call with bated breath.

But she knew it was falling down around her and she couldn't sit and pretend nothing was going on. The nonchalance, the time spent away from the flat, the interstate trips to which she was not invited anymore … They got into terrible arguments, when they would end up making love passionately, so much so that she began those fights just so she could be close to him, to feel his hands caress her body, to feel loved once more. The problem was, it was taking a toll on her brain. She thought about him constantly, called him incessantly, and felt alone and desperate when he wasn't with her. But now, she couldn't even talk to Karen about it. She couldn't talk to anyone about how things were. She was hanging on by a thread and knew something had to give.

Chapter 8

The night Terrence left, Ruth almost took her life.

He came home late after a boozy night with his friends, having secured a major deal at work, and Ruth had been looking out the window, waiting for his car to turn into the driveway. He hadn't called to let her know he would be late as he usually did, and Ruth had considered going out to find him when Karen called and asked her if she would like to go into the city to watch a movie. But she didn't want Terrence to come home and find her not there, so she refused, choosing to wait alone in the dark. She looked at the clock on the wall every few minutes and the smell of the fresh pasta she had baked some time earlier, which was left untouched, had already faded. The feeling was all too familiar to her.

She pounced before he even stepped into the flat, her ears burning, her fists already clenched for action.

'To celebrate,' he said, when Ruth asked why he had taken

so long.

'I waited for you,' she said, hating her own nagging voice, but powerless to stop it. 'It's past twelve.'

Terrence threw his briefcase on the sofa and raised his eyebrows in annoyance. She could see his jaw begin to clench.

'Really?' she said, preparing for another fight.

'Ruth, I'm tired. I just want to go to bed.'

'Maybe you already were. Just in some other woman's bed.'

'Ruth, enough.' Terrence continued on his way to the bedroom.

Ruth was behind him. 'You smell like her. What's her name? Who is she?'

'Stop already!'

Ruth could see him taking the bait and continued. 'Is it Samantha? I've seen the way she …'

'Ruth, stop it!'

He was taking off his shoes and Ruth knelt on the floor, facing him, looking into his face that bore annoyance, his gaze directed at the lamp that sat on the side table. She took his hands and stroked them. 'Just tell me. Don't do this to me.'

Terrence looked into her eyes and for a moment, she saw the guilt. He looked away again.

'It's true?'

'Ruth,' he said in a calm way, almost too calm, almost like Oliver.

Before she knew it she was begging. 'You can't do this to me.

Not again.'

Terrence squeezed her trembling hands. 'Maybe it's time.'

'Time? Time for what?' Ruth could feel her heart jump.

'To … to finish up.'

'You mean … us?'

Terrence nodded.

'No, don't say that. Just don't!' She shut her eyes tight, the world closing in on her. She heard him sigh.

'I don't want to fight anymore. I'm sick of it. Every day, every night, that's all we do.' His voice was resigned. He didn't want to argue and to Ruth this was worse.

'Don't you love me?' Her voice was small.

Terrence didn't answer and Ruth opened her eyes. She saw pity in his face, not love.

'Then go!' She jerked herself off the floor. 'Get the hell out.' Ruth knew she didn't mean it, she just wanted him to change his mind, make him think he was losing her and realise what that meant, what *she* meant, to him.

'If that's what you want,' he said quietly and got off the bed.

Ruth stormed out of the room and threw herself down on the sofa in the lounge room, hugging a cushion. A flood of thoughts entered her mind and she couldn't quite sort them out. All she knew was that he wasn't following her and her heart began to thump wildly at the possibility ... Maybe he was really leaving. She could hear things being moved around in the bedroom and she couldn't feel her throat, it seemed to be stuck. She stayed frozen for a few minutes and rushed back into the bedroom, where she found Terrence packing a duffle bag, the same one he had brought with him when he moved in.

'No. Don't go. I didn't mean it,' she pleaded. 'We can work it out.' She followed him from place to place as he took his shirts off the hangers and put them into his bag. He turned without a word and went into the lounge room. Ruth grabbed his arm and clung to him, trying to grab his bag, clutching at the shirts that were hanging out, taking them out of his bag and throwing them on the floor. He shook her off, but she still followed, still grabbing at things and throwing them away from him, all the while begging him to stay.

'Stop it, Ruth,' he finally said, stopping to face her.

'Just don't go. We can talk about it tomorrow. Let's make love. Like we always do. This is just another fight.' Ruth reached out for his neck, but Terrence ducked out of her embrace.

'No more, Ruth.'

'I hate you!' she screamed. 'You hear me?'

Terrence looked straight into her eyes. 'I'm not in love with you anymore.'

Ruth drew back in shock, unable to find words. She didn't expect him to just say it. So plainly.

'It's over,' he said, and turned away, heading to the door. 'I'll get the rest of my stuff later.'

'Who is it?' she demanded. 'I deserve at least that.'

He stopped but didn't turn to face her, his shoulders slumping. 'If you need to know, yes, there is someone else.'

Ruth felt her body go rigid. 'Who? And I don't care!' She just wanted him to stay. They could work it all out later when he realised it was really Ruth he loved.

'Ruth, please!'

'Terrence, don't do this.' She lunged at him again, clinging to his lapel, and stared into his eyes, as he averted hers. He tried to shake her off. 'Please. Stay with me. Don't leave, please.' She could hear herself and was disgusted with her begging, but all she could think about was keeping him there. He would realise he loved her and this would just be one of their usual fights.

He squeezed her quickly and extracted himself from her grip. 'Bye, Ruth.'

'Don't go.' She tried to grab onto him again, but with a shove, he pushed her backwards, driving her to the floor, and strode out.

A strange yet familiar feeling was back at her. She stayed on the floor for how long she didn't know, sobbing loudly, and didn't move until she felt her throat close from thirst. She shut her eyes and willed herself to sleep, to turn this into a dream, some nightmarish fantasy. No, this wasn't like it was with Oliver at all. With Oliver, she didn't want to die. Now, she did.

She lifted herself up slowly and dragged herself to the fridge, from which she grabbed a bottle of wine and made her way slowly to the bedroom. The room was spinning and she collapsed on Terrence's side of the bed and closed her eyes. She wished she could just sleep it all away, but sleep was eluding her. She sat up suddenly and opened the drawer of the side table where Terrence kept his sleeping pills. She had wondered why he needed them when he slept so peacefully, but never wanted to ask about them, to embarrass him about something that was not her business. She rustled around in the drawer, moving things about, hoping he hadn't taken them with him. And then there they were, the little grey pills, inside a bottle with his name on it. She sat on the edge of the bed now and threw the whole lot down her throat, following them with half the bottle of wine. Then she lay back on the bed to let whatever would happen, happen.

Terrence

There was no one else, not really, no one that he loved anyway. Ruth had been right though. There had been others; he knew it couldn't last with Ruth, but a part of him felt that maybe it could, maybe she'd be the one. Very soon after moving in with her, he knew she wasn't. But it just worked, the two of them enjoying life together, going out, making love, socialising …

He banged his fist on the steering wheel. He never wanted to hurt her, but it was just never the right time to leave. He wished he could have been a one-woman man, especially with Ruth. He had left Layla for her, Layla who had also given him everything. He hurt Layla badly and he knew it. He loved Layla, at least as much as he could love somebody else.

He thought he loved Ruth: she was fun, fantastic to look at, a great partner to show off to his friends and colleagues. She was so easy-going, so casual about life, didn't force the issue of marriage as Layla did. He wondered if it were him and before he could answer himself, he shrugged off the thought. He just didn't expect her to fall in love with him so quickly and he knew he was scared when he began to fall for her.

But in the end, they were all the same. Needy.

He hoped she was okay, again wishing he could have been happy with her. She was a cool girl, and they got along really well. Sure, they fought a lot, but in the end, they always made up, and in spectacular fashion. He knew it wasn't the sex, she knew her way around a bed, but he knew she had passed her use-by date. He hated to think of it like that, but it had been that way for as long as he could remember. He needed his independence and as hard as it was to leave them, as much as he hated these scenes, he went into the next relationship hoping that woman would be the one that would make him want to stay. He wondered if he would ever find her.

Now as she lay on the cool bed, a warm breeze gently

floating in through the open window, she was glad she didn't give the bastard her life that night.

After resting herself on the soft pillows, waiting for the pills to do their job, images of her father floated through her mind, a grin that spread all over his face, then her mother, that warm smile that creased her forehead, her friend Karen, throwing her head back with a laugh … She sat up with a start. What was she thinking? What was she doing? It was less than a minute later when she found herself bolting to the bathroom, leaving chunks of vomit along the way.

Oh, she paid dearly, her mind and body in knots for weeks afterwards, but she survived. She would again. She'd never let them take her again. She felt a tear begin to well and angrily brushed it away. She wouldn't give them any more tears, she couldn't.

Not even Paul.

Chapter 9

Ruth met Paul before Terrence came into her life. As she had told Terrence, she helped Marielle select him to manage the copywriting of the advertisements, but his eye for photography meant that he also helped Ruth with formatting work at Mari. Paul was a man her own age, serious and playful at the same time, whom Ruth felt quite at ease with. Still in a funk after Oliver had left, Ruth didn't have any interest in another man at the time she met him, although she did appreciate that he was good-looking and self-assured, but not cocky.

At this time, Ruth's new job was indeed a welcome distraction after Oliver's betrayal, as Karen had said it would be. Ruth was determined to repair her friendship with Karen and also set about sorting out her heart.

She dived headlong into her work, finding satisfaction from doing what she loved—creating. Marielle allowed her artistic control over the design process, and Ruth and Paul worked closely together to create advertising campaigns that they added to their portfolio. Marielle did not work with them in the office, which at the beginning was a little shed in the backyard of Marielle's parents' home.

Ruth found Paul to be fun and easy-going, so much so that there were times she almost admitted to him her despondent state of mind when she found her thoughts straying to Oliver. But she was trying to make an effort not to think or talk about him and it seemed to be working. The more she banished him from her mind, the less she wallowed in self-pity. But in those moments of self-indulgence, when Ruth gazed out the window feeling sorry for herself, she caught Paul's troubled face staring at her. When she turned to him, he'd look away guiltily as if he had been caught doing something wrong, and Ruth wondered if he sensed her gloom.

Paul's own life was not something he talked about either, both of them understanding that theirs was to be a professional relationship and even though they talked about their childhoods and other random events, significant others was not a topic they discussed. Nevertheless, Ruth found herself a little miffed when Paul mentioned leaving early one afternoon as he had to take his girlfriend, Moira, to a work party. Ruth wondered why her chest jumped and she felt a case of the green-eyed monster—she wasn't by nature a jealous person. She put it down to ego. Most men wanted to bed her, and Ruth had expected that Paul would be one of them, so the fact that he didn't make a move made him endearing, however rejected she felt about it. She caught herself admiring him, for his brain, his casual manner and his sense of humour, wishing she could meet a man such as this somewhere, sometime.

She found herself wanting to talk about him to Karen and did so on occasion.

'He is so talented and dishy.' Ruth's glazed eyes looked heavenward and she cleared her throat, quickly realising how it sounded. 'And we work well together.'

'Oh really!' Karen, who knew her friend too well, had raised her eyebrows in question and Ruth laughed it off.

'Well, you talk about workmates too!'

'Yes, but they're not attractive young men who I work this closely with!' Karen retorted.

'He makes me laugh, and I need that right now.'

'Uh-huh,' replied Karen, a smirk on her face.

In the second month, on a Monday, Ruth had come to work with her eyes red and swollen, and Paul asked her what the matter was.

'Nothing, I'm fine.' She moved past him to the kettle and turned it on. This morning was the first time she had seen Oliver since their breakup.

She had spent the night at Karen's house, both enjoying their favourite movie, *Beaches*, sipping on wine and crying through the film, trying to decide which character was which of the two of them.

'I'm Hillary,' said Karen. 'The reserved loyal friend, who is always there.'

'What does that make me?' said Ruth. 'The one who is married to her career?'

'Well, no, but you are the one who always has an audience. I'm the wind.' Karen smiled, her hands floating through the air.

'I want to be the wind,' retorted Ruth.

'Well, I guess you are too …' Karen stopped and let out a hearty laugh. 'Really, we want to be wind?'

Ruth laughed along, feeling better already. She had been feeling lonely and Karen suggested a girls' night to perk up her spirits. They stayed up late into the night, talking and laughing, and Ruth was slightly hungover when she awoke the next morning, cursing that it was a Monday.

'Should have done this on a Saturday or Friday,' she said to Karen as she sipped at the black coffee in front of her, her head in her hands.

'Well,' said Karen, nursing her own sore head. 'To be fair, it was a last-minute decision. But let's not do that again. Not on a Sunday night.'

'I know. But I had so much fun. I must call Paul and let him know I'll be a little late.'

Karen nodded and Ruth made the call, explaining that she would be coming in around midday. She still needed to go home, get changed and pick up her workbag. He told her to take her time and she was relieved that he was so understanding.

'I'll cover for you.' He laughed. 'Marielle's probably had a bender too. Her car isn't here. Seems I'm the only one without a life!' Ruth hoped Marielle would be just as forgiving.

As she got into her car, she looked into the rear-view mirror to reverse and there he was. Oliver, standing on the footpath, signalling for her to stop. Ruth's heart skipped a few beats and a lump of lead lodged itself in her throat, but she put the car in park and got out. She wished she looked a little more decent; her eyes were red, her hair was tied into a messy ponytail and she wore a large, baggy sweater. From the corner of her eye, she could see Karen come out and lean on the porch bannister, ever protective, ready to come to Ruth's rescue if necessary.

'Hi, Ruthy.' He smiled his lazy smile, one that she didn't find very attractive anymore. It just made her realise how boring he really was. Ruth hadn't seen him since the day she kicked him out of her life and her nerves were frazzled now, and not just from the over consumption of alcohol. But even through his composed smile, she could see he was just as nervous. He seemed surprised to find her there. *Well, my car should have given it away*, she thought.

'Hi. How are you?' Ruth smiled. She was determined to be mature about this. She knew it had to happen at some stage; she never really knew how she would react when it did.

'I'm okay,' he said. 'And you?'

'Yes, great,' she said. 'I've started working with a start-up. Doing something I love. It's going swimmingly.' She wanted to hit herself. *Swimmingly*, really! Wherever did she find that word in the recesses of her brain?

'I heard. You should be careful though. These things are everywhere—scams, they call them.'

Ruth felt the hair on the back of her neck bristle. The nerve of him. 'Well, I love it. I've got no commitments or anyone to answer to.' She wanted to slap him, but she also wanted to throw herself into his arms. She still missed him as much as she tried not to.

'No, that's not what I meant …'

'I have to go, I'm late for work.'

'Yeah, sure.' He leaned forward and gave her a quick hug.

When he released her, Ruth just stood there gaping at him.

'Do you think we could … I don't know, just catch up? Sometime?' He looked nervous again, his fingers tapping each other.

'I don't think it's a good idea.' Ruth wanted to say yes very badly.

'Not now, just whenever you're ready.'

'I have to go,' she muttered. 'See you, Oliver.' She rushed back into her car and drove, not allowing herself to look behind her, to her past.

'No looking back, don't look back,' she said to herself and then burst into tears.

By the time she arrived at her flat, Ruth was a blubbering mess. She took a long shower and considered not going in to work at all. She then realised that not only would she be letting Paul and

Marielle down, she would be allowing herself to be affected by Oliver again, and she had come so far. Or at least she thought.

Throwing on some make-up, trying to look as normal as she could, she headed off to work. Nevertheless, by the time she reached there, her mascara was smudged, her eyes red raw and her heart was breaking all over again. But by then she knew it wasn't Oliver that she wanted back, she was just reminded of how small she felt, how betrayed and broken her heart had been not so long ago.

Now, as she stirred the coffee, she could feel another lump settle into her throat and the urge to cry again.

'Want to talk about it?' Paul looked at her from the desk they shared.

Ruth shook her head, not trusting her voice.

'Well, let's get your mind off whatever it is,' he said, turning to the computer.

Ruth was grateful and took her seat by his side. His monitor already had the text and photographs ready to set out. It was a job for a small whitegoods company, an easy job that was just an income gatherer, and they weren't far off finishing it.

Ruth stared at the screen, her hand around the mug of coffee shaking. Paul glanced at it and moved his eyes away. As Ruth watched the screen, the images began to blur and she sniffed, trying to prevent her tears falling. She felt Paul's arm creep around her shoulders and let her head fall onto his chest. He stroked her hair while she sobbed uncontrollably, leaving mascara and tears on his white cotton shirt, which smelled of fresh detergent.

She stayed that way for a while, feeling his comforting embrace, and then he pulled her head up. 'If you don't want to talk about it, let's get out of here,' he said and grabbed her hand. 'Let's play hooky.'

Ruth had to laugh. 'I haven't heard that word from anyone, except my mum,' she said, and already began to feel brighter.

They went to Luna Park that afternoon, Paul leaving a note for Marielle, just in case she stopped in. Paul made her go on every ride there was and when it was getting to sundown, he took her to the beach across the road, where they sucked on iced sticks, watching the sailboats come in to dock. They didn't talk about anything too serious, just chatted about movies and music, something they both had very similar tastes in. He never once pushed her to tell him what was wrong and she didn't want him to know either; she knew she couldn't get emotionally involved with this man. She wanted him to be the one that cared for her as she was beginning to care for him and not complicate their friendship with unnecessary feelings of another kind.

Nevertheless, when they got back to the office to retrieve their cars, Ruth felt that she had fallen a little in love with him. But she knew it could never be, they had to maintain a professional relationship. She respected the fact that he had a significant other and never wanted to be the 'Suzanne' in any relationship.

When she got home that evening, the phone was ringing and for a terrified moment, Ruth thought it may be Oliver. It wasn't; it was Karen calling to see if Ruth was okay after seeing Oliver that morning. Ruth assured her she was and told Karen about her day with Paul. Karen aah-ed knowingly and Ruth felt herself blush, but she dismissed it, telling her that Paul had genuinely helped her to distract herself from the incident.

The next day, both Ruth and Paul went on with their work, albeit reliving the fun of the day before, laughing together about the little boy who had been left on the ride after the operator had packed up, and moaning about the massive traffic jam they'd been stuck in on the way home. It had certainly taken Ruth's mind off Oliver and given her hope that there were nice men out there and hopefully one day she would find hers.

'Thanks, I needed that,' she said, planting a kiss on his head.

'Anytime,' he replied softly, taking the hand that she rested on his shoulder and squeezing it lightly.

She tried for the next month to ignore the obviously mutual attraction and felt that Paul was doing the same, but their friendship was becoming important to her, and she didn't want to sabotage that. She really liked Paul and she hadn't had many friends of the opposite sex before. She just wished she wasn't attracted to him. Most mornings, she found herself at work earlier than she had to be, waiting for him to arrive, and there were times she had to remind herself to stop staring at him, his wavy brown hair that kept falling over his eyes and his bottom lip tucked into his mouth by his teeth as he focused on the computer screen. If he was aware of her scrutiny, he never let on, and Ruth, knowing that he had someone else, felt a tinge of jealousy towards that girl who got to run her hand through that hair and gaze into those amber eyes.

It was around this time that she had met Terrence and things changed for Ruth.

The three months that Ruth spent with Terrence were fraught with a range of emotions, and Ruth could not control how she acted or reacted to the people in her life. She found herself being short with Paul and distant towards him, so much so that it was too late when she realised that he had become different with her too. He refrained from their usual banter, focusing their discussions solely on their work, and Ruth, so lost in her own world of Terrence, didn't even notice.

Because Ruth spent so much time away from work, preferring to work at home or going off with Terrence on his trips, there developed an awkwardness between Paul and herself. But when her relationship with Terrence began to erode, Ruth wanted to turn to him for comfort or even just as someone who could take her mind off her problems, as he had done before. She knew it was selfish, but she really didn't want to discuss Terrence with anyone else, knowing that she was going down that path and falling into a slump again. She also felt it better not to talk about her personal life with Paul, realising how erratic and suspicious she sounded; for some reason, she wanted him to admire her, to think she was above all the pettiness that some women usually came with. Besides, she had never discussed anything so personal with him before and this had worked well for their relationship so far.

When Ruth realised how much it nearly cost her the day she swallowed those pills, she began to put all her energy into her work, trying to forget Terrence's existence. She found herself being irritable and finicky about details of work and began arguing with Paul more and more often, so much so that Marielle pulled her into the main house one morning to discuss the situation.

'Maybe it's time to keep work and play apart,' Marielle said, tapping the table with sharp red fingernails.

'What?' Ruth was startled. She had just pushed her own fingers into her coat pocket to hide her fingernails that were bitten to the quick.

'You and Paul.' Marielle crossed her long legs and leaned her elbow on her knees, looking Ruth in the eye.

'I still don't know what you mean,' Ruth said, a little intimidated by Marielle's steely gaze. But she always had been intimidated by this smart, stylish woman, who was, in fact, her peer.

'You know he's in love with you.' She leaned back and waved her hands about. 'And the way you two carry on, I get the feeling it's mutual.'

'No way!' Ruth retorted. 'As you know, I've just come out of a debilitating relationship and I can't even think about another man right now.' Ruth had to confide in Marielle about Terrence as she had taken a few days off after Terrence had left her. 'Besides, Paul has a girlfriend.'

'Oh, you don't know. Yes. Moira left him. Actually some time ago.'

'I didn't know that.'

'Yes, well … Anyway, I'm just saying that business and pleasure don't mix, especially as we work so closely together.'

'Well, I had no intentions with Paul. I still don't.'

'Okay,' Marielle stood up indicating the end of their conversation. 'Just ease up on him.'

'I'm sorry. I didn't realise I was upsetting him.'

'Oh, I don't know if you are, it just seems like you two are at loggerheads all the time, so …'

'It's me. I know it's me.' Ruth lowered her head, realising what she had been doing.

Marielle patted her on the shoulder and Ruth felt like a little child being chided. She didn't like it.

She walked slowly back into the shed, thinking of Paul and realising that he had indeed been subdued and off-handish. She shook her head at her own vanity; she had been so self-absorbed that she assumed it was all about her! She opened the door to find Paul taking a break, his feet up on the little chair, his head leaning back on the two-seat settee, his eyes closed. He looked as though he was asleep and Ruth felt a sliver of shame run through her. She sat by his side and he turned his head to look at her, a crease in his brow.

'I'm sorry,' she said.

'For what?' He sat up now and the crease deepened.

'Just the way I've been lately.' She tried to stop a tear that she felt fill her eye. 'I know we don't really talk about our lives, but after

Terrence, it's been hard to cope. I know I've been taking it out on you.'

'It's okay, I get it.'

Ruth placed her hand on his thigh and he jerked. She laughed. 'I'm not coming on to you, don't worry,' she said.

Paul grinned in embarrassment. 'I know you're not.'

'Anyway, I just want you to know I didn't realise how shitty I was being.' Ruth got up and went to the desk. She wanted to add, *I am here if you want to talk about Moira too*, but she felt that would be crossing a line.

Paul stretched and followed. 'No problem. Let's get to work.'

They resumed work and intermittently Ruth glanced his way to try to decipher any truth to what Marielle had said. No, it didn't seem like he felt anything for her apart from a good work partnership. Usually Ruth had good instincts about these things, but Paul seemed as normal as usual, so Ruth dismissed Marielle's warning. They could go back to being friends and Ruth smiled to herself; she could begin again to admire him from afar.

For the next few weeks, Ruth tried to keep herself focused on work. Marielle had moved them to a little warehouse, not far from Ruth's flat, a bigger place, with three desks, a bathroom and a kitchenette. Brand-new computers were bought, with high-tech programs installed, some of which they had to learn from scratch. She threw herself into her projects and realised how much she enjoyed her job, even the challenging tasks that had her glued to the computer screen late into the evening.

Paul and Ruth worked really well together by this stage, having gotten over their misunderstanding; they resumed their usual banter that helped the day go by in a much more pleasant manner. They played jokes on each other, laughed at stories of their lives and even talked a little about their lost loves. They went out for lunch breaks now, as there was a little café situated a block away from their office and it gave their tired eyes a rest from staring at the screens, which was how they were used to spending their break times.

'Moira was not the right one.' Paul smiled shyly, as he sipped on his long black. They had been lunching one afternoon and this came completely out of the blue. 'We met through mutual friends, but that's probably not the best way to go,' he said sheepishly. 'Now I try not to go out, so I don't have to bump into her.'

'I get it.' Ruth thought of Karen and Pete, Terrence's best friend, and she understood completely. On the weekends, she went out with Karen, who was now in a serious relationship with Pete, but Terrence's name at first was completely off limits. However, it was inevitable that it would come up every now and then and Ruth began to feel less angry each time she heard it. 'Did she break your heart?' Ruth was surprised at her boldness.

Paul frowned and looked into his coffee. 'I don't know exactly. I missed her at the beginning …'

'Why did you guys …?' Ruth stopped. 'Sorry, not my business.'

'It's fine. I don't really know. It was me, I guess. Not that she objected too much. After a few months, I think we both felt it had run its course.' He leaned forward and looked Ruth directly in the eyes, an expression on his face that she couldn't quite fathom. 'Sometimes you just know when you haven't found the right one.'

Ruth blushed and turned away from his stare. 'Sometimes it takes more than it just running its course.' She wondered if it really could be that easy for some people. She looked at her watch. 'Time to get back,' she said and stood up.

In the next few months, Ruth tried hard to ignore the burgeoning feelings she was having for Paul. She knew she had been attracted to him before, but continued to remind herself that it was not a good idea to get involved with him. It had been over six months since the end of Terrence, and Ruth felt she was well and truly over him, but she also wanted nothing more to do with men, at least for a while. She knew if she went to that place with Paul, it would be a rebound relationship, and she never wanted to hurt Paul like that. And anyway, he had never really suggested by his words or his behaviour that he felt anything more towards her than friendship and a good work partnership.

Besides, Ruth was having fun just being a girl and she went out often, exploring the city, going on overnight trips to wineries and spa centres with Karen and sometimes even by herself, where she met and befriended many interesting and some not-so-interesting people. She took a skiing trip with Karen, a holiday by herself to Fiji and spent her time off doing the things she used to love, like playing volleyball, accompanying her father to football games and visiting her parents on a more regular basis. She sometimes went out with Marielle and Paul, where she met exciting and not-so-exciting men, some of whom she kissed passionately and some of whom she saw a couple of times after. But Ruth knew she was still not ready to go further into a relationship. The scars of betrayal were deeply etched in her heart.

Chapter 10

It was one evening after a celebratory dinner, marking the anniversary of the opening of Mari, that Marielle, after getting very drunk, announced that she had a little crush on Paul when they first met.

They were all sitting on the balcony at a bar in the city overlooking the Yarra, where the light of the moon reflected on the water, concealing its usual colour of muck. It was a warm evening and little clouds were wafting slowly across the sky. *A night of romance,* Ruth had thought, wishing she had the romance that the evening offered. She sighed and looked to Marielle, who was chatting about something or other; Ruth had already lost track of what she was saying and tried to catch up. The place was beginning to empty and Ruth was ready to go home, having drunk a little too much, her head woozy.

'I thought you were a bit of a playboy,' Marielle slurred. 'Maybe why I hired you.' She giggled then stopped, realising what she'd said, realising who she was.

Ruth was stunned into sobriety. Marielle, the pristine

goddess, who held her head high and treated most people like commoners, was disclosing something of herself so intimate. And in front of Paul!

Paul shifted uncomfortably, laughed nervously, and looked towards the river, a funny little grin sitting on his lips.

'Really?' Ruth wanted to know more, but Marielle, recognising her gaffe, laughed and waved her hands about in dismissal. 'I want to know more,' said Ruth boldly, throwing caution to the wind. *Blame it on the alcohol,* she thought. *Marielle will sure have to.*

'Well,' said Marielle, standing up in a wobble. She held on to her chair. 'It's time I had a sleep,' she said. 'Jacob should be here by now.' She craned her neck to look over the crowd for her boyfriend, whom Ruth and Paul had met once when he dropped Marielle to work one morning.

'You can't leave like this,' said Ruth, reaching out to steady her.

'I'm fine,' she said. 'I see Jacob there now.' She gestured to an older gentleman who walked towards them. He greeted Paul and Ruth and took a stumbling Marielle out of the bar. Paul and Ruth burst into laughter once she had gone, and Ruth grabbed his hand in excitement.

'Wow, that was something. She had a crush on you!'

Paul shook his head in embarrassment. 'I promise, I didn't know.'

'And if you did?'

'If I did, nothing. She is still kinda my boss.'

'Well, I guess so.' Ruth was intrigued and more than a little curious. 'And if she wasn't your boss?'

'Still nothing.' He shook his head. 'She's not really my type.'

'And what's your type?'

Paul looked at her sideways and Ruth was suddenly self-conscious. 'Well, not her anyway,' he said and held her stare.

The mood seemed to change and although Ruth could feel her head still swimming from the amount of vodka shots she had consumed, she was suddenly aware of her proximity to Paul. That feeling of romance was back in the air and she felt it more vividly now. She wanted to throw caution to the wind again, to lean over and kiss those lips that seemed so very close to hers.

She took a breath. She promised herself she wasn't going to get involved with him but her mind was muddled. 'Blame it on the alcohol,' she said softly.

'What did you say?'

'Maybe it's time to go.' She sighed and he nodded.

'Need a taxi?'

'No, I'm right over there,' Ruth said, pointing in the direction of her street, which was only two blocks away.

'That's close! I didn't know you lived so close.'

'Well, I don't know where you live either.'

'Brighton,' he said. 'I'll taxi it. I left my car at work.'

'Why don't you just stay at mine?' Ruth said impulsively and then realised how it sounded. 'I just meant, so that you don't have to come all the way back from Brighton tomorrow to get your car from work.'

'I don't know …'

'Someone waiting for you at home?' Again, Ruth was aware of how it sounded.

'No, nothing like that.' He looked at her. 'Do you have a spare room?'

Ruth reddened. 'Well, no. But I have a sofa.' She suddenly wanted him to come over to her place more than ever.

'Are you sure?'

'Yeah, c'mon.' She took his arm and they walked back to Ruth's flat together, almost falling over on the way. It was a silent stroll, Ruth still wondering if it was a good idea, but not caring if it wasn't.

They entered the flat and Paul, coming in after Ruth, closed the door behind him, looking around. Ruth breathed a sigh of relief that the place was tidy.

'Welcome to my humble abode,' she said, bowing in exaggeration, but when she looked up, Paul was already in front of her, staring intently into her eyes.

Leaning up, Ruth kissed his lips. She could feel his hesitance and stepped back.

'Sorry,' she said and looked down at her shoes.

'Don't be,' he said, and reaching towards her, put his mouth on hers. Their clothes were already off by the time they had gotten to the bedroom.

Paul was tender and generous and Ruth felt a compatibility, awakening something inside her again. It wasn't wild like it was with Terrence, or calm and routine like it was with Oliver. It was sensitive and passionate, and it was, to her, making love. She lay awake until the early hours of the morning, falling in love with him.

When she awoke in the morning, the sun was streaming through the lace curtains onto Paul's still-closed eyes. Ruth leaned up on her elbow and watched as small puffs of air escaped his mouth. She wanted to reach out and stroke back the wisp of brown curls that sat on his forehead. She could still feel her body tingle when she thought about the night before, the way his hands, so gentle, yet forceful, covered her body, the way his lips lingered on her face, touching her forehead, her nose, her mouth. She had reached for him with hunger, wanting to consume him and be consumed by him.

Ruth felt that this was different and as much as she didn't want to keep comparing him to anyone else, she couldn't help it. But then she thought they were all different and they turned out the same, all cheating bastards who had hurt her terribly. How could she know Paul wouldn't do the same? Ruth's heart was suddenly heavy. She didn't know what this meant, for now, for later, but she didn't want to be in that horrible position again. She lay back and looked at the ceiling, wishing she could just trust him.

Feeling her movement, Paul stirred and she turned back to his sleepy, smiling face. She needed to make a decision about what she wanted from him. This could be dismissed as a mistake, a one-night stand, never to be thought about again. That may at least save their friendship. She had already weighed up the pros and cons. Paul was kind and gentle, but so was Oliver; he was good-looking, but so was Terrence. He talked to her like an equal, like he just liked being with her, but there was also their working relationship, which would be shattered if something further were to happen. She didn't know what this would mean for them working together.

'Hi,' he said, his eyes on her. He took the hand that lay on her pillow. 'You okay?'

'Hey, there, sleep well?'

Paul nodded and grinned. 'So well.'

Ruth could see that he wasn't quite sure what to do, so she sat up, crossed her legs and faced him. 'Listen, Paul,' she said and saw his knowing eyes turn from her. She paused and he looked back at her. 'Last night was …'

Paul sat up and shrugged, brandishing a fake smile. 'Yeah, yeah, I know the drill.' He stretched. 'It was great but … It's okay, Ruth, I get it.'

Ruth was taken aback and all of a sudden realised that she actually wanted to be with this man. 'Is that how you feel?'

Paul put his feet down on the floor, his head bent. 'Isn't that what you think?'

'Well … no. No.'

He turned to her now, hope lighting his eyes, and Ruth reached out to him and pulled him back into bed.

Chapter 11

Patty was in tears and Ruth was unsure of how to comfort her sister, so she just sat and stroked her hand as Patty sobbed out the story of how Mark had been cheating on her for the last year.

'Even before Fiona was born!' she hiccupped.

Patty had found images on Mark's computer, images of another woman, someone she had never met. But Patty wasn't blaming Mark. She kept putting the blame on the other woman, and on herself! When she questioned him about it, he came clean and told her he needed a break from their life with all their children—'All of whom he had asked for!' cried Patty, incoherently—and he was feeling stifled!

Ruth was horrified. 'But he chose this life, he was the one who wanted children, the one who wanted you to give up on your career to be a housewife.'

'That's what I wanted too,' wailed Patty, 'but now look at me: I'm homely!' Patty burst into a fresh bout of sobs.

Ruth didn't want to agree, so she remained quiet. She looked at Patty's once-luscious red hair, now a drab, limp brown. Her brown cardigan was two sizes too big for her and the black trackpants were a staple. Ruth wondered how many of the same kind she had in her closet. She looked harried, and it wasn't just today; it was every time Ruth saw her. Ruth put it down to the stress of having so many children, but she assumed it was always what Patty wanted and that Patty didn't really care about how she presented herself, especially after she had her first child. She raised her eyebrows at Patty's black trainers, which looked ten years old.

Patty looked at her, incredulous. 'See, you think it too!'

'Well, you do have four children. It doesn't leave much time for you to go to the salon.'

'I don't know what to do, Ruth.' Patty moaned and Ruth rubbed her back. She could hear the children play in the backyard with Roberta and felt a touch of sadness for them. She was also trying to control the anger she felt for Mark, another man who had betrayed a woman.

'I don't either, Pat.'

'Leave the bastard,' Gary's booming voice interrupted from the hallway.

Ruth and Patty looked towards Gary's voice, their eyes widening, and looking back at each other, suddenly burst into giggles as they heard their father shuffle away.

'Maybe Dad's right,' said Ruth. 'But what does Mark say?'

'He says it was a mistake and that it won't happen again.'

'Do you believe him?'

'I don't know. I want to.'

Ruth didn't know what to believe either, but she knew she was not going to put up with any of that. She had nearly let Terrence off the hook, was almost willing to look the other way to keep him. A shudder of shame ran though her.

Ruth left the house that evening in thought. She was angry with Mark, but she was more angry with Patty, who she thought should have been stronger. And Patty had asked Ruth for her advice because she knew what Ruth had been through. 'Like I'm the expert on cheaters,' she muttered to herself, irritated, as she drove home, where Paul would be waiting for her.

She smiled when she thought of Paul. These last few months had been the happiest she had been and they had spent most of their time together, with no ulterior motives, no questioning each other, not trying to change one another, just enjoying being together.

They had explained to Marielle the nature of their relationship and she had begrudgingly accepted it. They tried to keep work as professional as possible, but managed to dart into the bathroom together when the temptation to pounce on each other got to be too much. They spent most weekends together too, but Ruth never felt smothered. He was as happy to go out for a night on the town as he was to take a trip to the beach and when she needed to spend time with her friend, she never felt the need to make excuses about it. Karen was in a world of her own with Pete and both were excited about finally being in good relationships, and at the same time for once.

'What do you want to do today?' Paul asked Ruth one Sunday morning, after a late night watching old movies, which she actually enjoyed watching with him.

The radio was on, masking the city noise, and the sun spilling its rays into the bedroom made Ruth feel like she was in heaven. 'I want to stay in bed all day,' she said, stretching her arms skyward. 'With the music on, with you next to me, the phone off the hook and ignoring the world.'

Paul smiled. 'Just the thing I want too,' he said and snuggled back into bed with her. Ruth dived under the covers, waiting for Paul to pounce.

They managed to stay in bed until midday, falling in and out of sleep, content to just lie together, their arms wrapped around one another. Ruth felt a moment of panic when she looked to him at one stage, his eyes fluttering in a shallow sleep, and realised that she was already in love with him. *I can't be,* she thought, *but can I? And why do I fall in love so easily? What's wrong with me?*

'I can feel you watching,' said Paul, his voice husky and his eyes still closed, and Ruth was drawn out of her doubts.

'Mmmm, I could watch you all day.'

'Good,' he said and turned to her. 'I will hold you to that.'

'Come to me,' she said and Paul reached to her. She allowed herself to drown in him, letting her fears fly out of the window into the bright noonday sun.

'This has to be a record,' Ruth exclaimed afterwards.

'I love records,' said Paul. 'We can break this one too.'

Their need for each other was intense, it was plain to see, but right now their need for other sustenance was stronger.

'Coffee?'

'Yep, let's make brunch too,' said Paul, and kissing Ruth on her shoulder, jumped out of bed. They made hot coffee and toast with eggs and avocado and almost gulped it down in their hurry to get back to the bedroom, where they spent the rest of the day, Ruth reading a novel, something she didn't have much time to do lately, and Paul working on his photos on his laptop. They got up to shower together in the afternoon, had dinner that consisted of baked beans on toast, and ice-cream, and set straight back to the bedroom, where they made love, played a long game of Monopoly and continued with their activities of reading and photography.

'Stop that,' said Ruth when she realised he was taking a picture of her.

'I can't ignore beauty,' he said, winking, and kept clicking his camera.

'So cheesy!' she laughed, trying to duck under the covers, but when she emerged, Paul was waiting and began clicking again. She tossed her book at him and stuck her tongue out.

It was one of the most enjoyable days Ruth had ever had and she vowed that she was going to do it more often. She felt calm, at peace and completely in love, and this time, she didn't resist the thought.

****

Paul's parents invited Ruth to Brisbane to meet them the next month, and although she was so pleased that it had come to that stage of their relationship, she still felt nervous. She hadn't introduced him to her own parents, even though he had hinted at it several times and downright asked once.

'Maybe next week,' she said, hoping that by the next week she would be ready for them to meet him. But when the next week came and went and she hadn't said anything about it, Paul didn't either.

'When are we going to meet this man?' asked Gary one afternoon when Paul shooed her out of her flat for the day. He was planning a three-month anniversary dinner and told her to stay out until six p.m. Ruth had taken the opportunity to spend the day at her family's home.

'Soon,' replied Ruth, promising herself it would be just that. She wanted them to meet Paul so badly, but something held her back, what, she couldn't tell. She thought she felt secure with Paul and talked herself out of her fears when she was not with him, but she always made an excuse when it came to actually doing it. She knew she wanted them to meet him; she imagined Gary, a twinkle in his eyes, nodding to her that she had found the right one. And she knew he would love Paul, as would her mother. 'A strong young man, who has the right idea,' she would say. 'What denomination is he?'

'Are you happy?' Roberta, who was bustling around the house, stopped to ask. She had been babysitting Patty's children while Patty was at the salon and Ruth had been pleasantly surprised that Patty had let her children out of her sight, and to pamper herself, at that!

'Yes; oh Ma, I want you to meet him so badly.' She turned to her father. 'And Pa, you would really like this one.'

'As long as you do.' Gary didn't look very convinced. 'But we have seen very little of you lately, so I think he must be keeping you busy.' He winked.

'Oh Gary!' Roberta chimed in. 'Leave the girl alone. She will introduce us when the time is right.'

Gary laughed and moved past her mother, giving her a peck on the cheek and a pinch on the buttocks as he walked away.

Ruth, as she had been doing a lot lately, thought of her parents' love for each other and the affection they still showed to each other after so many years together and wondered if she would have that someday. She hoped she would and desperately hoped that Paul would be the one to give her that kind of security, that kind of love. But she still felt something was holding her back and had an idea of what it was.

It was the photograph.

When Ruth first visited Paul's house in Brighton, a large, stately house with the biggest garden Ruth had ever seen, she was charmed, not with its size, but the tasteful way such a grand house could be turned into a cosy home. From the outside it had looked ostentatious and intimidating, but upon entering it, she felt comfortable, at home.

The foyer just past the front door was spacious and Ruth stopped to take it in, her first time at Paul's family home. It was here that she saw it, the picture that would begin the end. The one on his wall, the beige wall that displayed his photography, next to others of his family and friends.

'That's my mother,' he said, pointing to one which displayed an elegant woman with a mischievous curve on her lips. 'With my father,' Paul said, smiling at the face of a jovial man with an outright laugh looking towards his mother.

'What's going on there?' she asked him.

'I think he was pinching her butt, to make her laugh too.' Paul smiled and Ruth was reminded of her own parents' amorous behaviour. He seemed to be very fond of his parents, whom he talked about quite a lot. They had moved to Brisbane to be with his divorced sister and her toddlers.

'You miss them,' she said. 'Will you go there too?' she asked, suddenly afraid of his answer.

'Why would I do that?' He pulled her close and kissed her. 'I have everything I need and want here.'

Paul continued to tell her about the people in the pictures, family friends, cousins, childhood friends, but Ruth's eyes had already fallen on one she couldn't tear them off. It was separated slightly from the family photos, with other random subjects, but mostly people, young, old, beautiful and plain. He had a knack for capturing their essence, not just their actions, and this one stood out.

'Who is this?' she asked Paul, as she scrutinised the picture, ignoring others that had more obviously attractive people.

This one was different. The woman in it wasn't beautiful, not in the traditional way; she just had a slight smile, her fingers on her lips, her hair light and thrown across her eyes, which were gazing at the camera with tenderness, yet she seemed somewhat aloof, distant. It was a mesmerising picture, the sepia tint creating an effect of old-fashioned love.

'One of my subjects,' he answered, and putting his hand on her arm, moved her along.

Ruth resisted. 'She is stunning.'

'I guess so.' Paul was not as enthusiastic and he tried to move Ruth away again, but she stood put.

'Did you know her well?'

'Not really. Just someone I knew from uni.'

There was something about his forced coolness that pricked up Ruth's ears, but for the moment she chose to let it go. There were people in her past that she hadn't fully discussed with Paul either. Sure, he knew a little about Oliver and Terrence, but she never harped on about them. They were the past and should remain so, yet Ruth found her stomach tightening and a slight ringing in her ears. She tried to shake the feeling but couldn't, and when she went home the next morning, after a night of love and contentment, the photograph returned to her mind. She couldn't put her finger on it, what she had seen in the picture that caused her to react this way. She tried to put it out of her mind and Paul's phone call to tell her he already missed her allayed her fears.

Ruth removed the crease on her forehead and shook her head, trying to get rid of the insecurity she was feeling. Paul had been perfect. He hadn't been too nosy or demanding yet gave her just the right amount of attention without crowding her. Ruth, for her part, wanted to be with him at every waking moment, but knew she couldn't jump headlong into anything as she did in her first two relationships; she knew what they ended up being—disasters. She loved Paul, she knew that, but she still hesitated when she thought about him in the long term and wouldn't allow herself to think about a future. She was almost waiting for the other shoe to drop, for the inevitable to happen.

She smiled again now, as she drove home after having spent the day with her parents. She was looking forward to their dinner that evening, and she'd missed him since seeing him that morning, even though she had had such a lovely time at her childhood home. She frowned when she thought about Patty. She had come home after her visit to the salon and her dowdy brown hair that usually fell down in rat tails was set with blonde highlights and ringleted curls. Ruth had forgotten what a beauty her sister had been when she was younger. Ruth worried about Patty and considered her dilemma. Was every man a cheating bastard? Not Paul, she tried to reassure herself.

'I think I'm going to leave him,' Patty said to her when they had gone out onto the porch, just before Ruth had left the house. The children were playing inside, followed everywhere by Roberta, and Patty had taken the chance to have a cigarette, another new habit that she'd seemed to embrace. Ruth was beginning to feel close to her sister, something she hadn't felt in all her years. She thought that perhaps it was because she understood what Patty was feeling now: betrayal. They finally had something in common. Ruth sympathised with her, just wishing she didn't have to go through this and knowing how much it would take to overcome it.

'If you think you need to,' replied Ruth, taking the cigarette out of her hand and taking a drag.

'I still love him though.'

'I know.' Ruth looked into the darkening evening and felt a sense of foreboding. 'But this too shall pass,' she said and laughed. It was one of her mother's favourite biblical phrases.

'You are turning into Mother,' said Patty.

'I hope so,' Ruth replied.

'I see them,' said Patty, throwing a glance through the window at her mother's bustling figure. 'They are so happy, so good together. Why can't we have what they have?'

'We will, some day.' Ruth sounded surer than she felt.

****

Ruth neared the flat and looked at the clock on the

dashboard. It was nearly six. Well, he should be done by now. She parked her car and headed to the door.

Soft music was playing as she opened the door, and the smell of something scrumptious wafted towards her. As she stepped in, she felt something soft crush beneath her foot and jumped. Looking down, she saw a sprinkling of rose petals that led into the dining area, where she found Paul, wearing an apron with nothing else and holding a ladle, looking sheepish.

'Ready?' he said, and Ruth moved towards him.

She took the ladle from him and threw it onto the table, kissing him as she did. She grabbed the apron string that was around his neck and led him to the bedroom.

'Dinner can wait,' she said, pulling the apron from him.

Dinner was perfect. A platter of antipasto for starters and fettucine carbonara was the main. After their strenuous workout in the bedroom, Ruth was hungry and almost gobbled the food. It was as delicious as it smelled. She told him about her day with her parents and he didn't mention anything about going to see them.

It was at dessert when the feeling came back. As she lapped at the pistachio ice cream—store bought, he confessed—Paul leaned in and took her hand across the table.

'I love you,' he said, an intensity in his gaze.

And that's when it hit her.

The photograph, the look, the something she could not put her finger on. It was one of intimacy, the same expression on Paul's face right now. Now she knew why she was jealous of that girl. She had been looking at Paul with that same intent look, the look … of love.

'Ruth?' Paul's eyes creased and Ruth realised her jaw was dropped and her eyes wide. She straightened her face.

'I … I have to … go to the bathroom,' she said, and Ruth jumped up, dropping Paul's hand.

She reasoned with herself. So what? She had loved Oliver; she had loved Terrence. Why couldn't Paul have loved someone else too? But he kept the picture. So why couldn't he? It was a beautiful photograph. Yet she didn't have any constant reminders of her past lovers on her wall.

She stopped pacing the bathroom floor. He just told her he loved her. She looked in the mirror. 'He loves me,' she announced to her reflection. She smacked her forehead. And she had just left him hanging … There he was, just sitting at the table, probably wondering if he had scared her off by saying those words. She loved him, she felt it, but couldn't bring herself to say it to herself, let alone to him. It was too soon. It would be making a commitment to say it already. She knew she still had some baggage in her heart to sort out before she could do that.

But, yes. She did love him. Ruth sat on the edge of the bath, relieved that she could admit it to herself. Yet, if she went in there and said it to him now, it would sound ridiculous, like she had rehearsed it, like it wasn't natural. But how could she tell him what she was thinking when he said it to her? She would sound like a jealous girlfriend, which, of course, she was. *Oh, why am I making this so complicated?*

Returning to the table, knowing she had a sheepish look on her face, she observed Paul, who had already started clearing away the dishes. His back was to her as he put the ice cream bowls in the sink and Ruth straightened her eyebrows and put a smile on her face. Putting her arms around him and leaning her head on his back, she felt him stiffen. But then, he turned around and enveloped her in his arms.

'I'm sorry,' he whispered through her hair. 'That was probably too soon.'

Ruth shook her head and turned to look at his face, which had an expression she couldn't quite fathom, his eyes creased but a straight smile. She leaned upwards and kissed his lips.

The next day, she took him to meet her parents.

Chapter 12

It was at Karen's engagement party where Ruth came face to face with the men that had deceived her.

Karen and Pete had fallen in love and Ruth felt guilty that she had been so wrapped up in her own love life to even notice how far her friend had gone until Karen stopped over at Ruth's one afternoon after work to show her the emerald ring that sat on the third finger of her left hand.

Ruth screeched with joy when she opened the door to find Karen's hand entering the room before she did.

'I said yes!' Karen squealed as they jumped up and down, holding each other's hands.

'Of course you did,' Ruth cried and hugged her friend. She really was happy for Karen who had now been with Pete for nearly a year.

'And please be my maid of honour?'

'Who else?' said Ruth, hugging her friend again. 'Yes, yes, yes!'

Ruth helped her friend prepare for the engagement party which was held at Karen's house where she still lived with her parents. 'I can't live on my own like you do,' she had said to Ruth once. 'I'm not leaving here until I'm married.' Ruth marvelled at how she had stuck to it. For that matter, Ruth had done the same, married straight out of her parents' home; it was just unfortunate that she had no choice in the matter when she and Oliver parted, but by then, she was too used to living by herself. She just hoped that Karen was luckier than she.

'This is happening so quickly,' said Karen, as they hung yellow streamers along the back porch, which was now paved. 'Not just the party tomorrow, but the whole thing.'

Ruth had a flashback to when she met Oliver, in this same backyard, some three years before. She couldn't believe it had gone so quickly and so much had happened since then. A stab of pain hit her heart when she looked over to the spot at which she stood when he had made his move. 'Yes, it is. Are you sure about this?' Ruth wished the words hadn't jumped out of her mouth the way they had. 'I mean ...'

'I know what you mean,' said Karen. 'I know that I want to spend my life with Pete.' She paused and looked over to Ruth. 'You know Terrence will be here tomorrow.'

Ruth nodded and swallowed. She hadn't seen Terrence since he left her on the floor more than a year ago and didn't know how she would react. 'I know. I'll be fine.' She smiled broadly, with more confidence than she felt.

Ruth already expected to see Terrence at the party but with Paul on her arm, she felt that she would be fine. What she didn't expect was to see Oliver there too. He was a last-minute addition, a favour to Karen's brother, and when Ruth caught sight of him through the glass doors, standing in the backyard, almost exactly where she had first noticed him those years ago, she felt like she had gone back in time. A time when Oliver had shyly approached her, where she, bold and popular then, had toyed with him, a time when she had been a different person, unafraid of life and love.

Paul squeezed her hand, sensing her dread. Ruth had already warned him that Terrence would be there and he knew he needed to be her moral support, and by the way she leaned on him, her physical support as well. Ruth looked at him in dismay and he smiled warmly down at her. She felt some of the butterflies subside and took a deep breath. How she wanted to turn around and run, but she knew that would be an awful thing to do to her friend. Besides, she knew it was eventually going to happen, that she would see Terrence and Oliver again, so she may as well kill two birds with one party.

She still steered away from the backyard, opting for the kitchen, but she quite literally bumped into Terrence, and he at first looked shocked to see her. But he quickly recovered, and plastering on his usual playful grin, he gave her a hug.

'Great to see you, Ruth,' he said emphatically, and Ruth

stood as stiff as a board, trying to find the words to say back to him.

Paul came through. 'Hi, I'm Paul,' he said, reaching his hand out to Terrence, who shook it heartily.

They made some conversation, which seemed a blur to Ruth, and she soon felt Paul's arm on her lower back, steering her away again.

'Are you okay?' he asked when they had gotten into the hallway where Ruth took an audible breath.

Ruth nodded and observed Paul, marvelling at his composure and demeanour towards Terrence when he met him.

'Should I be concerned?'

'Oh, gosh, no!' Ruth found her own composure had returned and hugged him. 'Thanks for that.'

'Well, at least that's done,' said Paul. 'So we can enjoy ourselves now.'

Ruth hesitated.

'What is it?' The concern was back on his face.

'I just saw, um ... Oliver, my ex-husband.'

Paul threw his head back. Then he laughed. 'A reunion for the exes? Well, they're the past and I'm the present ... hoping never to be one of them.' He took her hand. 'C'mon. Let's get this over and done with.'

Chapter 13

It was not to be the end of the exes. The next week, on a balmy Friday evening at a work get-together, which included Marielle and held at a pub in the city, Ruth would meet Anna, the girl in the photograph.

Arriving together, after quickly changing at Ruth's place after work, where Paul now kept some of his things, they headed to the city on foot. Ruth was in a good mood.

After seeing Terrence and Oliver at Karen's party, she thought that the meetings would affect her, but she realised that although she still felt a dart of attraction to Terrence and a sliver of sympathy for Oliver, there wasn't much else. Oliver had been alone and after a brief smile of excitement when he saw Ruth approach, his face changed upon seeing her hand in Paul's. He had waited for them to near and prepared his ever-so-calm face. It was then that Ruth realised that it had been an act all along. She wondered why she hadn't seen through it before. Clearly the man bore so many insecurities that he needed a façade most of the time.

She came away from the party with a mixture of feelings: joy at not being drawn to any of those men anymore, but also a feeling of bitterness that they could do what they had done to her and then be quite okay about it afterwards, expecting her forgiveness. Well, she had to forgive, she had no choice, but she was not going to forget.

'Closure,' she had said out loud after she had gotten into the car and felt a warmth flood her body. She knew Paul wouldn't ever do anything to hurt her.

'Closure,' replied Paul. He took her hand and kissed it.

****

But now here was Anna. Sultry, that was the word for Anna, and goddess. Yes, that was another word. Ruth was by no means a shrinking violet and knew she was attractive to men and women alike, but when she saw Anna, she felt like a wallflower that had long withered. Again, she realised that Anna was no great beauty, not in the traditional sense, but there was something so attractive about her, even Ruth felt a magnetism—a person who just seemed to draw people to her without even realising it.

When Anna, dressed in an oversized cardigan, tight jeans and blue boots, first walked into the bar quite late into the evening and with a friend on her arm, Ruth had looked closely, trying to figure out where she had seen this woman. But then Paul turned to follow her gaze and his expression changed; his eyes became wide and his lower lip dropped slightly. Ruth didn't miss it and when Paul turned away from Anna, and back to Ruth, his eyes were troubled. He clearly saw the question on Ruth's face and gave her a lopsided grin.

'Time to go?' he ventured.

'Isn't that …?' Ruth figured it out and wondered why it had taken her so long. That face was etched in her brain.

'Who?'

Ruth rolled her eyes. 'Don't be ridiculous, Paul. I just saw you look at her.'

'Erm …' He took another quick glance in the direction of Anna, who was now laughing lightly at what the bartender was saying. Her hand was in the back pocket of her jeans and she had one of her legs hitched onto the leg of a barstool. She looked like something on the cover of a magazine. 'Yes, I think it's Anna.'

'That's her name then.' Ruth was watching Paul closely now and he seemed frazzled.

'Yes, I thought you knew that.' He attempted a smile.

'Why haven't you told me about her?'

Paul laughed, a weird little gurgle. 'Nothing to tell, I told you before.' He gulped down his beer.

'Okay,' said Ruth, a little hammer beginning to batter at her brain.

'Should we go then?' Paul repeated.

'After this.' Ruth held up her glass, which was nearly empty, wanting to stay on, even if it was just out of morbid curiosity.

'Hi, Paul,' a husky voice said behind him and Paul almost jumped.

'Hi, Anna,' he said, turning around.

Anna put her arms around him and observed Ruth over his shoulder. She smiled and stepped back.

'Hi, I'm Anna. You must be Ruth.'

Ruth was surprised that this woman knew who she was and smiled back, but all she wanted to do was gouge out her beautiful eyes.

'How is the new job going, Paul?' Anna asked, sipping on a beer.

'Yes, good. Not so new though …' He looked in the direction of the door. He seemed lost for words and Ruth just stared at him. She had never seen him behave this way before, so unsure of himself, so oddly rude.

'Good, good,' Anna replied. 'How are your parents? And Jamie? Is she still up north?'

Now Ruth was becoming incensed, but she knew she shouldn't be. It was natural to ask about his family, but Ruth was upset because Anna knew so much about Paul. He had acted as if she was nothing more than a subject for his photography.

'Give them my best,' Anna said, while Ruth watched her gracefully touch Paul on the arm, give him private knowing smiles and nudges.

'Ready to go?' Paul turned to Ruth and took her arm.

By now, Ruth was more than ready to leave. She was not enjoying the feelings that were arising in her, feelings of rage, of jealousy, of hate, and although she realised she was being unreasonable, she couldn't stop it. She got up and felt a pang of pain through her bladder. She had been holding it up for a while not wanting to leave them alone but she knew she wasn't going to hold it in until she got home.

'Excuse me,' she said to Paul and Anna, as she wondered where Anna's friend had disappeared to. 'I'm ready, but I have to use the ladies' room.' She shrugged, wishing she didn't have to leave them alone, even for a moment.

Paul kissed her full on the lips, a little too passionately, something that he didn't do much when they were in company, and Anna raised her eyebrows with a smirk.

It was the quickest visit to the toilet that Ruth had ever done, but the line had been long and by the time she got back to where they had been sitting, more than five minutes had gone by. It was not quick enough though, for as Ruth approached them, Anna was leaning into Paul, her lips already locked on his.

Ruth stopped in shock and it seemed the scene had turned into something like a movie that was playing in slow motion. She stood frozen to the ground and watched the horror show, waiting for the climax. Someone bumped into her and Ruth blinked. She saw Anna open her eyes and look at her, while she still had her lips on Paul's. Then Anna closed her eyes again and lazily pulled her head back. She looked at Paul and nodded in Ruth's direction. Paul jumped off his bar stool and quickly turned around, his dumbstruck eyes finding Ruth's own dazed ones.

Ruth gawked at him for a second, turned around and walked quickly out of the bar, her back straight. Then she was running, running home, ignoring the people whom she bumped into and the obscenities they threw at her as she raced past, and ignoring the ringing of the phone, which was still in the pocket of her jeans.

'Don't think, don't think,' she cried out loud as she ran past the entry to her street and kept running. 'Home, home, go home,' she said, puffing as she ran into the road where cars whooshed by and screeched as they tried to avoid her. She heard their beeping but didn't care. She kept going until she could go no more and collapsed outside a block of flats, where she slumped on the little brick fence that surrounded the complex. She coughed and wheezed, trying to catch her breath, and fell onto the cold ground in a heap, her arms wrapped around her knees, her brain in a haze. She welcomed it. She didn't want to think about what she'd just seen, something she knew in her heart was eventually going to happen anyway.

'Are you okay?' A couple walking past her stopped and the woman bent down, putting a hand on Ruth's shoulder.

Ruth looked up in surprise and, with the help of the woman, raised herself from the ground, suddenly aware of her appearance. She nodded to the concerned faces of this young couple who seemed to be on their way to the city. Then she burst into tears and the woman pulled Ruth into her arms where Ruth sobbed noisily, while she softly patted her hair.

'Thanks.' Ruth pulled back and noticed a bit of mascara that she'd left on the woman's light-blue top. 'Sorry,' she said, trying to wipe it off.

'Are you okay? Can we do anything?' the man's brusque voice piped in.

'I'm sorry,' she said again, looking up at the tall man with a goatee, who looked like he rode motorcycles for a living. He smiled down at her.

'Can we take you anywhere?'

Ruth realised what she must have looked like and stared down at her black suede sandals with the little red heel, which was a mushy brown now. She nodded.

'Where?' said the woman.

Ruth shook her head. She meant to say she was okay with the nod. 'No. I'm fine,' she said as her phone began ringing again. She took it out. 'I'm going to be okay.' She saw Paul's name flashing on the screen and hung up. She smiled widely at them.

The man and woman were still standing in front of her, concern and more than a little confusion written on their faces.

'Thank you,' she said. 'I'm going to be just fine.'

She watched them walk away with a couple of backward glances and Ruth hoped that they would be happy together. She sat again on the wall and called Karen. Her keys were in her jacket that she had left hanging on the barstool and she hadn't had the presence of mind to pick it up as she dashed out. Even if she did remember it, she didn't want to be anywhere near Paul or Anna. It would just give them time to lay their excuses on her and she knew what she had seen. There was no explaining that away.

'Where are you?' Ruth could hear Karen already moving about, getting ready to pick her up. Ruth hadn't even told her what the matter was.

Ruth looked up at the sign. 'Waverley Street, number nine.'

'Stay there, get in the shadows,' Karen ordered and Ruth obeyed. It was late now and who knew what was out and about at this time of night, especially such a gorgeous night as this, with the moon shining clearly without any clouds to impinge on its glow.

She ducked behind a bush next to the fence and looked at her phone. Already twelve missed calls from Paul. And a message: *Where are you?* She deleted it and wished Karen would hurry.

'Where to?' Karen said as Ruth got into her car.

'I don't have my keys,' Ruth said softly, childishly.

'Paul has a set?'

Ruth nodded. 'But I don't want to see him.'

Karen seemed to understand. 'Mine then,' she said and drove in the direction of Rivera.

After spending the night in tears at Karen's house, Ruth steeled herself for the message she knew she had to write. She realised now that it was never going to work with Paul. She hadn't given herself enough time to heal from the relationships that had hurt her so badly and from the way this turned out, it seemed to be heading that way again. Paul had been calling all night and even resorted to messaging her, something which he was not fond of doing.

11.08 – *Ruth, please call me.*

11.24 – *Ruth, I have your jacket, please call.*

11.38 – *I'm outside your place. Where are you?*

It had gone on for most of the night between unanswered calls, but Ruth had been strong and turned off her phone after two in the morning, when Karen convinced her to try to sleep. Poor, innocent Karen, who never knew what it was like to feel this way. Of course, she had been much more crafty in her choice of men, rarely jumping into any relationship willy-nilly, and Ruth hoped Karen would never have to feel as she did now.

She knew Karen meant well, but Ruth knew there would be no sleep for her tonight. She thought about Anna and Paul and their kiss, and tried to remember every detail, so she would hurt, and hurt so much that nothing could hurt her again. Her tears stained the pillow on Karen's bed and she felt Karen's hand on her shoulder. Karen knew Ruth was all talked out so she didn't try to make her discuss it anymore.

They had sat on Karen's bed, drinking hot chocolate after Karen's mother had come in to check on them and insisted it was what the doctor ordered. Nothing could make Ruth feel better, as much as she appreciated the gesture, and her heart hurt more badly than she ever thought it could. Even Terrence's betrayal had not hurt like this.

Ruth put her hand on Karen's and wiped her eyes. She

looked at the clock—four in the morning. She squeezed her eyes shut and vowed never to shed another tear on a man.

When she turned on her phone in the morning, a slew of messages came at her from Paul and she read through them, this time not with tears, but with a steely resolve. She took specific notice of the one that told her he had left her keys in the letterbox. She replied to this one asking him to remove his things from her flat, that she wanted him gone before she got home that evening. Paul's messages had stopped by then but he replied immediately to this one.

I'm staying until you get home.

Please be gone by the time I return, she typed into her phone.

We need to talk it out. You don't understand.

I don't want to, she replied. *It's over.*

Just come home.

It's my home, not yours. Ruth knew she was being unkind, but she just wanted this done with, and the sooner the better.

She is nothing to me.

Okay, I'm about to block you, so please just be gone when I get back tonight. I don't think I really want this to go anywhere, anyway.

I told you I loved you, was his reply.

And there's a reason I didn't say it back, was hers. Ruth squeezed her fist tightly so the tears would stay away.

Your keys are in the mailbox.

Ruth spent the afternoon visiting with her parents.

'How's Paul?' asked her father. 'You two are usually joined at the hip.'

'We're done,' said Ruth and hoped Gary wouldn't push it.

'Want to talk about it?'

'Nope,' said Ruth and bit into the chunk of steak her mother had put in front of her. She was pleased her father knew better than to urge her to discuss it.

It was late and Ruth didn't want to leave. She thought for a moment about moving back home, she loved being here so much, but Roberta had come in and waffled on about Patty and Mark and how they were working it all out. Ruth just didn't want to be reminded of her sister's own heartache and how she had forgiven her philandering husband. She took a deep breath and decided to go home to her flat, one that was devoid of Paul and his things. Karen dropped her home and wanted to stay with her, but Ruth had already decided that she was not going to break down into bits of nothing as she had with the last two.

Yet, as she walked around the empty flat, looking for anything of Paul's that he may have left behind, she felt a sadness creep into her. She had a shower, put on a dress that she had been planning to take to Brisbane and went to town.

Paul

He couldn't understand it. He pushed Anna off him and rushed behind a retreating Ruth, but by the time he reached outside she was nowhere in sight. He stormed back inside the bar and found Anna sipping on her beer.

'There goes your girlfriend,' she smirked.

'What the hell did you do that for?' he yelled and people around him turned to look. Paul ignored them, his rage deafening him.

'I just needed to kiss you,' Anna said casually and took another sip.

'Why can't you just leave me alone?'

'She knew who I was,' said Anna, raising an eyebrow, and leaned close to Paul, who was looking at her with a combination of indignance and anger. She had tried to hurt him before, but he knew what she was about and left her before she could.

'I didn't waste my breath explaining you.' Paul turned around to leave.

'Wait,' said Anna and Paul clenched his fists. 'I'm sorry.'

'You're sorry?' Paul turned to her again. 'That is the woman I love, the one I intend to spend the rest of my life with. You're sorry? Take your sorry and ...' He took a deep breath, clenched his fists again and walked out.

'Paul!' Anna called, but Paul kept walking.

She was behind him and he turned around to face her again, fire now in his eyes. He saw her shrink back for a moment and then her façade was back. 'I think this is hers,' she said and handed Paul

Ruth's jacket. He grabbed it from her and stormed away.

He called; all night he called and messaged. But there was no response. He went back to Ruth's place but she wasn't there and Paul spent the night on her sofa, hoping she would come home and he could explain Anna.

Anna! He could kill that woman right now. Theirs was a fling. Sure, she photographed well. The picture! Why on earth had he kept that goddammed picture? He wanted to get rid of it, but his mother had liked it and since it had no meaning to him, he left it up. He barely knew it was there; it wasn't as if he stopped to stare at it and ponder over their lost romantic thing, whatever that was. He knew even after they had spent only a couple of weeks together that she was not the right one, that she just liked the power she held over people. But when he had gotten out before it was too late for him, she had persevered, calling, texting …

He realised he was doing that right now with Ruth, but this was different; he was in love with her and couldn't bear to think about life without her, especially because of Anna.

When dawn crept through the window, Paul knew Ruth wasn't coming home and put her keys in her mailbox. He messaged her to let her know.

The last message from her stung. He knew she loved him, but to hurt him like that … There was no turning back for her. Yet …

Paul sighed and did what she asked. He would find time to explain later. He would leave her alone for now; all his frantic messages explained his side, but she clearly didn't want to believe him. He didn't want to message her again just in case she was good on her word and blocked him.

'If I wanted to be with Anna, I would be,' he muttered to himself as he picked up her favourite cup, the one with the little daisies around it, and dropped it into his bag.

He would give her time to settle down and give him time to calm the feeling of dread that had tied knots in his heart. She had to come to work, after all; they could talk it through then. He thought about Ruth's exes and for a moment, hated them with an unfamiliar fury.

As he turned to survey the flat, he saw his grey-and-black-chequered scarf with a thin line of green thread running through it. It was one of his favourites as well as one of Ruth's, and lay beneath one of the cushions on the sofa, its short tassels hanging out. He left it there.

When he went in to work on Monday, Marielle told him that Ruth had quit.

And Paul knew it was over.

'Maybe I was too hard on him,' Ruth said to herself as she picked up a grey scarf, buried between the cushions in her sofa. She held the soft wool to her face and inhaled deeply, feeling tears spring to her eyes. Maybe this could be the reason she needed to see him again, to return his scarf; she desperately wanted to find a reason, but she shook her head free of the thought and even managed to keep the tears where they belonged. She knew she had to stick to her guns.

Getting off the sofa with a renewed sense of determination, she walked to the rubbish bin and flipped the lid. She let the scarf hang over it for a moment, then shut the lid and went into her bedroom, which now looked cold and forlorn. Paul's things had gone and although there weren't a lot of his things to begin with, there still seemed an emptiness just at the thought. She opened her closet and a lump lodged itself in her throat. A little space remained where his shirts and pants once hung. She moved her own clothes together to fill the gap and shoved the scarf deeply into the recesses of the top shelf.

Well, that was that. She knew she needed to harden up. She knew it was time to be one of them; she couldn't be the sucker anymore. She knew she had to be ruthless with men; she smiled at the irony.

Ruth undressed and took a long shower, trying not to cry. She had cried enough over these men. She was not going to do this again. She got into her cold bed and reached out to the empty space beside her and she could again feel her heart begin to beat fast. She looked at her phone, wanting to call Paul, and hoping for a message or a call from him, and then grateful that there weren't any, especially now, in a moment of weakness. She turned off her phone, swallowed the lump in her throat and tried to sleep.

Chapter 14

When Ruth met Derek, she thought him quite ordinary. In fact, she couldn't remember the particular moment she met him; he was just … there. Dark-brown hair that was cut close to his scalp, he resembled someone who had just returned from army training. But even though Ruth wouldn't have taken a second glance, when he smiled it seemed that Ruth was the only person in existence, it was so warm and genuine. At Marks and Sons, the firm where Ruth now worked as an assistant designer, Derek was an executive assistant of the chief designer, and their exchanges in the large staff lunchroom were at first brief and lacklustre. A hello, a wave and some small talk about projects were their only interactions during the first four months, when they just happened to be sitting at the same table.

Ruth enjoyed it here at Marks and Sons, a large firm with more than forty employees. She knew she had to leave Marielle and when she called her the day after Paul's indiscretion to discuss her resignation, Marielle asked her to come in to talk about it. Ruth was hesitant, but Marielle had been good to her and she knew she owed her at least that much.

'Well, don't say I didn't tell you so,' said Marielle the moment Ruth stepped into the building.

Ruth nodded, waiting for more words of disapproval, but Marielle just linked her arm in Ruth's and led her to the little coffee table.

'Tell me all,' said Marielle, crossing her legs and leaning her shoulder on the back of her chair. She looked like a catwalk model, poised and lanky.

'Marielle, there's nothing to tell, but I know I need to go now. I'm so terribly sorry.'

'We can't lose you!' Marielle leaned forward and looked like she was going to bang on the table, like she was on a midday soap opera. But she didn't, even though her fists were curled in readiness and her heavily mascaraed eyes bore through her.

'There are plenty of me out there; in fact, there are much better versions of me.' Anna's smirk floated in front of Ruth and she quickly rubbed the face from her mind.

'Yes, maybe. But you know how we work, what we do,' Marielle said earnestly. 'And we are a great team!'

'Not so much now,' said Ruth dryly.

'Well, I love Paul, you know I do, but if someone has to go …' Marielle left the sentence hanging.

'It has to be me.'

'Ruth, no. Please, reconsider.' She stretched her hand out, placing it on Ruth's.

'I can work from home until you find someone else. I won't leave you hanging.'

Marielle pursed her lips, considering. After a moment she sighed. 'So your mind is made up then. Okay, well, as you know, I have been looking into hiring another graphic artist, so now I can just look for two.' Ruth admired Marielle's ability to look at things in a positive way. 'Will you give me a couple of weeks?'

Ruth smiled. 'Absolutely. I can take some stuff now to work from home and perhaps I can use some of the work I've done as part of my resume?' She looked hopefully at Marielle.

Marielle got up and hugged her. 'Yes. I will even keep a lookout for something for you. And who knows, maybe one day you will return to us.'

Ruth nodded but knew she wouldn't be returning, not with Paul here.

It was less than a week later when Marielle was at Ruth's flat with an advertisement. Marks and Sons were looking for an assistant designer and Marielle had collaborated with them on one of their bigger projects. She shoved the ad at Ruth and insisted on helping her apply for the job. Ruth was not one to pass on an opportunity and she and Marielle worked late into the evening working on her application and her portfolio.

'Why did you let that man go?' Marielle said as she stretched lazily on the sofa, taking a little break with a glass of wine. She saw the look of surprise on Ruth's face. 'I know, it's none of my business, but I just see him looking so …'

'Marielle, please don't talk to me about him.' Ruth had gotten so lost in the excitement of planning for her new job, Paul had sat in the corners of her mind, rather than taking up the amount of room that he usually did. Now the thought of him hit her again, just when she felt she was being satisfactorily distracted by something else.

'Have you even talked about it?'

'There's nothing to talk about. It's done.' Ruth pulled the papers and brochures together and began to slip them into the large plastic sleeves of her portfolio.

Three days later, she had the job and Marielle let Ruth go with many kisses and a bonus cheque.

Paul had not contacted Ruth in all that time and Ruth was grateful; she knew it would set her back if she had any contact with him. It was way too soon for what she called closure, but she did feel a sliver of sadness when she went in to collect the rest of her things from Marielle's office, and had not seen him there. She found herself running her fingers over the keyboard, taking a last look at his unfinished projects that were scattered over the table and closing her eyes; she sniffed the air deeply, trying to hold the scent of him in her nostrils for as long as possible. She jerked her eyes open, suddenly realising what she'd been doing, and turned on her heels and left.

By this time, Ruth had decided that moving to a new house

would create a new atmosphere, a fresh start for her. This flat, and she needed to blame something, had brought her nothing but heartache and she wished she hadn't wanted to keep it after her split with Oliver. Besides, she had outgrown it. She was a new person now, not the same little weak woman who fell into a heap when push came to shove. She was determined she would be.

She soon found a two-bedroom apartment on the outskirts of the city, which cost a pretty penny, but Ruth thought it was well worth it. She had saved a lot of money, as much as she thought herself a spendthrift, and with her new job, she would be earning so much more. A new place, a new outlook, a new space: that's what she needed and she decided it was something she had to do—spoil herself. After all, there was only herself to think about now.

She turned the music up loud and sang loudly while she packed her belongings, convincing herself that her new life was about to begin. As she was about to close the door of her old home for the last time, Ruth felt a sense of emptiness that was reflected in the flat that was once filled with so much of her. She was tempted to go through it once more, walk around each room and reminisce, just to remember the things that happened there, but she quickly spun around and turned her back on it.

'Onward and upward,' she said to herself and had a little giggle at the words that could have come straight out of her mother's mouth.

She spent the weekend after her first pay cheque from Marks and Sons decorating her house in her own way, not as Oliver,

Terrence or Paul would have liked. She was free of men for the moment and she wanted to make her life her own. Still, when she found Paul's scarf while she packed, she shoved it in with her things and buried it again behind her clothes in her new wardrobe.

But Ruth was lonely. After a long day of work, she would unwind with a shower and eat dinner by herself, usually easy, quick frozen meals from the supermarket. She'd spend an hour on the spacious balcony that overlooked the park, reading a book, enjoying the space that was all hers. Then she would turn on the television or the radio, or read about love and happy endings.

'There are no happy endings,' she said angrily one day, as she finished one of her novels and threw it to the floor.

Karen, of course, tried to be the good friend she had always been and helped Ruth with the move. She stayed with her on the first night, talking about her wedding that was planned for the next year. Ruth had reservations about it, but she knew it was her own views on love that had been altered and she would hurt Karen if she voiced her concerns to her friend. Besides, any man these days seemed to be philandering scoundrels, and even though Pete seemed like a genuine man, albeit a little rough around the edges, he was still a friend of Terrence and she hoped that Terrence wouldn't steer his friend in the wrong direction. Ruth really hoped that things would work out for Karen and that she got the happiness she waited for; she deserved it.

But Paul hadn't seemed that way inclined either and look where that went. Ruth knew she had no idea of how to judge or to even trust anyone anymore. She had sworn off men for now and she had already thought about living in singledom for the rest of her life. It wouldn't be that hard. She could still have short-term relationships and she just would not invest her heart in them. For the moment that thought satisfied her.

After a few months, Ruth allowed herself to think about Paul now and then, when she felt the coldness in the bed beside her, and she often took out his scarf, spreading it on the pillow where his head used to lie. She wondered where he was and what he was doing, whether he had rekindled his love with Anna, and felt a surge of rage at the thought. She wanted to ask Marielle, who called to check in a couple of times a month, but she could never bring herself to ask about Paul, even though Marielle tried to hint at it.

'Don't you want to know how the company is doing?' Marielle said.

'Yes, I do. I miss being there, even though it's so busy here,' Ruth replied.

'You know you can always come back, I would make room for you.'

'I know and I appreciate it but you know I can't.' Ruth missed the familiarity of the place, the comfortable surroundings, the chats and …

'Because of Paul.' Marielle sounded sad. 'Well, he is the …'

'I don't want to know, Marielle,' Ruth pleaded. 'Please don't ask me about him or him about me. Please.'

'He says as much as you do anyway,' Marielle replied in a

sulky voice. 'Anyway, I just miss going out with my friends. All together!'

Ruth missed it too. Karen was always busy and Ruth missed just going out to a garden café, a bar, a club, even a movie, and she took to doing these things by herself, but it was not the same. Besides, every place she frequented reminded her of Paul and she'd come home and feel the emptiness surround her again.

Now there was Derek who was worming his way into her heart from his spot at the lunch table. He was quiet, yet chatty when given the chance, and seemed nervous at times, and in fact, Ruth found him a little dull in the beginning. But after their initial brief interactions, it seemed that every time Ruth popped her head into the staff lounge he was there, and that smile would appear on his face at the sight of her. She knew what the smile meant; she was used to it but she was still flattered and found herself drawn to it.

'Made you coffee. I know how you like it,' he'd call and Ruth would smile and sit with him, not really enjoying the coffee, which was too weak for her liking, but appreciating the effort.

She soon found herself wanting to talk to him, even though she decided she wanted nothing more from him than friendship. Yet in the pit of Ruth's stomach, she knew this was different to other men in the office she had friendships with. Like Mel, the jolly man with hair that looked like Ronald McDonald, who sat next to her and talked non-stop about his wife and children, or Daly, who came to her every Monday with a hangover and tales of his wild weekend. Ruth knew that she was safe with them. There was no attraction whatsoever and she would laugh along with them, sympathise with their blues and talk of inconsequential things like the weather or the latest movie they had watched. They were fun, but Ruth knew they were just that. With Derek, it was a little different, and Ruth suspected that it was because he already had her in his sights.

It started with the chance meetings in the staffroom, progressed to Friday night drinks after work at the bar on the ground floor of their building, and then to movie nights every two weeks. Even though Ruth didn't find that she had much in common with Derek, she liked his reliability, his stability in her life. He also seemed lonely, not having many friends outside of work, and he had a sister who was erratic and spoke to him once every six months. Yet he was an optimistic person, cheerful to a fault and seemed to adore Ruth. And more and more Ruth looked forward to her day at work, with the thought of Derek waiting for her in front of her desk, a cup of coffee in hand and a smile on his face.

'I can't let this go any further,' she said as she pulled away one evening as he deposited her at her car and had leaned in to kiss her. They had just been to see a movie and Ruth had expected this might happen. She felt it, in the dark theatre, a little rumble going through her stomach, when Derek glanced her way and leaned closer; it was all too familiar. They had both walked out of there a little tense and somewhat uncomfortable. So when he tried to kiss her, Ruth was not surprised.

'Why not?' he asked, quite seriously.

Ruth giggled now. She felt nervous. She had had a couple of flings lately, but nothing too serious and she liked it that way, but she knew that Derek was off limits. He was her friend and she hoped he would remain so. To go any further would complicate things between them and she didn't want them to end up like she and Paul. She certainly didn't want to start looking for another job.

Ruth could see that her giggle offended Derek when he frowned. Even when he was angry, or hurt, the most he would do was frown. He never uttered a nasty word to her, ever.

'No,' she cried. 'I'm just a bit nervous.'

'Why?'

'Because I don't want to go there, Derek. I just can't lose your friendship. It means a lot to me.'

'Why would you lose my friendship?'

'You know, just in case it doesn't work out.'

Now he laughed. 'I'm not proposing marriage, Ruth. I just want to see how we can be as a couple. I already love you.'

Ruth was aghast. 'Love me?'

'I thought you would have known by now.' His brow creased again.

'You never said …'

'I was giving you space … time. I know that you've been through a few relationships that haven't really worked out.'

'But …'

'I know. You haven't told me everything and I don't want to know, that's your business. But I think you will really be able to be who you are with the right one.'

This was a bit much for Ruth, this presumption completely out of the blue, but she was already warming to the idea, as much as the voice in her head was yelling for her to run.

'We're perfect for each other, don't you see?' he went on. 'We have a great friendship; we work in the same place. We get along. It's the perfect partnership.'

It sounded like a business deal, but Derek was right. 'Can I think about it?' asked Ruth, wondering if it was a good idea to date someone from work. It hadn't worked out so well the last time.

'Yes, but now that it's out there in the ether, don't keep me waiting.' He pecked her on the cheek and Ruth wasn't sure that she should have felt so absolutely nothing. She hoped it was just because it had come at her out of the blue.

Ruth, already knowing that their friendship was doomed after this incident one way or another, pulled him to her and kissed him full on his mouth. She felt his warm lips on hers and she closed her eyes, waiting for the fireworks to begin. She didn't feel anything again, except his hip squashing her stomach when he pushed her up tight against her car.

The music played softly as Ruth's head lay on her pillow that night and tears tried to spring to her eyes as she thought of Paul. She pictured him beside her, his eyes closed, his mouth in a slight smile, the little snore she still missed. It had been months; she should have stopped thinking about him by now. But she remembered his every feature so well, his lick of hair, his soft, cool mouth as it lapped hers. She squeezed her eyes tight, not allowing the tears to fall; she had to move on, not just with her mind, but with her heart. Yet as she lay between consciousness and slumber, she whispered, 'I miss you.'

A month after Derek kissed her, they had gone to bed together and still Ruth had not felt the spark that she had with Paul, Terrence and even Oliver. It happened after a night of watching old movies, something that Ruth had now gotten quite used to and she smiled ironically that Oliver was not around anymore to appreciate her new pastime. After the movie had finished, Ruth found Derek asleep on the sofa, his head in her lap. She tried to remove it slowly but he opened his eyes and gently pulled her face to his. She let him take her in his arms and carry her to the bedroom, where they made love, sweet and tender, but which left Ruth wanting more. She woke up the next morning accepting that every man she went to bed with was not going to make her toes curl and that there were other qualities that Derek possessed that were more important: patience, friendship and common interests.

Ruth liked Derek; they had been going on dates to the movies, enjoying long drives and went out with colleagues at times after work. Ruth was having fun again, enjoying the company of a man, and she felt special again, had someone who made her feel that way. But Ruth refused to let him move in with her; she knew she wasn't in love with him, not yet. They had been together, not really knowing what exactly they were, for more than six months and Derek had been dropping hints about living together.

'It's so lonely when I spend the night without you,' he said one evening, and Ruth immediately knew what that meant.

'It just gives you time to miss me,' she replied, a quiver of apprehension creeping up her spine.

And another time: 'It's such a waste to spend money on a flat when I'm here so much anyway.'

'But when you get sick of me or we have a fight, you have somewhere to go,' Ruth said and gave him a peck, knowing well they never fought or even argued about anything. They seemed to agree on everything, giving them no reason for a fallout of any kind.

And yet another when they had popped into Derek's flat some twenty minutes away from Ruth's place: 'My place is so poky; I wish we could spend more time here, but there wouldn't be anywhere to put your things,' he said, looking around the place that really was quite cramped. Even the lights were dim, making it look like a little toilet cubicle.

'We don't have to spend any time here if you don't want to,' Ruth said, wishing he didn't bring it up so often. 'You can just come and stay at my place at any time.'

'But you don't really want me to be around all the time.' He looked sulky.

Ruth knew he was pushing for her to suggest he move in altogether and she was adamant it was not going to happen. 'I just think it's too early to take another big step.'

'Early? I don't know about that.'

'C'mon, we'll talk about it another time,' Ruth said, grabbing his arm and wondering how long she could put him off.

Ruth knew she wasn't ready for that kind of commitment from Derek. She still didn't know if she could trust him and she didn't know what it was going to take for him to gain that trust. She understood she was being unreasonable, but she was not ready for more heartbreak. She was happy with the company, even feeling like she could love Derek at times, but her heart was never fully committed to him.

'Has he asked you to marry him?' Ruth's father, who could see the hesitancy in his daughter, asked one evening when she visited her parents' house after work.

'No, and I certainly hope he doesn't!' Ruth almost slammed the spoon into her soup and was a bit surprised by her vigour.

'But you have been together for a while now. Surely you must … you know,' piped in Roberta, who believed that it was about time Ruth settled down with someone whom she had been dating and was probably doing the deed with.

'Mother!'

'Bertie!'

Ruth and Gary looked at each other and laughed. They were on the same page, as always.

'Laugh at me if you will,' grumbled Roberta. 'But it's not right to just go from one person to another so often.'

'Well, it's not like I'm dating a different man every weekend,' Ruth retorted, thinking about how much simpler it would be to do just that.

'I'm just saying, you're nearly twenty-five and still no serious match. That Paul fella was a winner. Why ever did you leave him?'

'Mother …'

'Yes, call me old-fashioned, but I think you really should start thinking about a serious future. Or else your time will run out. Have you even thought about children?'

'A bit hard to, without a sperm donor.' Ruth wanted to shock her mother into silence and it seemed to work.

Roberta put her hand on her chest. 'Ruthy, please!'

'Sorry, Mum,' said Ruth and looked at her father, who was trying to mask a laugh with a cough.

'Sorry, I know you don't want my opinion,' Roberta continued. 'You have your own ideas, you've always been the independent one. But I just look at Patty and she has already had her children …'

'And a cheating bastard for a husband,' Ruth cut in. 'Is that what you want for me?'

'No, no.' Roberta reached out and took Ruth's hand across the table. 'I don't want that. I think it's … just that now, look at her. She's doing a course online, getting her science degree; have you seen the way she looks now?'

Ruth had noticed that Patty had been taking care of herself lately. Every time she'd seen her, Patty had immaculate nails on her fingers and toes and she'd even highlighted and cut her hair to a cute, shoulder-length bob. She looked completely different from how she'd looked when Ruth declined to comment on her appearance, the day she found out about Mark's infidelity. 'I think she's doing great. I love how she's come into herself,' Ruth replied.

'It's about time. But to keep a husband?'

Roberta and Gary looked at each other quickly.

'What am I missing?' Ruth cocked her head.

'Nothing,' said Roberta and rose to put on the kettle. 'Coffee before you go?'

'That would be great. Thanks, Mum.'

'Well, she is doing great at work, aren't you, honey?' put in Gary.

Ruth sighed. Work. Yes, that must be the consolation prize. But work did invigorate her. 'Yes, it's great. I get to fly to Sydney next week. I may even have to set up there.' Ruth could feel herself getting excited. They were right. Work made her happy, sometimes happier than the time she spent with Derek.

Roberta spun around. 'You're moving to Sydney?'

'No, no! I may have to go there a couple of times a month. That promotion I told you I just got, well, that's part of the deal. It works well if I don't have anyone who is waiting at home and nagging at me.' She smiled at her father who shook his head at her in resignation.

Roberta sighed. 'Okay, you win.'

Ruth went to her mother and put her arms around her back. 'Love you, Mum. That's for sure.'

Roberta leaned her head on Ruth's and closed her eyes.

She waved goodbye to her parents, and as she drove away,

the image of the two of them, Gary's arms wrapped around Roberta's waist as she leaned into him, in her head. *How I wish I could have that,* Ruth thought, and the image of Paul sprang to her mind. She hadn't thought about Paul for a couple of days and she smiled, pleased with herself. It was progress.

She had seen him in a bar with friends a couple of months ago when she had stopped in after work with Derek, and her heart had beaten so hard, she walked out, Derek following lamely, asking her what the problem was with the place. She kicked herself then. She wished she could have just had closure as she had with Terrence and Oliver and perhaps talking to him would have done the trick. She hoped she would have the opportunity soon, especially as there was every chance that he would frequent the places she did; they were always in agreeance about where they went and what they liked.

Ruth had even seen Terrence on a number of occasions since meeting him at Karen's engagement. It was inevitable considering Karen was engaged to Terrence's best friend and whenever the group of them, which now included Derek, went out together, she felt no lasting impression, just a sliver of resentment and a resolve never to trust and love anyone like she had done before. She knew it was why she kept Derek at a distance, as sweet and as committed as he was.

Ruth nodded to herself with purpose, shaking her head to rid the image of Paul from her brain. She knew she was not ready to fully commit again.

Chapter 15

Derek couldn't be at Karen's wedding. Work had taken him to New Zealand, where he would be for two weeks, and as much as he had wanted to stay to attend the wedding with Ruth, it was an important convention—a promotion at Marks and Sons depended on it. Ruth was disappointed but understood how important his work was to him, and a week into his trip, she was already missing him.

'I wish I was there with you,' he said as Ruth lounged in the seat on the balcony, feeling a little lonely. He had called every day for the first week and Ruth enjoyed the calm of the evening as she settled in to await his call, which came at the same time every day.

'Same, I don't want to go without you. Everyone will have their partners there,' she grumbled. She wasn't used to being away from him for so long and even though she went to Sydney at least once a month, it was not for more than a couple of days at a time. But this trip of Derek's was for two weeks and she missed him more than she wanted to admit to herself, wondering if she was indeed in love with him.

'I could come back?' Ruth could hear the concern in his voice.

'No, of course not,' she said, feeling selfish. 'I'll be fine. The wedding's only three days away. Don't you have a big dinner or something that night?'

'No, that's tomorrow. I don't really want to go but …' He sounded frustrated.

'Just go. You'll be back in a week. Don't miss me,' she said, then smiled. 'On second thought, miss me like crazy.'

'Talk tomorrow. Love you.'

Ruth was taken aback. 'Yeah, we'll talk tomorrow. Have a good night.' She hung up quickly, wishing he hadn't said those damn words.

The next day Ruth didn't hear from Derek and tried calling at their usual time, but his phone switched straight to voicemail. She figured he had run out of battery or something like that. She shook her head in exasperation; she usually had to remind him to charge his phone, so that was the most likely cause. The day had been tiring anyway; she had spent it at Karen's place and was expected to be there early the next morning for a rehearsal lunch and a bridal get-together.

When she got home the next evening, it was late and Ruth was exhausted. The day had been a flurry of activity with so many little meals set out that she was full and worn out by the time she returned to her apartment. She planned an early night, with another big day on the horizon. She still hadn't heard from Derek and tried calling him again, but there was no answer and Ruth wondered if he was upset with her for not having returned those words to him. She thought about whether she loved him, *really* loved him, and figured that perhaps she must if she was missing him so much.

'Then why can't I say them?' she said tossing herself onto the sofa and turning on the television. 'Just say it,' she said, sitting up suddenly. 'Practise.' She cleared her throat and imagined Derek sitting in front of her. 'Derek, I love you.' She smiled. It sounded silly and she thought that if someone was watching her she would have looked ridiculous. She tried again. 'I love you, Derek,' she said and saw Paul in the place where Derek was supposed to be. 'I love you,' she said sadly. 'Derek.'

She got out her phone and messaged Derek, telling him she loved him. At least she could do it as a text message, if not directly to him. She watched TV for a little while and there was still no response. She opened Facebook and scrolled through her news feed while she waited.

She stopped and scrolled backward. Derek had been tagged in a picture with a small group of people and beside him, an arm around her shoulder, and his head leaning slightly into her, was an attractive blonde, someone Ruth had never seen before.

An involuntary tremor shook her body and she quickly clicked away from the picture. She turned off her phone and stared at the TV that was showing a couple of people dancing in the rain, but she couldn't hear anything, her ears were buzzing so loudly. She shook her head clear and turned it off, sitting there in silence, frozen. She had been waiting for something like this to happen through all the time they had been together, waiting to see how she would feel about it when it did, when the betrayal finally came.

She felt the same annoying tug of fear that she had felt when she saw Anna in that photograph on Paul's wall and now she wondered why Paul had kept that picture. Yes, it was a beautiful shot, but to have someone he probably loved on display all the time would just have been tempting fate. It was the reason why she got rid of all Oliver, Terrence and Paul's memorabilia.

She guiltily thought of the grey scarf of Paul's that had been tucked in her sofa. The one she pulled out every now and then when Derek was not staying over, the one she lay next to her as she slept. She rested her head on the sofa and wondered how it would have been if they hadn't bumped into Anna that evening. Would she still be blindly trusting of him? She thought he was the one, that he was different, but he hadn't turned out to be different at all. They were all the same. Even Derek.

She absently wondered why she was thinking about Paul's betrayal when she had just been dealt another blow, by the man she had just realised she was in love with. Heading for the fridge, she poured a glass of wine and walked into the cool air of the balcony, feeling the warmth of the alcohol sliding down her throat. This feeling was now too familiar, and Ruth didn't like it; it reminded her of someone she once was, who she said she never would be again. Weak.

Taking the glass of wine back to the kitchen, she poured it down the sink and went back to the sofa again, picking up her phone. She had to face it head-on. She scrolled back to the picture of Derek and kept her eyes on his face, trying to be okay with the fact that this was just the way it was. She could feel her temper rise, the heat in her face, the same feelings cloak her body. She clutched the phone and stared intently into his eyes that she enlarged on the screen, looking for the betrayal that she already knew had happened. She glanced again at the woman next to him and quickly looked back at Derek. She couldn't fathom his expression, he just had the awkward smile he usually used in photographs.

Ruth sat back in her chair and considered what to do. She so badly wanted to text him again, to break up with him, to let him know she knew. But then she realised, what for? This was the way it was, with all of them. She may as well get used to it; she had already resigned herself to it and this latest betrayal was one she was well prepared for. She turned off her phone and took herself to bed, grabbing Paul's scarf out of the closet and laying it on her bed. She didn't feel guilty about it tonight.

****

The day started out beautifully. The sun was high in the sky and a warm breeze wafted through the window, swaying the white lace curtains that waved around Karen's figure. Karen looked the picture of bliss, a fitting sleeveless bodice that flowed into a rounded, full-length princess skirt. A smile was plastered on her face and it was infectious. Ruth beamed back with love for this wonderful friend who had been around for as long as she could remember. She felt a pang of happiness mixed with a tinge of envy and as she leaned forward to fluff Karen's veil, which dropped to below her waist, Ruth impulsively hugged her friend and took a moment to hold close the person who would never be disloyal to her.

She let go and held Karen's shoulders. 'Let's go. You can't look any better. No one in the world could look as beautiful as you do, right now,' she said as she gazed into Karen's smiling eyes.

They walked together to the door and Ruth opened it, but Karen, hurrying forward, shut it again, leaning against it.

'Am I doing the right thing?' Her eyes were now looking at Ruth with a real fear in them.

'A little late for that thought, isn't it?' Ruth, feeling the same pang of fear for Karen, tried to mask it with a laugh.

'No, I mean it. You're my best friend. Tell me I'm not making a mistake.' Her trembling hands grabbed Ruth's and Ruth squeezed them.

As much as Ruth didn't want to do it, she had to tell her. 'You are. You are doing the right thing.'

But as Karen walked down the aisle, a teary smile on her face, Ruth wondered if she really was. And as Karen kissed Pete at the altar, she thought about Paul and wondered why it wasn't Derek that came to her mind. She looked at the man standing beside Pete, his best man, Terrence, the man who had crushed her heart, and she felt a shock of rage at him, at what he had been part of turning her into. She looked back at the couple, intent on not making this day about her. It was her best friend's wedding.

****

'Where's Derek tonight?'

Ruth had seen Terrence saunter over to her, his hands in his pockets, a wicked smile on his still beautiful face. She had taken a moment to herself, feeling a range of emotions that had left her drained. She wondered if there would ever be a day where she would be a bride again, whether she could trust someone enough to let them in; more importantly, would there ever be a man who was trustworthy?

'Work thing.' She waved her hand in dismissal and looked away, ignoring the temptation to look at his face.

Terrence stood next to her, so very close, she could feel his elbow rub against her arm. When Terrence leaned over to kiss her, as they stood together in the gazebo, admiring the night sky, Ruth stared into those shining eyes, and almost let him. Just in time, she realised what was happening and jerked backwards.

'Terrence!'

Terrence lazily laughed. 'Just for old times' sake,' he said.

Ruth laughed back a little uneasily. She was taken aback at her instincts. She had almost let him kiss her, without considering the fact that she had a boyfriend, albeit a thousand miles away. She hadn't even stopped herself because of Derek, she had stopped because she realised it was Terrence and she couldn't stand the thought of falling under his spell again.

'That's crazy,' replied Ruth, nervously.

'Well,' he said and raised his eyebrows. 'You still find me attractive?'

Ruth found him so very attractive right then and it wouldn't require too much more temptation to throw herself into his arms, but she knew that it was just because she was feeling insecure. She had just been thinking about her current cheating boyfriend, and one of her old cheating boyfriends was putting the moves on her. She cringed when she thought about the night she begged him, literally on her knees, to stay with her. She was damned if she was going to give him the satisfaction.

'I am not about to stroke your ego,' she said laughingly. He was still the playboy she had fallen in love with, but she was not falling now. 'Go back in there. I'm sure there are plenty of good-looking women who will do that for you.' Ruth was surprised at how blunt she was with him.

Terrence turned away and looked into the distance, Ruth following his gaze to the lake, where the water glistened from the reflection of the little lights that surrounded the large garden. It really was romantic; if only she had the right person beside her.

Paul's smiling face came to her mind again … and then Anna's.

'I'm sorry,' he said softly, putting his hand on hers that rested on the railing.

She almost removed her hand from his, but she left it there and he squeezed it. Ruth felt tears begin to spring in her eyes and remained silent. Terrence leaned over, kissed her cheek, and walked away. Ruth couldn't bring herself to look after him and swallowed hard. She had made it a point not to waste her tears anymore and she hadn't so far. Terrence was not going to break her again.

It was after Karen and Pete had been waved away that Ruth sat at one of the empty tables, the one that had just been vacated by her parents.

'Come home with us,' said Gary before they left, 'spend the night at home. We can have snacks and stay up late. Mum will make pancakes tomorrow, or maybe I will cook scrambled eggs.'

Ruth knew they were feeling sorry for her. They had met Derek and seemed to like him well enough, although there hadn't been any definitive comments on him. Not a yay or a nay, but they seemed a little miffed that he had let her attend the wedding on her own. 'Thanks, Dad. I'm tired too, but I'll just stay for a bit more.' Ruth was dreading going home to an empty apartment but she wasn't relishing the thought of being woken up at the crack of dawn by Gary singing in the shower.

She kissed her parents goodbye and sat at the table alone, looking around at the stragglers, some too drunk, and others swaying on the dance floor that was now devoid of music. The night was getting cold but was still as beautiful and Ruth looked up at the stars which filled the sky. She wished Derek were here and hated herself for still wanting him.

She took out her phone and her finger hovered on his number. She wanted to call him so badly. No, there was not much on Facebook about him when she checked this morning. In fact, there hadn't been much on his page and when she looked for the photograph again, it was no longer there. There had been no messages or calls from him today either and Ruth wasn't going to keep trying him; she needed to retain at least a little self-respect, and hopefully when he returned, he would have the guts to break up with her.

Ruth sighed and stood up, ready to leave.

'Hey, there,' a low voice said behind her.

Ruth jumped and looked at the owner of the voice who had his hand stretched towards her.

'Mike,' he said, and Ruth took the offering.

'Ruth,' she said, smiling at this attractive, dark-haired man, whose even-toothed grin made her think twice about leaving.

She had seen him through the evening give her furtive glances and once, even a broad smile, but Ruth had not taken much notice, except to feel flattered by the attention. She got enough of it, so this one was no exception, but there was something about him. She did like his smile though and sat back down, gesturing for him to take the seat beside hers.

'Were you about to leave?' he asked, sliding into the chair after turning it towards her.

Ruth nodded. 'It's about that time,' she said, refilling her glass of wine. 'How about you?'

'Yes, I was, but I didn't want to leave without meeting you.'

Ruth turned to Mike, whose now teasing smile disarmed her for a moment. She giggled and took another sip of wine. 'That's a line.'

Mike laughed too and Ruth noticed his laugh was as attractive as his smile, his whole face lighting up, little creases forming in the corners of his eyes.

'Okay,' said Ruth, leaning back into her chair. 'Tell me who you are.'

'So, you know my name,' he said, flicking back his wavy hair; taking her glass from her, he took a sip. He handed it back, ignoring Ruth's indignant glare, and continued. 'I'm going to lay it straight. I am divorced, I have two children, four and three. They live with their mother half the time and with me the other half. I've had an amicable divorce and I get along with my ex quite well.' He paused and rubbed at his goatee and Ruth found herself wanting to get closer to him. 'I work with a real estate agency; actually, I part-own it. Zephyrs. Heard of it?'

Ruth shook her head, amazed at the candid summary of his life.

'Up past Geelong.' He took another sip of Ruth's wine and Ruth didn't mind this time. She liked his easy manner, his relaxed way, like he had known her forever. 'There's not much else really. Born and bred in Carlton, my parents still live there and I moved to Geelong, where I now live in my big beach house by the sea with my children.'

'Aha!' Ruth replied, leaning forward. 'There it is.'

'There what is?'

'The kicker, the hook.'

'Well.' He smiled sheepishly. 'I was just giving you information. Now it's your turn.'

Ruth stood up and her head spun. She wasn't sure whether it was from the wine or from the touch of Mike's hand on her arm as he tried to steady her. But as she turned to face him, she could see his look, an expression not of concern but of want. He kept his hand on her elbow and Ruth slid into his embrace. Even as she kissed him, she knew she could fall for him. The tingles in her stomach and the quick beat of her heart told her it would be very easy to do with this man.

The phone rang and Ruth ignored it, holding Mike firm with her lips, feeling his arms around her, and more importantly, feeling her body spark in anticipation.

The ringing continued but Ruth didn't care.

'Are you going to get that?' Mike moved back and removed a stray hair that had fallen on her face.

'No,' she said.

PART TWO
FINDING RUTH

Chapter 16

She knew it was a juggle, but Ruth was not ready to give up either one. And why should she, she asked herself every morning as she got ready for work and when she went to bed at night, the only times she had a moment to think. She wanted both of them and had had them both, quite successfully, for the last three months.

Mike was sexy, a man in every way, and he knew how to curl her toes in bed. Derek was kind and sweet and didn't push her to do anything she didn't want to do. Mike was authoritative, taking her arm, leading the way whenever they went out. Derek let her lead, let her guide him. She got her satisfaction from telling Mike about her job and hearing about his, a real estate representative, with a stake in an agency on the greater coast, while she was happy to talk shop with Derek, helping him with his work and he helping her with hers. They were chalk and cheese and although she couldn't decide which was which, she was happy to feast on a bit of both.

But none had committed to her and she was unwilling to commit fully to them either. And for the first few weeks, it was terribly convenient. Mike had his children quite a lot of the time and could only make time for Ruth on the weekends, and Derek was trying to climb the corporate ladder, which meant schmoozing with potential clients on the weekends.

'I don't know what I'm doing!' She looked at Karen's blank face and laughed. She was exhilarated, on a natural high for most of the days and most nights, hardly having a moment of downtime.

Karen had stopped at Ruth's apartment on her way home from work and they were having drinks on the balcony overlooking the park, where joggers and dog walkers meandered each day. Ruth had kept her secret to herself, not wanting to divulge it to Karen, knowing quite well what her strait-laced friend's response would be. But she couldn't hold it back anymore, she needed to talk to someone about it. She'd even considered talking to Patty, but her sister's newly busy life didn't leave her much time to sit and have conversations with Ruth. Besides, she rarely had time to go anywhere anymore, not even her parents' house, and she certainly heard about it from them.

'Ruth! You have to make a choice,' said Karen, still wide-eyed in shock.

'Do I?' Ruth leaned forward playfully. 'So, why do I?' Nothing Karen said was going to get her down.

'Because'—Karen paused, clearly not expecting that question—'because, for one, you'll get into a whole heap of trouble.'

'How?' Ruth was curious. She wanted to know exactly how she would pay, just to prepare herself, not that she hadn't thought about that before.

'Well, if either one was to find out …' Karen stopped.

'Yes, what?' Ruth leaned further forward in anticipation.

'Well … well, you will be alone again,' said Karen, flustered.

'And, what difference would that make?'

'But if one of them finds out …'

'For starters they won't.' Ruth leaned back and sipped at her wine. She looked up at the evening sky, tinted pink, and felt warm, safe. 'And you know what? I'm so sick of bearing the brunt of these cheating men. I think I just wanted to know what it would be like to be on the other side. And honestly, it's not bad at all.' She smiled and winked at Karen.

'Ruth!' said Karen her hand on her mouth. 'This is not who you are.'

'Who am I?'

'You're a good person, someone who has wanted to have a good life, a committed relationship …'

'What exactly has that gotten me? A cheating husband and more cheating men.'

'But Ruth …'

'Well, it's my turn,' said Ruth adamantly. 'All men are cheats, so why should we sit on the sidelines and wait for their loyalty?' She saw Karen's face go dark and realised what she had said. 'Not all men, Karen. I didn't mean Pete.' Karen nodded, but Ruth knew her sensitive friend was already upset. 'I just meant that I am happy. I haven't been happy for so long, and right now if one of them strays, well, I'm prepared for it.'

'You can't live like that though,' said Karen.

Ruth now wished she hadn't said anything to Karen, but she was her best friend. Who else could she confide in?

'What about Paul?'

'What about Paul?' said Ruth, feeling her heart beat a little faster.

'Have you seen him?'

'No, why should I?'

'Because you loved him too, and you haven't made your amends with him, like you did with the other two.'

'What does that …?'

'Come on, Ruth. If you can do this with both of these men, you don't really want either of them. You are just playing it safe, having fun. But at whose expense? You already said that Derek didn't do anything to hurt you. Why would you hurt him?'

'I can't keep up.' Ruth was confused with Karen's spiel. 'And what does this have to do with Paul?'

Karen smiled. 'Funny that's what you took out of that.' She rose to leave. 'I have to go.'

Karen kissed Ruth on the way out. 'Just be careful. You're the one who is going to end up with a broken heart … again.'

Ruth sat back down and looked at her view. She loved the

tranquillity, even through the noise and hustle and bustle of city life. She watched an older couple, hand in hand, walk around the park in loops. At one point, the man stopped to straighten the woman's shawl, which had slid off her shoulder. She kissed him and nestled into his arm and they kept walking. Ruth couldn't understand why she felt a teardrop try to well and she angrily squeezed her eyes shut, not allowing it to fall.

A broken heart. Well, she already had had her share of those and she knew she was protecting herself from another. Again, Paul came to mind. She had a sudden urge to call him and she picked up her phone. Her fingers hovered over his number but she tossed it on the table just in case she was too tempted; she couldn't give in to her thoughts about Paul. Besides, she had to leave in an hour. Mike would be waiting for her and it was a long drive to Geelong.

It was starting to get a little tricky with Derek. He had wanted to take her out on Saturday, and she had to make an excuse about visiting her parents. He'd offered to go with her, but she told him she wasn't ready for them to get too comfortable with each other.

'We've been together for nearly a year,' he said. 'I have already met them and they seem to like me.' He stopped. 'Or maybe they don't?'

Ruth suddenly had a thought at this. 'Um, they are okay with you. But … I think they just think that I …'

'What?'

'Never mind. I think they are just old-fashioned, you know.'

'What do you mean?'

'Nothing. They just think it's bad to be living in sin.' She shook her head in mock-exasperation.

Derek laughed at this. 'We aren't even living together. You refuse to move in with me.'

'Yes, well …' Ruth nodded sagely. 'They aren't silly. I'm pretty sure they don't think I abstain.'

Derek shrugged and hugged her, Ruth feeling nauseated with her treachery. She felt terrible that she had given him the impression that her parents didn't like him, but she needed a good alibi for when she was with Mike.

The drive on a Friday evening was a long one, but it gave Ruth time to think and be with herself for a little while. Between work, Derek and Mike, her time was never her own. Her parents complained that she didn't visit often enough and Ruth had declined attempts from Karen to catch up with her on numerous occasions. At times, she just wanted to push thoughts of all of them aside and just have a moment to contemplate her own feelings about everything that was going on in her life. But there were also times she was glad she didn't have that time; she knew what she would be telling herself and she couldn't give in to her old-fashioned version of morality.

Right now, as she sat in her car, bumper to bumper, listening to the evening news on the radio, she wasn't upset with the amount of traffic and the amount of time it was taking to get to Mike's house. She knew he would be waiting with a chilled bottle of wine and perhaps a lasagne or some other delicious meal for her. She twisted the dial and heard a version of 'Baby I Love Your Way', and tapped her fingers on the steering wheel, the anticipation of seeing Mike escalating.

She smiled to herself and a rush of emotion went through her body as she thought about the night she met him, under the stars at Karen's wedding. His kiss and his arms around her left her weak, almost making her knees buckle. And when he asked if he could drive her home, she refused. She couldn't bear the thought of having him in the bed she lay in with Derek. That would really be hitting below the belt and she hadn't lost that much respect for herself yet.

'I don't want to go home tonight,' she said, still looking into his brown eyes, creased with a smile. She liked that, it made him look mature, but also made him more knowing, someone who knew who he was, not someone who would rely on her to make him something. 'But I am excited to see that house of yours.'

'You work quickly,' he said, leaning over and kissing her again.

Ruth smiled back coyly. She felt dizzy but she didn't know whether it was the wine or the kiss, and right now she didn't care. She just wanted to stay in this man's arms, just for tonight. *While Derek is probably canoodling with some other woman in some other country,* she thought, even knowing she was justifying her decision. *Besides, one night won't hurt anyone, and I'm feeling so lonely right now.*

'It's a long drive.'

'Good,' she said boldly. 'More time to get to know you.'

They almost ran to Mike's yellow Mustang and Ruth stopped, putting her hand on her mouth.

'Wow,' she said as Oliver's Chevy came to mind. Later, she wondered why she had thought of Oliver at that point in time. Perhaps it was their shared love of classic cars, but she took an immediate dislike to the thing Mike called his 'baby'.

Mike, mistaking her remark for a compliment, smiled and bowed chivalrously as he opened the door to let her in. In that instant, she forgave his taste and happily jumped in. The drive had taken too long, with Ruth not wanting her conscience to catch up with her, but Mike passed the time by sharing the stories of his life with her.

'My marriage broke up because she was unfaithful,' he said quite matter-of-fact, as he gazed at the long, dark road ahead of them.

Ruth, who was just watching his face, his furrowed eyes as he talked, swallowed hard and looked away.

'But I know why, and it was all too late. I was the classic husband, spent so much time working myself up the corporate ladder and ignoring the things that were important. She got sick of it, even though she tried to …' He looked at Ruth and smiled cynically. 'I shouldn't be talking about my ex-wife, should I?'

'No, it's fine,' said Ruth, not really wanting to know more about this man who she just intended to spend the night with. She just wanted to feel the touch of his lips on hers again, to feel the shiver down her spine, the butterflies in her tummy, something she hadn't felt in a long time. She leaned over and ran her lips along his neck.

'Mmm,' he murmured. 'Still twenty minutes away.'

'Sorry,' she said and sat back in her seat.

'But don't stop,' he said and Ruth leaned over again and nestled her head in his neck. It felt snug, like it belonged there.

They didn't speak the rest of the way and Ruth tried to ignore the warnings that were banging at her brain. When they pulled up into Mike's driveway, she stared ahead of her at the enormous rendered house with large glass windows that stood before her, her mouth agape. A path of red bricks led a short way to a double wooden door that Ruth could see had an old-fashioned door knocker on it. She could already smell the sea air and breathed it in as she opened the car door. Then the sound of lapping water hit her.

'Are we very close to the beach?'

'At the beach.' He smiled and shrugged. 'Perks of being a realtor.'

Mike took her hand and led her in, Ruth a little struck by the house, its size, its style, its proximity to the water. Even though it was so big, it had a cosiness to it, a set of tables in the foyer, large and small photographs displayed on them, making it feel like a family home, and Ruth had a warm feeling like that of when she entered her childhood home. She looked at the aquamarine plush settee sitting in the centre of the living area, offset by a tinted glass window that took up a whole wall, and felt like she was in the middle of an advertisement. She felt her arm being taken and she let herself be led to the doorway. Mike pulled open the light-blue curtains and for a moment Ruth caught her reflection in the glass, a still innocent woman, her cheekbones high, her eyes wide, her body poised in hesitation.

It was gone in a moment as Mike turned on the outer light, which glowed a muted yellow, and Ruth found herself staring at a vast expanse of sand with water that seemed to be crawling up to them. The only thing that kept it at bay was the mahogany decking, where stood a set of deck chairs and a coffee table, with an unopened yellow umbrella in the middle. Green plants with yellow flowers surrounded the pergola, and Ruth could see that little drops of rain were beginning to hit the flowers.

'Wow,' she said, 'you live here.' It wasn't a question and for the first time in her life, Ruth wondered what it would be like to be away from the city, her beloved playground.

Mike kissed her neck gently. 'I'll be right back,' he said, leaving her on her own while she took in the scene, the light-grey clouds, barely visible in the thick of the night, the moon invisible. Raindrops tickled the ocean, the sound of the patter giving Ruth a feeling of serenity, and she exhaled.

'It's raining,' she said as she turned to Mike, and found him right behind her, a glass of wine in his hand and a smile on his face. He reeked of seduction.

Ruth knew this was it. She could still change her mind; it

wasn't too late to go back. She found herself taking the glass, setting it on the table beside her and pulling Mike to her.

****

As the dawn crept into the room, disturbing her eyes, Ruth thought about what she had done. A tight knot was pulling at the pit of her stomach and she wanted to cry. She didn't feel that way last night, when she had made love to Mike, over and over again, and then finally had nestled into his arms, tired but exhilarated, the longing sated. She had managed to keep Derek from her mind; she slept soundly.

Derek's face came hurtling into her mind now as she lay motionless, wondering if Mike was still in bed with her. She opened her eyes to take in her surroundings and found herself looking at a beige wall, on which hung a giant painting of an Australian landscape. The side table held a framed photograph of two little boys and Ruth picked it up, scrutinising the faces of two smiling children who looked like miniature versions of Mike. A wave of guilt swept through her and she put it back softly. She eventually risked turning her head behind her to see if Mike was still in bed. She found crumpled sheets but no Mike, and she looked up at the ceiling, feeling terrible guilt and an anger with herself for stooping to the level of the men who had betrayed her, doing exactly what they had done. *Had they felt the same way she was feeling right now?*

'No harm, no foul,' she said softly to herself. She could keep this secret; she never had to see Mike again. She wondered about his attendance at the wedding and resolved to ask Karen who he was. She wished she had just gone home with her parents last night when they offered, then she wouldn't be in this position; she never would have met Mike. She rubbed at her eyes, wishing it was all a fun little fantasy that she played in her mind on occasion, when the monotony of Derek got to be too much.

But now, she just had to get out of here as soon as possible. Pulling the light linen sheets up to her chin, she could feel her nakedness and wondered where her clothes were. Oh yes, they were still in the living room, probably dumped around the carpet, where they had started last night. Ruth clenched her fists, irritated at her impulsiveness. What she should have done was break up with Derek first before getting into bed, literally, with another man.

'Awake?' Mike, his tousled hair falling over his eyes, poked his head through the door and seeing her awake, smiled, letting himself in with a tray of toast, coffee, tea, jam and butter. 'Breakfast,' he said, placing the tray on the side table. Then he sat on the bed, his eyes uneasy now.

Ruth, whose hands were clutching tightly to the sheets that were protecting her modesty, suddenly let go and rose up, letting them fall, and put her arms around him.

Chapter 17

Now, as she reached Mike's house, she pushed aside Karen's warnings and thoughts of Derek. This was her time with Mike, when she was a different person, one she didn't even recognise herself, sure, but one that was happy and fulfilled.

The weekend with Mike was wonderful, as usual. The long summer Saturday was spent at the beach, literally Mike's backyard, and he was happy to have Ruth strut about on the sand in her bikini. He didn't want to hide her from the world as Oliver had and he played with her, chasing her on the sand into the water, hugging and caressing her in the salty sea, while she hungrily devoured his kisses, the heat of her passion tempering the cold of the water. When the sun began to set, they clambered to the house and made love, barely stopping to have dinner, and made love again.

Lying in Mike's bed that evening, his arms wrapped around her, Ruth was happy. A wind had suddenly come through the coast and Ruth watched through the window from where she could see the waves, rough and demanding. She shivered and Mike's arms tightened around her. She knew she was in love with him.

Ruth thought that perhaps it was time to end things with Derek. She tried to think of why it would be best not to keep him hanging on, but the thought of Mike hurting her and leaving her alone again terrified her. The man would surely have women throwing themselves at him on a regular basis, with his dashing looks, his quick wit and his candidness, as he had been when she first met him. She wondered for how long he would be able to resist temptation.

The only problem was that when she was with Derek, she thought of ending things with Mike. She knew now that Derek had not been unfaithful that night. He had come home from New Zealand two days later, a few days earlier than Ruth had expected. She had gone to Mike's place straight after work on the Monday and had already blocked Derek's calls and messages, knowing in her heart it was over with him. As she was used to doing by now the way she did with the others, she dismissed him when he appeared in her mind. She returned home at seven in the morning to get ready for work, deciding it was time to pack Derek's things, a routine she was getting used to. She sighed and tried not to think about what she would say to him when they came face to face, and they certainly would. She cringed at the thought of finding a new job again and briefly wondered if Marielle would take her back. And that's when the pesky, lazy smile of Paul's jumped into her brain, replacing the forlorn one of Derek. No, she would have to look elsewhere; she couldn't imagine what it would be like to see

Paul again, let alone work alongside him every day.

She shook her head free of the things she had to do and focused on what needed to be done right now. And for now, she had to get ready to go to work. That was all her mind could take for the moment. She unlocked the door to her apartment and heard the hum of the TV, a reporter on the morning news. She frowned, confused, and followed the sound which came from the dining room, where she found Derek at the table, a cup of coffee in one hand and his head in the other.

'Where have you been?' he yelled and jumped up. 'Are you okay?'

Ruth was dumbfounded at the sight of him. He was supposed to be away for another few days and she really didn't expect him to come back to her. 'What are you doing here?' she asked, not quite sure how to act.

'I came early. I've been calling you, messaging. What's going on?' He moved towards Ruth and she backed away. 'Ruth, what's wrong?'

'Did you have a good time in New Zealand?' She put her hand on her hip and screwed her eyes at him.

'Yeah, sure, well, not really …' He paused. 'But I was so worried about you. I even called Karen.'

Ruth didn't know that. 'I thought you had moved on from me,' she said in a small voice.

Derek just stared at her and then burst into laughter. 'You daft woman, I love you, you're never getting away from me.' He drew her to him and Ruth leaned her head on his chest, breathing in his scent and knowing how much she missed him and also knowing now he would never have done anything to hurt her. The ghosts had just come back to haunt her in her moment of weakness. And she had jumped at the chance to be one of *them*.

She knew that this was the time to tell him what she'd done. She had to if there were to be any future with this man, and right now she wanted there to be.

'So,' he said leading her into the kitchen and turning on the kettle. 'Where on earth were you? I've been waiting here for hours. I was going to drive to your parents' house, I was so worried, but I didn't want to worry them.'

'Well, you should have,' replied Ruth. 'I was a little lonely last night, so I stayed the night with them.'

The moment had passed.

As Ruth sat at the table, a cup of coffee in hand, wishing she could just have a shower to wash Mike off her, Derek told her all about the annoying blonde who wouldn't leave him alone.

'And then to top off a disastrous trip, she took my phone, actually took it, and I didn't even realise until I got home. Then she sends it to my room with a smiley face on a Post-it, after I made a complaint to the hotel.' He was indignant and Ruth knew he wasn't lying. Why else would he have been so panicky trying to get in touch with her? 'Speaking of, why didn't you answer my calls?'

'Funny story,' said Ruth. 'I lost it at Karen's wedding.' She tried to think of something that would make sense and she got up and began to wash her cup. 'That's why I was over at my parents' house. I went to pick it up last night and couldn't bear coming home to an empty place.' She hated herself so much right now, but the excuse seemed plausible and Derek had no reason to suspect anything else. *Until now*, she thought wryly.

'Well, I'm home now.' Derek came up behind Ruth, wrapping his arms around her, and she squeezed her eyes tight. How could she be this person? Ruth wished Derek had betrayed her, it would have been so much easier; it would clear her conscience. She knew she had to stop seeing Mike. She pulled his arms tighter around her.

****

Now, as she drove home from Mike's place that Sunday afternoon, she had a new resolve. She was going to end it with Derek and she would have to come clean with Mike. She knew he would understand. He just had to. Karen was right; if she didn't, it would all end in disaster.

She was glad Derek wasn't coming over tonight; he was going out with his old high school mates for drinks and she had encouraged him, knowing he had so few friends. She was relieved now; it would give her some time to think about how to say what she needed to say to him. But even as she thought about it, she felt a flicker of sorrow run through her body and she clutched at the steering wheel, trying to convince herself that it was the right thing to do.

She had barely walked into her apartment and thrown her overnight bag on the bed when Derek called.

'Open the door,' his laughing voice said, and Ruth felt a stab of guilt, a thrill of fear and also a slight irritation at his unexpected visit.

She was just about to jump into the bath to rinse the lingering scent of sex and Mike off her and now here was Derek.

'I'm in the bathroom,' she said. 'Let yourself in.' How she wished she hadn't given him the key to her apartment.

She hurriedly shed her clothes, dumped them under a pile of others in the basket and tucked the bag under the bed. Wrapping a towel around herself, she thought about how she was neglecting everything, including her chores, and shook her head to dismiss the thought. She didn't have time to think about that right now.

She found Derek in the kitchen, a bunch of flowers in his hands. She felt a flutter in her heart and pulled him to her, kissing him deeply. She realised she had missed him more than she realised.

'Why do I deserve these?' she said, guilt flooding her body.

'Can't I get flowers for the woman I love?'

'Yes, yes, of course.' Ruth smiled. 'Just settle yourself. I need to have a shower.'

'Strange time for a shower.' He shrugged.

Ruth felt an unnecessary need to explain herself. 'It's been such a warm day and I'm a little, you know … yuck.'

'How was it with your parents?'

'Um, yeah. They're good. You know the usual. Make yourself a drink. I'll be back in a minute.'

The shower beating down on her, Ruth struggled with how she was going to do it, how she was going to break Derek's heart. She felt a shudder of indignance. No one seemed to have cared when they broke hers! But Derek, innocent, sweet Derek, who would give anything for her. No, she knew she needed to make a decision. She couldn't keep stringing them along the way she'd been for the last few months. But it was a hard choice, especially with the way she was feeling now as she was about to end it with Derek.

She thought she could love both of them but what was more important was that she was not making either of them the centre of her life. She was the important one now. What she needed mattered. A nagging guilt hit her heart, but she took a deep breath and got out of the shower.

Derek was waiting for her on the balcony, two glasses of wine cooling in ice on the little table in front of him.

'We're working tomorrow,' Ruth said, eyeing the glasses.

'A celebration,' Derek replied and held out his hand, guiding her to her seat, next to his.

'What are we celebrating?'

'Well, do you know what I did this weekend while you were gone, while I was missing you?' He reached forward and kissed her ear.

Ruth was on alert. She was nervous all the time, wondering when her little web of treachery was going to tear apart. 'Um?'

Then he was down on his knee in a second, a little red velvet box materialising from nowhere. 'Marry me.'

Ruth's eyes widened and she leaned back in her chair. She didn't say anything, just stared wide-eyed at the box, which was now opened, revealing a solitaire diamond set in a band of gold.

Derek's eyebrows narrowed. 'Not the reaction I was expecting.'

'Um … I don't know what to say,' Ruth muttered, her mind awhirl. 'I didn't expect it.'

'We've been dancing around it for a while now.' He sat back in his chair, his head low. The silence that was momentary seemed to last forever. 'You don't want to marry me?'

Ruth thought he looked like a little boy who had just been rebuffed by his sweetheart, but how could she say yes?

'You said that your parents would be happy … I thought that you were hinting …'

'No! I wasn't hinting …' Ruth was aghast. This was the last thing she expected … or wanted.

'Then you don't want to?'

'I didn't say that.' Ruth realised she would lose him if she said no, and this was the second she knew she wasn't ready to lose Derek yet. She knew somehow she really did love him. In that instant she made her decision. She had to leave Mike.

'Yes.' She put out her hand and Derek, his eyes now ablaze with excitement, slipped the ring on her finger.

Chapter 18

She lay on the bed facing the large glass windows and watched the water lap at the sand. It was so serene, so calming and Ruth wished she could seize it and make it part of her. She was so overwhelmed right now, her mind constantly creating believable excuses for Mike or Derek, her conscience in a continuous battle with itself.

Mike was already taking his morning swim in the cold ocean water, something she still couldn't get herself to do. She wondered if she could just sneak out and text him later to tell him that something came up and she had to leave. And she needed to leave in time; Mike's children were coming home early and he had urged Ruth to finally meet them, but she was nowhere near ready to meet his kids. So far she had managed to avoid seeing them, thinking she would be long out of his life before the time came, but now, four months later, Mike was getting impatient. This was getting too serious and Ruth now had to figure how she was going to deal with it all. This was an unexpected complication, well, another one anyway, something else she needed to store in that muddled brain of hers.

'If we are serious, then you will need to meet them at some stage,' he had said last night, when he had taken her out to dinner. If she had known, she would have made an excuse and wouldn't have come at all this weekend.

'But what about your ex? Maybe she's not comfortable with it.'

'I've already talked to Eve about you. She's fine. She has her own life too.'

'I'm just nervous, Mike.' She took his hands, hoping to make him feel her discomfort.

'They are little things!' He laughed. 'They don't need to see you as their new mother.'

The word jolted her. *Mother!* 'I don't know if I'm ready to take on that kind of responsibility.'

Mike frowned. 'You knew the deal from the moment we met.'

'I know, I know.' Ruth saw she was getting in too deep; the waters were getting too wavy and she knew she would soon find herself in a rip. She could feel it coming.

Mike put his arm around her. 'We are getting serious. Don't you think it's time we become a bigger part of each other's lives?'

'I guess. It's just that work is …'

Mike sighed. 'Work is always the problem for you. You're always jetting about. I barely get to see you. Remember what I said about work taking over my life … just be careful.' He cocked his head. 'Hey. Maybe I can come with you the next time. I may have some leave …'

Ruth was alarmed at the suggestion. 'Well, you can.' She tried to think fast. 'But you will probably spend most of your time without me.' She hated herself for this, she hated lying so much, but it was becoming second nature to her now. She did it easily and without too much thought. For all Mike knew, Ruth still lived at home with her crabby parents, who she disliked, and nothing could be further from that truth. 'It's like concentrated work, you know. Meetings, dinner with clients, more meetings, then sleep and repeat.' She laughed, trying to make it sound silly.

'Yeah, but I can make you sleep so much better,' he said, a sly smile on his face.

She had relented and agreed to meet his children, but Ruth was still hoping to make a quick getaway before they came over. She had already texted Karen, who was not happy about being her excuse. But she agreed to call Ruth at eleven in the morning with an emergency, telling her it was the last time she'd cover for her.

Unfortunately, they arrived at ten, when Ruth was still showering. She came out of the bathroom in a towel, her hair wet and dripping, to find two wavy-haired little boys already in the kitchen making a noise. Eve, Mike's ex-wife, a tall and stately blonde, upon seeing Ruth frozen at the bedroom door, smiled an amused grin, and crossed her arms. She called out to Mike, who was busy running back and forth trying to pick up garments that were strewn all over the lounge room floor from their previous night. His arms full, he stopped and glanced at Ruth with a look of alarm, seeing the awkward position she was in. Ruth ducked back into the bedroom and quickly threw on some clothes, cursing herself for not leaving earlier.

Ruth heard a knock at the bedroom door and she sheepishly called out, 'Come in.'

Eve entered, the same look of amusement on her face. 'Sorry, we were early,' she said. 'I'm Eve.'

'Ruth,' said Ruth still trying to shove her foot into her shoe.

'I've heard all about you,' said Eve, reaching over to grab the second shoe that lay at the other end of the room. She sat on the edge of the bed next to Ruth and dropped it on the floor next to Ruth's foot. 'You make him happy, I can see that.'

Ruth wanted to curl up and bury herself in the sand that she could see through the open window. She smiled unsurely.

'Are you nervous about meeting the children?' Eve spoke to her like a child, but instead of resenting it, Ruth welcomed it. She was anxious, and terribly guilt-ridden. How could she do this thing that was such a massive part of a relationship when she had no intention … She nodded.

'Don't be. Just be yourself,' said Eve and swished out of the room with a wink.

'Be yourself,' Ruth repeated to herself. 'I don't even know who the hell that is.'

Ruth liked Eve. She never would have thought an ex-wife

could be so welcoming, so sweet. She wished she was the typical ex, the jealous monster, threatened by the newcomer, a great excuse for Ruth when she finally left. What a thought! Ruth winced at her deceitful thoughts.

She sighed and looked out of the window again, contemplating escaping out of it. But she knew she couldn't do that. Besides, the screen was too tight and would take too long to unscrew. She shrugged and rose, ready to meet the family.

Alex and Bradley happened to be lovely little children, immediately pulling Ruth along to the beach, chattering away with her, while she chased them around the beach, built sandcastles and held their hands when they wanted to walk in the sea. And when she looked over at Mike, who sat on the step of his deck, watching them in amusement and what Ruth could only describe as love, she flinched.

When Karen's call finally came through, she didn't want to leave.

Ruth stopped in at her parents' house on the way home. She needed something familiar, something safe, and always found it at her childhood home. And when she walked into the little house, with her mother's lamps creating a homey glow that bounced off the familiar surroundings, Ruth almost cried.

'Are you okay, girl?' her father said when she threw herself into his arms, burying her head in the safety of his chest.

'I'm good,' she mumbled. She hoped he would never have to find out what she had become. She couldn't imagine her father accepting that this was what had become of his precious princess.

After a thorough dressing down about her weight—'You have gotten so thin,' complained Roberta—Ruth just wanted to stay there.

'I think Patty has a new man,' said Gary, and got a look from Roberta.

'What? She left Mark?'

'No, but I think she might.'

'Now, now.' Roberta frowned at Gary. 'I think it's just a thing. She's just getting it out of her system.'

Good for Patty, thought Ruth, but a sad feeling ran through her. *Was everyone in the world doing this?*

Her mother asked her about Derek, while her father rolled his eyes.

'Derek's fine,' she said. She didn't want to tell them about his proposal yet. She was still in two minds as to whom to get rid of.

'I liked Paul,' her father butted in.

'She's with Derek, Gary!' Roberta looked at her husband in exasperation. 'Really, love, you must learn to filter what comes out of your mouth.'

Ruth wanted to giggle, but her mother was too vexed. 'It's okay, Ma. I know Dad had a thing for Paul.' She winked at her father.

'You did too,' said Gary stubbornly.

Ruth sighed. 'I have to go,' she said, picking up her handbag.

'Stay the night. It's getting late,' Roberta urged.

'Work tomorrow, early,' she replied, wishing she could stay in this home, her safe place.

'You're working too hard. We barely see you anymore,' complained Roberta but Ruth was used to this complaint from everyone. If they only knew it wasn't work that was keeping her from them.

'Well, at least stay for dinner,' said Gary.

Ruth left the house with a tear stuck in her eye and a doggy bag. She couldn't tell them the way she felt about Derek, the constant state of uncertainty she was in. Even Mike, as secure as she felt in his arms, the moment she left, she was worried about whom he was talking to, whom he was seeing.

When she arrived back at her apartment, she parked her car, leaned back in her seat and took a deep breath. Then she reached over to the glove box and pulled out Derek's ring, slipping it on. She was more conflicted than ever.

She was leaving for Sydney again the next week and Derek was unhappy that Ruth had not spent much time with him lately. This was a longer trip but Ruth thought that leaving both of them for a full week was just the thing she needed. She had to have some time to figure out whom she wanted to be with, if any of them. She had already told Mike that she wouldn't be seeing him for a couple of weeks and when she realised that, she already missed him. It was getting overwhelming, and Ruth knew she would probably be best with both of them out of her life. But she couldn't do that, not yet.

A night out with clients was organised for Friday evening at a restaurant, the day before Ruth was to leave, but she didn't have much to plan or pack as she was used to these trips by now. She went to Sydney almost every month and even though she always told Mike it was for longer it usually wasn't for more than a couple of days at a time. She knew things had to come to a head, she couldn't go on like this forever …

The evening began well, Ruth wowing their new clients, with Derek contributing to the conversation as if he were a third party, and they both knew it was a successful meeting. After bidding goodbye to them, Ruth and Derek were elated and moved from the restaurant to the bar next door, staying on to toast their success. Ruth just wanted to remain out here, in the midst of the throbbing crowd who were celebrating the beginning of their weekend, rather than go home to be alone with Derek. She knew it was ridiculous that when she was with Derek, all she thought about was Mike and when she was with Mike, her thoughts automatically reverted to Derek. She loved them, but in her mind, they were always going to do the same thing to her—cheat. This time, she would be a step ahead of them. She now tried to drown out the thoughts that were always hammering her brain with a bourbon, but it didn't seem to work.

After a couple of drinks, Derek suggested it was time to leave and Ruth reluctantly agreed. She had a big day ahead of her and swallowed the last of her shot with a heavy heart. She waited at the door of the bar, envying the people, young and old, laughing and drinking without a care in the world, while Derek went to empty his bladder.

'Hi, stranger.'

Ruth turned around and her stomach went to jelly. Paul was standing in front of her, his smile, the same one she remembered and loved so much, planted on his face. On his arm was a woman, not Anna, but a pretty young brunette, with a large grin and a ring in her nose.

'Hi … er … Paul,' Ruth stammered.

'Don't even remember my name?' He reached in and pulled her to him.

Her senses were overtaken by him, the sight of the skin on his neck; the scent, the familiar scent that she tried to keep on his scarf, engulfed her. She breathed it in deeply and let go of him.

Derek was by her side now and he put his hand out to Paul, who shook it.

'This is Danni,' Paul said, and the young girl smiled at Ruth warily. 'Danni, this is Ruth.'

Ruth smiled at her and introduced Derek. 'And this is Paul, my, er, I used to work with Paul before I came to Marks and Sons.'

Paul raised his eyebrows and Ruth didn't miss the small smile that rested on his lips.

'Have a drink with us,' Paul offered.

'We were just leaving,' said Ruth, and Derek nodded.

Paul and Danni said goodbye and went inside.

'I'll get the car if you want,' said Derek and Ruth nodded, hoping for a minute by herself to regain her composure.

She stood at the front of the bar, amidst the tables of people who were enjoying the unusually warm weather for April, and waited, trying to breathe slowly to slow her racing heart.

'Is this closure then?'

She turned to see Paul at her side and again, her heart began to beat so fiercely, she thought she may faint. She didn't trust herself to say anything, so she just stared into those piercing eyes of his, which seemed to understand. He took her hand and gently squeezed it before walking back into the bar.

Her heart was racing now and she wished Derek would hurry, wished she had just gone with him to the car. She looked up to glance into the bar and saw Paul's face staring straight back at her, a crease in his brow.

That was not closure, she thought, as she lay next to Derek that night. She thought she was done with Paul, thought she would feel as she did when she had seen Oliver and Terrence at that party which seemed so long ago, but if Paul had tried to kiss her as Terrence had tried to at Karen's wedding, she would have happily melted into his arms. And as much as she didn't want to, thoughts of Paul kept returning to her through the night, thoughts of love, affection and betrayal.

It was three in the morning when she checked her phone, which she always kept on silent. A missed call from Mike and a message, telling her he already missed her and to be careful in Sydney. 'Don't get snapped up by a handsome stranger,' said his message with a smiley face.

Chapter 19

That handsome stranger was Jerry. Tall, dark and very, very handsome, his looks a mixture of Hugh Jackman and Clint Eastwood, Jerry was rugged, but with an air of nonchalance. In fact, when she thought about it later, he was more like Mike, Oliver and Terrence all rolled into one. Perhaps that was the attraction, she surmised, when she wondered why she had been so impulsive. Or maybe it was that she didn't have to be somebody important to Jerry.

It was at her hotel, the same hotel she frequented when she spent time in Sydney, where the clerk knew her by name and Ruth was still smarting over her 'closure' with Paul. No, she knew after that restless night that she wasn't over him and spent the plane ride allowing herself to escape into the world that used to be theirs.

'Hello, Daisy,' the clerk said and she always managed a laugh. On her first visit, Ruth's reservation was mixed up with someone called Daisy and through some wrangling by the clerk, he managed to get her a suite with an upgrade to make up for mixing up her booking.

'Hi, Dario,' she replied and took her room card. 'Can you check for any mail? Some work stuff may have come through.'

'Sure thing,' he said and turned to go into the back room.

'Hello, Daisy.' Low, soft and throaty.

Ruth turned to find a man of around thirty staring intently at her and she smiled at the name again.

'I'm Jerry.' He reached his hand towards her and Ruth took it, allowing hers to be held for longer than necessary.

'Actually, it's …' she started and stopped. 'It's good to meet you,' she said, wondering and also knowing why she didn't reveal her name to this man.

Dario was already back at the desk and he raised an eyebrow at Ruth, who ignored it. He handed her an envelope and turned down his brow at her. Dario was acting like a protective father and Ruth wanted to laugh at the little man, who couldn't possibly be more than five years her senior.

'On business?' asked Jerry, walking her to the elevator; even his walk was one of self-assurance, a man who knew who he was and revelled in it.

'Yes,' she replied. 'I'm in town for a couple of days.' She wondered why she needed to lie to him and again, marvelled at the easy way the lies came out of her mouth. 'How about you?'

'I live in Sydney. I'm just here for a meeting,' he replied and looked skyward. 'The top floor.'

'Ooh, luxury,' said Ruth.

The elevator opened and they both stepped in with another man, who had a very serious look on his face and was mumbling to himself. Ruth and Jerry stood behind the man in silence, and glanced furtively at each other, giggling when the man burst into another bout of mumbles. Ruth had pressed the button for the eleventh floor and Jerry had clicked on the topmost button on the panel. Ruth couldn't believe what she was feeling. Her senses were heightened and there seemed to be an electricity in the elevator. All thoughts about Derek, Mike and even Paul had completely vanished from her mind.

When the mumbling man exited on the fifth floor and the door closed behind him, Ruth and Jerry stood staring at the reflection of each other through the steel doors. She scanned his filled-out physique, covered by a loose shirt, the first two buttons undone, a little pop of hairs protruding from beneath it. He half leaned on the handrail and his head bent as he looked down at her through a set of curled eyebrows, a glint of a smile on his lips. When she caught his eye, she turned to him and in an instant, they were in each other's arms, her back leaning up against the cold steel panel of the elevator. Jerry's lips were on hers and her hands slid against the muscles of his back, pulling him to her. Then his lips had moved down to her neck, and her leg was hitched up around his thigh, which she could now feel his hands on, raising her skirt higher. Suddenly there was a 'ding'.

They both jumped out of each other's arms and Ruth managed to straighten her skirt before a woman stepped in. The woman, older, reserved, raised an eyebrow and pursed her lips, then turned to face the door. Ruth cleared her throat and patted her hair, which, she could see in the reflection of the door, was mussed, a curl fallen out of her tight bun. She looked at the panel which was approaching the eleventh floor and took a sideways glance at Jerry, who had a playful smile on his face, but his back was straight and he was back to looking like a professional gentleman on his way to a meeting, albeit in that ever-so-cool shirt.

When the lift dinged on Ruth's floor, the doors opened and she looked at Jerry, who seemed to be challenging her. She stepped out of the elevator and turned back to him, reaching out her hand. He took it.

An hour later, sated and spent, Ruth lay on the mauve shag rug in the centre of the living room and stared at the ceiling. She heard the door shut and Jerry was gone. She idly wondered if she'd see him again and somehow knew she would. She reached over to the table and grabbed her phone. A missed call from Mike again. She needed to return his call from the previous night and had not done so yet; she hadn't had a chance. Derek had dropped her to the airport, and as she was already late, she boarded immediately. She intended to return his call as soon as she got to her room, but now after Jerry, she just couldn't. She flung the phone on the floor and continued to survey the ceiling, letting a nothingness take over her. But the soft ticking on the clock alerted her to the time and she realised she was running late for her meeting, which was to begin at noon. She quickly dressed and rushed out the door.

Throughout the meeting, where she was briefed of her duties while in Sydney, she could think of nothing but Jerry, his large, tapered hands caressing her, his lips that touched her body so tenderly, so masterfully. She thought about Mike and how he was just as satisfying in bed but she suddenly realised what she was doing again.

No, there would be no comparisons. They were different and she was different with each of them.

But she did compare them; it was impossible not to.

There was Derek, safe, calm Derek, who she felt she loved, and Mike, the family man who made her feel safe, who she also felt she loved. But then there was Jerry. Ruth knew she couldn't love a man like Jerry. He had been around the block, one could easily see that; he could give Terrence lessons on charm!

Ruth wondered why she had behaved so impulsively. Just a couple of years ago, she was a different person, someone who was a one-man woman, someone who wanted stability, marriage, a future with someone she loved, someone who loved her back. She regarded the ring which was still on her finger and wondered if Jerry had noticed it. She knew it wouldn't have mattered and that thought made Ruth smile.

It was six in the evening when Ruth got back to the hotel and found herself looking around for Jerry. She saw him immediately, sitting in an armchair beside the elevator, scrolling through his phone, and Ruth made a mental note to call Mike back, and soon. There were already three more missed calls and another message, disappointed that she had not spoken to him. She smiled at Jerry, if that was his name, and took a seat next to him.

'How was your, er, whatever you were at?' he said and opened his mouth in a smile that revealed his white, even teeth, and Ruth felt a tingle in her tummy. He could certainly buckle her knees.

'Work meeting. Don't really know if I remember anything that went on.' She shrugged.

Jerry laughed. 'Hmm, well, mine was about the same. I couldn't think of much else.'

Ruth smirked. Yes, that was how a player talked. 'Yes, me too.' There was a sudden realisation. Ruth was a player too! And she also realised she liked how it felt. 'You busy tonight?'

'What have you got in mind?' He crossed his legs and cocked his head in a teasing way.

'Well, dinner for starters,' Ruth laughed. 'I'm starving.'

'Sure. Let's go.'

'I have to drop my work stuff off and freshen up first. Do you want me to meet you there?'

'I can come up with you and wait. I don't mind.'

Ruth leaned back. 'Really!'

Jerry held up his hands. 'Just wait, I promise.'

Ruth felt herself redden, but as the elevator rose to her floor, she knew there would be no waiting. In the end they had to settle for room service.

'Who are you really?' she asked as she lay in his arms that

evening.

'I'm Jerry, just Jerry.' He kissed her ear and rose from the bed, and Ruth watched as he picked up his clothes and put them on, glancing her way and grinning as he did.

'Bye, Daisy,' he said, as he leaned over and kissed her lips. Then he was gone.

Ruth lay in bed and turned on the TV. She liked Jerry, but she knew what he was. A distraction from her web of lies, even though the irony was not lost on her. He was now part of the secrets and lies she offered to everyone she cared about. She wished she could call Karen, talk to her about it all, maybe get her head straight, but she knew what her friend would say and she wasn't willing or ready to give up anything she had right now. *It will work out*, she thought, but she reluctantly looked at her phone.

She walked over to the balcony, still in her slip, and looked down at the little people and cars on the road below, still heading home from work. She leaned on the railing, admiring the pink sky and the clouds that floated by, enjoying the cool breeze that wafted past, and she let herself think about Jerry—not Mike, not Derek, just Jerry. This moment she gave to her own thoughts about the man who had made love to her and left without asking for anything. Before she knew it, an hour had passed and Ruth reluctantly walked back into the room, feeling goosebumps on her arms. She hadn't realised how cold it had become.

Mike had to be the first call, his messages were beginning to sound angry, and she felt a stab of irritation. But once she had spoken to him and put his mind at rest that she had arrived safely, she found herself wishing she was in Geelong with him.

'Jerry,' she said aloud to herself, for no particular reason, but wondering if that was that with Jerry, a one-time fling, never to be repeated.

She quickly called Derek, who was used to not hearing from her for a couple of days at a time, but she just wanted to treat them equally.

'About to go out with Sam,' said Derek, clearly getting ready. Ruth could hear the keys jingling in his hands already. At the same time as she felt relief at his doing something rather than waiting for her call, she also felt a stab of jealousy, a stab of wonder, but she suppressed her fear and told him to have a good time. Sam was a good guy, one of the people at work Derek had bonded with, and anyway, she certainly wasn't in any position to suspect Derek of anything. If he was up to something, well, she probably deserved it.

That week that she spent in Sydney was a wonderful one for Ruth but also the most exhausting, her limbs aching from the amount of exercise she had gotten in the arms of Jerry. He had shown up at the dot of six p.m. every day, and after the first couple of days, she found herself looking forward to the self-assured, relaxed man, who sat waiting for her outside the elevator. And on the stroke of nine, after they had had dinner together, drank wine on the balcony while they talked about the state of the world and made love, he would leave and Ruth was left to contemplate her actions, and make her phone calls. She wanted him to stay the night but never asked and was a little relieved that he clearly had his own life to deal with. She didn't want him to disclose too much about where he was going every night and who he was with. When she thought about it later, Ruth was afraid of being told she was the other woman, and that, to her, would have been worse than being the cheater.

She considered what on earth she was doing with Jerry when she had two men waiting for her in Melbourne. Then she realised. She had no expectations of Jerry and he had none from her either. Both didn't want to know more about each other, other than what they felt when they were in each other's arms. When Ruth tried to tell him her name, he stopped her. 'I like Daisy,' he said and Ruth liked that. And when she told him she was leaving the next day, Jerry stayed until late in the night, holding her close.

'I'm gonna miss you,' he whispered, as she thought the very same thing.

'Same,' she said. 'It's been fun.'

Ruth felt Jerry tense and relax almost imperceptibly. 'It was the best week I've had,' he said and kissing her, he left the bed. Ruth wondered if she would ever see him again. She couldn't process how she felt about that but refused to think about it.

As the plane touched down in Melbourne, Ruth felt the same guilt that always came upon her when she arrived home from Mike's place, but now she was feeling guilty for both Mike and Derek. She had spoken to Derek a few times and to Mike even less, but Derek was the one who always called her. Mike had been patient after his initial panic.

Derek met her at the gate and she hugged him, happy to be in his arms. She realised she had missed him, his steadfast nature, funny but not loud, interesting but not arrogant. She was glad she was engaged to him.

Marrying Derek was a different matter. She knew she had to hold off for as long as possible. She also knew at some stage before they got there, she would have to come clean. About everything. Karen had warned her it would come to this and when she told Karen of her engagement, she assumed that Ruth had made her choice and didn't even ask about Mike. She decided not to enlighten her; she felt like the most rotten person in the world as it was and she didn't need it confirmed by her best friend.

Chapter 20

'How are you?' said Paul, as Ruth looked blankly at him through the mist that had just fallen over her eyes.

She recovered quickly and regained her composure. 'I'm well. How about you?' She could hear how inane that sounded.

Paul looked at the empty chair next to her and raised his eyebrows.

'Yes, please, sit,' she said.

She had stopped in at a café on her lunchbreak, needing to take a few moments away from Derek at work. She just needed a little bit of space, some time to clear her mind.

The wedding was getting closer, just three months away, and her nerves were shot. It had been nearly a year since he had asked her to marry him and the situation hadn't changed for Ruth. She knew she had to tell him something soon, but she wondered if she could just break up with Mike and stop seeing Jerry, who was like a magnet to her, still available, still so very handsome and mysterious, and still wanting nothing more than she could give him.

Luckily, Ruth was now in a position at work where she could decide when she travelled to Sydney and although she had tried to be strong, whenever she felt too closed in by either Mike or Derek, she fled into Jerry's arms. And he almost always seemed to be there, knowing she was coming to town, Ruth never stopping to understand how. There was one trip when he was a complete no-show and Ruth spent the week angry and irritable, going to work in a foul mood and going to bed early, wishing for the first time she had his number, but there had never been the suggestion of exchanging details about each other, which was part of the attraction, the charm of Jerry. When she saw him the next time, she didn't mention she was ever there.

It had to end eventually: her limbs were tired, her brain was battered and emotionally, she felt like she was on the edge of a cliff. Her parents were concerned, but Ruth let them believe that it was pre-wedding jitters. They accepted Derek now, especially because of the way he seemed to adore their daughter, and even her father tried to get to know him better, watching football matches with him and asking him to help with barbeques on special occasions. Of course, this meant that time with Mike was limited and Ruth missed him terribly, but what was even worse was finding excuses for not being able to visit him. She could see that Mike was running out of patience.

Karen was another matter. She knew Ruth better than anyone and when Ruth was ambiguous about who she was with or what she was doing, Karen questioned her. Karen also had a baby to contend with now and Ruth, happy that her friend had exactly what she wanted, also missed confiding in her. Karen was only going to tell her to do what Ruth knew she should have done a long time ago. But how could she tell Karen how she felt, how every moment of the day her brain was ready for attack, her nerves raw with the thought of betrayal finding its way to her door again. How could she tell anyone how things were, who she was and what she'd become, knowing in her heart of hearts that it wasn't just revenge, it was selfishness.

Now, here was Paul, sitting beside her, three months before her wedding, making her feel like a teenager. Paul, the man who throughout this time had always been the one her heart longed for. She still had his scarf, although his scent was lost, Ruth having to wash it eventually. She looked at the one he was wearing now, green-and-grey chequered, around his skin, leaning just below his Adam's apple.

'Ruth?'

She raised her eyes to his in embarrassment; she didn't realise she had been staring at his neck. 'Sorry, I'm a million miles away.' She straightened herself and cleared her throat. 'How are you anyway, still working with Marielle?' She knew he wasn't. Marielle had already told her that Paul had left more than a year ago to begin his own website design company.

He shook his head and grinned. 'No. I have my own business now. A start-up, so it will be a while before it really gets going. But it's looking good. Hey, you need a job?' He laughed.

Ruth actually stopped for a moment to consider. How wonderful it would be to just go away from her increasingly busy job and life, leave it all behind, go to Paul. Anna's face came to her mind, not the mesmerising photograph, but the image of her kissing Paul. 'I'm doing really well at Marks …'

'I was joking. I know you are. I still speak to Marielle. We work together sometimes too.'

'Speaking of … did you finally give her what she wanted?' She still found it so easy to play with Paul.

'Honestly, that woman has been nothing but professional with me. Even now that I've left.'

'Are you still with … what was her name?' Ruth knew her name.

'Danni. Yeah.' He raked his hands through his hair and leaned back in his chair. He didn't look very enthused. 'How about you? I hear you're engaged.'

Ruth nodded. She didn't know what to say.

'Are you happy?' Paul leaned towards her.

Not as happy as I'd be if it were your ring on my finger, was what came to her mind. She nodded again.

Paul looked at his watch. 'Hey, I have to go. Do you think we could catch up?'

'Yeah, sure,' said Ruth, feeling the urge to grab his arm and hold him there for as long as possible.

'Can we really though? Not just say it?'

'Yes,' Ruth blurted. 'Maybe get some of that closure.' She

smiled.

Paul cocked his head. 'Okay, let's name a time and place. Just so we can't make excuses. How about this Friday?'

Ruth couldn't do Friday. She was going up to see Mike. She still needed to find an excuse for Derek, but she was used to coming up with things by now. 'How about Sunday evening?'

Paul nodded. 'Yep, about sixish?'

'Sounds good,' said Ruth and now wished she could put off seeing Mike.

'Place?'

'How about Mosby's?' She smiled flirtatiously and stopped, suddenly self-conscious.

Paul laughed. 'Sure. Same place we …' He leaned over and kissed Ruth on her cheek.

Ruth wanted to stay there next to that warm cheek and leaned into him. Paul didn't move away immediately either and the electricity she always felt when she was near him was there still.

She watched him walk out of the café and he turned at the door and gave her a small wave.

She put her head in her hands. Now she had to put off Derek on Sunday night too. He had practically moved in with her and would want to know where she was. At least there was Erica.

Erica, her old high school friend, the same one that had stolen her boyfriend, had become Ruth's alibi. While lunching at the beach with Mike one afternoon, Ruth heard a shrill voice call her name and when she turned around it was none other than her old friend. Ruth greeted her as such, understanding that high school was a long time ago and kids did silly things to each other in the throes of adolescence.

'I thought that was you,' Erica said and grabbed a chair from the next table and placed it at theirs, smiling at a slightly irritable Mike, who finally had Ruth come down to be with him after a two-week absence. He was already beginning to hint that she should quit her job as it was taking her away from him.

That was a few months ago and Erica and Ruth stayed in touch, although Ruth felt that she still couldn't completely trust her. She noticed that some things didn't change, as Erica flirted openly with Mike, right in front of her. But Erica had her own issues, a broken marriage and a string of failed relationships, so Ruth chose to ignore her behaviour, especially when she saw that Mike had eyes for no one but herself. And Erica had come in handy, providing her with an alibi, the lonely old friend who needed someone to talk to, when Ruth took off for a day or a weekend at a time.

Derek was becoming more possessive lately, not in a threatening way, he just seemed jealous of the time Ruth spent at work, at her parents' house and with her old friends, but Ruth knew it was natural. She was to be his wife soon and he'd always wanted more from her than she could give.

Ruth decided to tell Derek the truth about meeting Paul, she wasn't going to hide him. He was, after all, a friend. And Derek, although jealous, knew Ruth had male friends and colleagues, and it was just something he would have to deal with.

She stared at the door. 'I'd give it all up for you in a heartbeat,' she said to nobody in particular. Then she got up, paid her bill and left.

****

'Again?' Derek was not happy. 'I think Erica is using you.'

'Erica needs me. I know you don't like her very much, but she's been my friend since childhood.'

'She lives so far away. And why do you need to spend the whole weekend?'

'It's been two weeks since I've seen her! And we have a bit of a drink and it's just nice to know that I don't have to drive all the way back, so I can just relax, you know.'

'Well, I'm not really fond of her.'

'I know, I know. But I can't desert her. Jason is treating her terribly.'

'Fine, but this has to stop.' Derek crossed his arms like a stubborn child.

'Oh, really?' said Ruth, her hands on her hips. 'Does it?' Derek knew Ruth wouldn't put up with being told what to do and when she challenged him, he immediately backed down. Usually, he was just trying it on. 'Oh, also, I bumped into Paul.'

Derek leaned his head to one side, trying to recall who Paul was. Apart from their brief meeting, Ruth had never mentioned

Paul to Derek.

'A colleague I worked with at Marielle's.'

'Oh. Okay?'

'Anyway, he's starting up a company and wants to run some ideas past me.' Ruth was again appalled at herself, at how the lies could just fly from her mouth without a thought, even when she didn't need them to.

'Okay, is he coming over?' Ruth could sense his annoyance, and she was suddenly defensive of Paul.

'No. We are meeting at Mosby's …'

'The bar?'

'Yeah. It would be weird to bring him here.'

'Why would it?'

'Because … I don't know.' She thought quickly. 'It would be weird to bring a colleague home.'

'You brought me home.' Derek laughed.

Ruth laughed back. 'So very true.' She leaned over and kissed him. 'And look at how that ended up.'

'So, did you get the email about the flowers?'

'I haven't checked yet.'

'What about the priest? He said he tried to call you. Did you call him back?'

'No, I will. Actually can you just deal with it?' Ruth replied and looked at Derek, who was frowning, and gave him a sweet smile.

He shook his head in mock annoyance. 'Okay, fine. But it

seems that I'm more interested in organising this wedding than you are. Very unusual for a couple. I thought you'd be all over it.'

'But you're doing such a wonderful job, why would I interfere?' Ruth laughed again, knowing she should have been taking so much more of an interest, as brides-to-be usually did.

****

She rushed to the bar. It was six thirty and she hoped that Paul hadn't left. By the time she returned from Mike's place, it was five thirty in the afternoon—the traffic had been crazy—and by the time she left her apartment, it was past six. Luckily Derek had been at his own place, a rare occurrence these days, and she didn't have to feel the guilt she always felt when she faced him after seeing Mike.

Ruth had had a terrible night at Mike's place; he was acting suspicious lately, not about anything that would alarm her, just a constant probing as to why they hadn't made more plans for their future yet. More to the point, why Ruth was skittish about moving in with him.

'Is it because it's so far from your work?' he had asked, just as they were going to bed.

Ruth wasn't expecting the question, but as usual, he gave her the answer. 'Well, yes. I guess. Work is so busy right now. I'm going off so often and to go there and back every day, it just doesn't make sense right now.'

'So what are you waiting for? For the work to calm down? For a promotion that won't take you away?'

'Yes, I think that would help.'

'And when do you think that might be?'

'Soon, hopefully,' she replied, hating herself more and more. 'Let's not talk about this right now.' She pushed him on the bed and lay herself atop him, looking into his loving eyes, feeling a sadness that when it came down to her choice, Mike would probably be the one to get the chop.

She lay in bed that night thinking about how it was so unfair on Mike, but she just hadn't had the heart to focus on him the whole weekend. Her heart was already at Mosby's with Paul. She wondered, as Mike snored gently beside her, whether she would do the same thing with Paul. She knew she couldn't. Even though he had hurt her the most, she could never do that to him. But she knew she could give up everything else for his love alone.

She didn't stop to consider that she was going to be married to another man within three months.

****

Ruth found Paul sipping on a beer, his eyes on the door and his furrowed brow straightened, and a smile appeared on his face the moment his eyes fell on her. The relief she felt when she saw him waiting for her flooded her body and Ruth knew there was no such thing as closure for her, not with him. She knew she would never stop loving him. All worry about Mike and his suspicions vanished, all guilt over hiding the truth from Derek flew from her mind. All that stood in front of her was Paul.

'Sorry I'm late,' she said as he rose from his seat at the bar and placed a kiss on her cheek.

'That's okay. I had a beer to ease my nerves,' he said, shaking the empty bottle at her.

'Well, you're a step ahead of me.'

'I'm already on it,' he said as the waiter placed a glass of tequila in front of her. He nodded to the waiter who nodded back with a wink. 'Still your favourite, I hope.'

'Are you trying to make me drunk?' Ruth batted her eyelids at him and he craned his neck back slightly.

'There's something new,' he replied. 'A flirtatious side I didn't get to experience.'

'Oh, stop it,' she said, waving her hand at him, embarrassed that her new habits were presenting themselves. 'Where's Danni?'

'At home, catching up with her brother. He's been away for a while and he's staying with us for a bit.'

Ruth felt a stab of disappointment. 'So you live together?'

'We've been together for a while now, so it was inevitable. You live with … what's his name again?'

Three names flashed through her mind before she picked the right one. 'Derek. No, we don't live together. We're … waiting.'

'For?'

'I'm getting married in three months,' she said and put her

left hand forward, suddenly realising her ring finger was bare. In her rush to get here, she had forgotten to put it back on. She was slipping. She had done this a couple of times already but had always remembered in time for Derek not to notice.

Paul raised his eyebrows.

'I … um, took it off to … wash up,' she said sheepishly.

Paul cleared his throat. 'Congratulations,' he said and leaned forward again.

Ruth turned to him and he brushed his lips on hers.

'Sorry,' he said.

Ruth's head was already swimming and Paul looked away.

'Are you happy, Ruth?'

Ruth took a moment to think about it. She never really thought about that question all that much. Was she happy? She had a great job, a fiancé, and people that fulfilled parts of her that others couldn't. But she still didn't feel secure. None of these men completely fulfilled her; at least, that was what she told herself when she tried to justify what she was doing.

Paul was looking at her now, his eyes creased. 'Ruth?' He took her hand.

Ruth realised a tear had fallen and she quickly wiped it away and nodded. She was angry for letting it fall. She had fought against them for so long and had won.

Paul turned his chair towards hers and took her hands. 'You can talk to me, you know.'

Ruth sniffed. 'I haven't seen you since … since our encounter with … her.' Ruth chose not to tell him she had seen him that one time and had bolted.

'I need to explain that.'

'No, really, you don't. It helped me a lot.'

'Really, how?'

'I don't want to talk about it, Paul. I just want to share a drink with you … for old times' sake.' She smiled shakily and raised her glass. 'To closure.'

Paul nodded and clinked his bottle with her glass. 'Okay, to brighter topics. How is life at the top?'

Ruth told him about her job at Marks and Sons and how she had no reason to complain about anything. She was now one of the head designers and was fulfilled with her career.

'Yet, there's a sadness in you that I've never seen before, not even after your split with Terrence.'

'Haha, Terrence. I see that guy so much these days. I can't believe I fell for a lech like that!'

'At least you're over him.'

'What do you mean?'

'Nothing,' said Paul. 'Well, I've told you about my new venture. That's all my life is at the moment. It takes every ounce of time from me. Sure, there's Danni, but …'

'But?' Ruth's heart caught. 'Do you love her?'

'I think so.'

'You think so? You've been with her for ages, you live with her! Are you going to pop the question?'

Paul laughed. 'I don't know. She does keep dropping hints, but I still don't know if she's the right one.'

'When will you know?' Ruth leaned on the bar with her head in her hand and looked at Paul, his eyes looking a little lost. He was wearing another scarf, brown and green, and she wanted to put her nose to it and take a deep breath. She cleared her throat and sat up. She had enough on her hands without complicating her life further. She could never hurt Paul, even though …

'Ruth?'

'Okay,' she said and motioned for the bartender to get her another tequila. 'I want to know.'

'What?'

'About Anna.' Ruth needed to hear it all, to move on from that fateful evening.

Paul looked into his beer and nodded. 'Anna and I were a thing. Before you. You already guessed that, I suppose.'

Ruth nodded but still felt a stab of jealousy that ran up her spine and exploded in her ears.

'I had to end it. She wasn't the girl in the picture. That allure, that appeal. It was all for show. She just photographed well.' He stopped.

'What happened?'

'I was with her for all of a couple of months, about the time I began working for Marielle. It was a working relationship that turned into a romance of sorts. But I never truly loved her. I didn't know what that really was until …' He looked at Ruth. 'Until, well, you know. You.'

Ruth blushed but the muscles in her back relaxed.

'Well, anyway, I ended it and she … I guess she liked a challenge.' He turned and looked deeply into Ruth's eyes. 'I didn't kiss her, you know.'

Ruth broke his gaze and looked down, picturing the moment that played in her mind so many times, she could write it down, word for word. 'From where I was standing …'

'You weren't standing there at the right time, that's all. She saw you come back. She saw you were threatened. She went in for the kill. And it worked.'

'You had your arm around her.' Ruth knew what she saw.

Paul laughed. 'You girls are tricky. She grabbed my arm and before I could do anything, she just … you know. Do you know what happened next, after you left?' He laughed without humour. 'No, you don't.' He took a deep breath. 'By the time I turned around, you were gone.'

Ruth could still remember the feeling, the utter betrayal, the humiliation, the heartbreak that she tried not to let herself feel. She now felt a tear slide down her cheek and Paul reached out to wipe it away. She put her hand on his and leaned into it.

'I'm sorry,' he said.

Ruth shook her head and squeezed her eyes shut. 'I still miss you,' she murmured.

'Same,' he said, leaning his forehead on hers.

She smelled it now, his scent, and she tugged on his scarf.

She lifted her chin and felt the brush of his face stubble, her lips lightly touching his.

Paul was the first to pull away. He cleared his throat again and forced a laugh. 'And we haven't even had many of these yet,' he said, raising his beer. Then he cleared his throat and took a long swig.

'Sorry,' said Ruth, even though she wasn't really sorry. She would have happily melted into his arms.

'Anyway, that's the story. I never had the chance to explain it, but I guess now we can call it the C word.' He smiled. 'You know, closure.'

'Yes, I think we can,' said Ruth, not terribly sure that it was. She felt closer to Paul than ever at this moment and closer to Paul than any of the men in her life.

Ruth sighed, her mind suddenly going back to Derek, safe Derek, oblivious to what she was doing to him. Poor Derek, the man she had also assumed was cheating on her, who she knew would never hurt her.

'You okay?' Paul was asking.

Ruth felt a gush of tears roll down her cheeks.

'What's the matter?' Paul took her hand again and Ruth shook it off.

'Nothing, nothing.'

'Ruth, please, tell me. It's not me, is it?'

'No; yes and no.' She looked at Paul now, who was leaning forward in concern. 'I've just messed everything up.'

'What? What have you messed up?'

'Oh Paul, if you only knew what I've become …' Ruth shook her head and gulped the last of her tequila.

'Want another?'

Ruth shook her head again. 'No.'

'What have you become?'

And she found herself telling him everything she'd done since she left him. Derek, Mike and Jerry. All of it, Paul listening without expression or interruption. And Ruth cried, heavily, sloppily, all the tears she had tried to keep from falling all these years.

Chapter 21

Ruth wondered if she'd made a grave mistake.

There was enough on her plate without adding another man to the pile. But Paul was different. Paul was the friend she could tell everything to now, and as she adjusted her white stocking, she wondered still whether she was doing the right thing. He would be there too today and she thought how it was crazy to look forward to seeing him more than seeing the man she was going to marry.

She slid her foot into the pink-and-white stiletto and stared at her feet. She could hear bustling outside the room and knew Karen had arrived. Sure enough, a moment later, Karen barged in, her hair in a tight bun and wearing a pink organza dress that Ruth thought looked quite ridiculous, but was perfect for a wedding and for Karen.

She held a number of bags which she tossed on the floor beside the door and as Ruth stood up, Karen rushed into her arms.

'I'm so happy! You're finally doing it. Welcome to the

happiness club,' Karen squealed.

Ruth squeezed her eyes tight, her head still on Karen's shoulder, and Karen pulled back and looked into her eyes.

'Hey, hey. Are you okay?'

'I think I'm still in love with Paul,' Ruth blurted.

Karen's eyes widened and then she laughed. 'Remember what I asked you on my wedding day?'

Ruth nodded. 'Am I doing the right thing?' She wondered whether she was really asking it of Karen now.

Karen nodded back. 'Yes. This is the wedding jitters. Look how it turned out for me.' She stepped back and, surveying Ruth, laughed again. 'Well, it would be better if you were in more than a bra and panties and stockings! Come on, let me help you put on your dress.'

'Can I have a few more minutes?' she asked Karen. 'By myself.'

'You're a strange one,' said Karen. 'I have to touch up my make-up anyway. Stupid make-up lady made me look like a raccoon. Trouble is trying to get Patty out of the bathroom.'

Ruth smiled. Yes, Patty had become quite the beauty queen. She was constantly grooming herself, a compact mirror a fixture in her purse. Ruth still didn't know what to make of it, except that the shoe was certainly on the other foot now, with Mark the one running around her, fawning over her, while Patty walked around like a queen who treated him like a gentleman-in-waiting. At least she had stuck by him in the end. Maybe it did work out for some.

Ruth collapsed on the bed and remembered lying here when she was a teenager, when she thought the world was complicated. Oh how she wished for those days back. She wondered what Mike was doing now.

She had tried and tried again to avoid him, making excuse upon excuse, but when she felt too closed in with Derek, especially with the wedding coming upon her so quickly, she would escape to see him. But when she got to Mike's place, the same issues would arise, the 'when are we going to live together' question. Mike was still trying to get her to move in with him and the last time she saw him, three weeks ago, Ruth was sure that he was about to pop the question. She knew the time had come to make the break.

It was after coming home after watching a romantic movie, which Ruth had been wanting to see for a while. He succumbed and spent the entire time in the theatre with his head snuggled into her neck. Ruth was feeling a range of emotions and only wanted to go out so that she wouldn't have to have any serious conversations with him. She knew their time was running out, that she had to end it now, or at least very, very soon.

When they arrived back at Mike's house, she watched as he poured them drinks and took it onto the decking, where the air was cool and the breeze was soft. They sat together, Ruth taking glances at him, trying to remember the lines at the ends of his eyes, one of the first things she noticed about him. She loved those lines. She rose and took his hand, leading him to the bedroom, where she tried to etch in her mind how he made her feel when he touched her, caressed her and made love to her.

Afterwards, he sat at the edge of the bed and leaned his head into his chest. 'Seeing you a couple of times a month is not enough anymore.'

'I have a busy life, Mike; you know how much I have to travel.' She despised herself. She got out of the bed and fumbled around for her clothes.

'But I know nothing of your life outside of your friend Erica. I know you hate your parents, but I think it's time I met them. We can even go to Canada to meet mine.' His eyes lit up. 'Yes, we can take a long trip, a holiday, a ...' He stopped. 'But you don't even live that far. I can even ask them ...'

Ruth was sick of the strands of the web that were turning into knots. She had invented this ridiculous life to be in this relationship and sometimes she didn't even know what the truth was and what were lies. 'We will, one day. Work is so busy now.' She slid on her blouse, tucking it into her jeans.

'But we should be together. I can even give all this up. If you can't move here because of your job, I told you I'm happy to move in with you, even if it is the city.'

Then he had gotten on one knee.

Ruth felt a flash of anxiety and slid her feet into her shoes. 'I have to go,' she said, heading for the door.

'Where?' Mike looked confused and Ruth stopped.

This had to end.

'Mike,' she said, walking back to where he still knelt. She sat on the edge of the bed and he joined her. Taking his hands in hers, she laid it out. 'I think it may be time to …' She hesitated

'To?'

'I think it's time to end this.' She looked away from his questioning eyes, the eyebrows that curled down in confusion. 'I just don't think I have what you need. Mainly time. I have too much on my plate right now. Too many things I need to do before …' She paused again. 'Before I can make a full commitment to you.'

'You just figured this out?' He stood up, looking down at her, and Ruth felt a sliver of fear. She knew he had a temper, but he never lost it often and never on her. But she just didn't know.

Ruth took a deep breath and felt a stab of pain in her gut. 'I just hoped …'

'Fuck that, Ruth!'

'I'm sorry,' she said. She got up and began to gather her things.

Mike put his hand on her arm. 'Ruth, please. Tell me what's going on.'

Ruth was already in tears by now, never realising how much this would hurt. But better that she hurt now than Mike knowing the truth. That would hurt him so much more.

'Ruth, forget everything. Stay, just stay here.'

'I can't,' she said. 'I'm so sorry.'

Grabbing her keys from the table, she dashed out the door. On her way home, she heard her phone beep. She pulled up on the side of the freeway and burst into a fresh bout of tears again. She looked at her phone. She had to do it, she had to delete him from her life. It was the only way. Without even opening his message, she blocked his number. It was the only way they communicated. He didn't even have her home number, which had been too dangerous for her to give him. She drove home in a state of angst and when she arrived, she pulled out her engagement ring and slipped it on. She was glad Derek was not home to see her pain. That would take some explanation and she couldn't do that right now. No amount of lies would cover how she felt about hurting that man.

That was three weeks ago and Ruth had tried not to miss him; she'd put all her energy into the wedding and endeavoured to focus on the man she was going to spend the rest of her life with. Now, as she was getting ready to attempt the biggest lie of her life, marriage, she was thinking about Paul.

Paul had been just wonderful, had even become friends with Derek, who at first found him a threat, but soon grew to enjoy his company and that of Danni, who Ruth couldn't stand to see snuggle up to the man she felt she really loved. But that boat had sailed, and Ruth knew it. Friendship, like the one they first shared, was the only thing they could offer each other, and both were happy to settle for it.

Ruth confided in Paul about everything and it was at his insistence that she had decided to give Mike the boot. She knew she would have to anyway, but Paul made her stronger. He was the friend she needed, not judgemental, but understanding. She even told him about Jerry, who she was determined not to see anymore.

The last time she had seen Jerry was two days after she walked out on Mike and he seemed to ease the pain. He didn't ask her what the matter was, but just let her lie in his arms while she sobbed and told him it was their last evening together. Then, after three days, she returned to Melbourne.

Jerry

'I could have married that girl and lived happily ever after,' Jerry said, as he tucked his father into bed.

'Why didn't you, Rod?'

'Because she didn't love me,' Jerry replied simply. He smiled at his name. Rod, a strong name given to him by his father. Jerry, a strange name, but one that sounded like the name of a player, just popped out of his mouth when he introduced himself to Daisy. Oh, he was quite aware that Daisy wasn't her name either, but it was a fun charade in the beginning. He just didn't expect to fall in love with her.

'How do you know that? Maybe she did.'

'I know. I knew from the beginning.'

'You have to get a good woman, someone who can make you happy. You love her. Tell her.' The old man broke into a series of rasping coughs and Jerry leaned him forward, rubbing his back. He knew there was not much else he could do for him. His time was nearly at an end.

'I could never have told her that.'

'How was work?'

'It was fine,' Jerry said, thinking about how close Daisy could have come to finding out who he really was. He worked at the twenty-four-hour café literally across the road from the hotel and he was in the middle of his shift when he had first seen her. Then he kept an eye out for this woman who happened to frequent the hotel on a regular basis.

The day he introduced himself to her, he had just finished his shift and was about to walk home when he saw her go in. On impulse, he followed her in. He waited every day to see when she may come and was disappointed when she didn't.

He thought about what his life could have been, what he was about to become, before his mother got sick and his father followed soon after. He had all the hours and loved being up there in the air, above the clouds, guiding his aircraft through the emptiness. But he had to put it all on hold to care for his parents and even with their insistence that he continue, he stopped, taking a job at a café less than a block away from his house, so he could be close to them in case they needed him. He didn't resent them for it at all. He owed them everything he had, and he knew it wasn't the end of his career. It was just on pause.

But Jerry was still lonely and he knew he didn't have time for a relationship; his parents needed him more than ever.

When Daisy came along, he couldn't resist, and his need for

a woman with no strings attached was perfect. He just didn't expect to fall in love with her and when he held her in bed, he could see the fear, the uncertainty, the vulnerability in her. He hurt, knowing he couldn't be more to her than he was. Yet, every time she arrived, he was there, making love to her and savouring it until he saw her next.

The time he didn't see her was when his mother had passed and he had taken time off work to settle things, console his father and prepare her funeral. But his thoughts were with Daisy and he wished so very badly he could tell her how he felt. He saw the ring on her third finger, and she knew he saw it, but to her it didn't matter. To her, he was a player. He was okay with that at first; it was quite clear she was in love with someone else, that her life was complicated, and he certainly didn't want to be the one to further complicate it.

He knew it was the last time he would see her. He had held her tight while she sobbed in his arms, and tried to remember everything about her, the way she looked, her hair splayed around her, her smell and her feel, tucking it safely away in the back of his mind. Then he had left.

'Goodnight, Pa,' Jerry said and leaning over, kissed his father's rough cheek.

She was going to miss Jerry. But Jerry knew what they were to each other. He knew she was a cheater, the same as him, and Ruth was happy that she could be who she was with him. She could never do that with Derek. To Derek, she was perfect. She could never make a mistake like that, she could never be any less than he thought she was or expected her to be.

Paul had questioned her impending wedding and Ruth explained that it may be what she actually needed. Someone who she knew would commit to her, someone who could possibly stray, but hadn't. She still had her moments of doubt, but Paul reminded her of how she had suspected him of cheating, when he never had.

She just hoped that once she was married to Derek, her suspicious mind would be calmed. Why would he marry her if he wanted anyone else? She tried to ignore the irony of what she had been doing all along.

'If you love him, you should be with him,' said Paul the afternoon before the wedding, when Ruth had called him in a panic. She'd been getting ready to go to her parents' house and the enormity of what she was about to do suddenly struck her. 'Of course it's never too late to back out, but I think you never would have said yes to him if this isn't what you wanted.'

'But I promised myself to come clean before the day. I just never got the courage.'

Paul was silent.

'Paul, you there?'

'Ruth, for that, it's probably too late, but if you need to

unburden yourself, then just do it. Just don't go into this with doubts.'

Ruth couldn't tell Paul the only doubts she had now were about him. She felt that once she was married to Derek, she would totally commit to him, she could even live with Paul being around at least as her friend. Paul was more than a friend, he was a confidant, and Ruth didn't want to lose him again by blurting out her feelings for him, which she kept in check.

After she hung up, she felt calmer; he could always do that for her and she went to her closet, which by tomorrow would be Derek's closet too, not that he didn't have most of his things at her place anyway. She reached up into the top shelf and pulled out Paul's scarf, which she buried her head into. She took it to the rubbish bin and held it above the opening. She couldn't let it go and after a few moments, went back to the closet and tucked it up there again.

Her phone flashed and she saw Karen's message; she was downstairs waiting for her. Ruth was spending the night at her parents' house before she went to the church the next morning and Karen was looking forward to spending Ruth's last night of freedom talking the night away.

Ruth had already packed her overnight bag and headed to the door. She turned around to survey her apartment. 'The next time I'm here, I will be a married woman.'

She closed the door.

Chapter 22

Her head was thumping and she couldn't move. She tried wriggling her fingers and was relieved when they stretched outward. She tried to move her toes but couldn't feel anything and her pulse began to race. She lifted her head and saw her body lying on a bed. It was a strange place to her, completely unfamiliar, and Ruth looked around to see a little window that had little pots of flowers on the sill. The light that entered the room was a dull grey and Ruth wasn't sure if it was because it was a rainy day or whether it was late in the evening. An armchair sat next to the window, and Ruth's eyes widened at the figure sitting in it, his eyes closed and a soft snore coming from his open mouth. Something about him was familiar, and Ruth tried to rack her brain to understand who he was.

'Hello?' she called out softly, but the man didn't budge. 'Hello,' she said a little louder, and the snore turned into a gurgle, the man opening his eyes.

'Ruth,' he said, jumping up and rushing to her side.

Ruth shrank back and the man stopped, seeming to understanding her apprehension.

'Ruth, it's me. Do you recognise me?' he said, speaking to her like she was a child. 'It's me, Paul.'

Ruth looked at the unshaven man, his amber eyes that pierced through her, and she knew that she knew him. She tried to smile and encouraged, he neared, but as he did, her eyebrows narrowed. She wasn't sure now.

'I'm sorry, but who are you?'

'I'm a friend,' said Paul, and pulling up a wooden chair that sat beside a bedside table, he seated himself on its edge. He put his hands on the side of the bed and Ruth shrank away again. 'A good friend.' He took his hands away and buried them between his legs.

'Where's my mother and father?'

'You remember them?' His face lit up.

'Yes!' Ruth was indignant. Why wouldn't she remember her own parents?

'We're, er, taking turns. They left a couple of hours ago.'

Ruth seemed to be a bit surer now. He knew her parents too. 'Where am I?'

'Your apartment. I …'

'I have an apartment?' She looked around at her surroundings now. A white wardrobe, which took up a whole wall, was slightly ajar and Ruth could see a flurry of colourful clothes gathered together. A dresser lay to its left, with an array of make-up, perfumes and other grooming products. Her eyes widened. 'That's all mine? I don't remember.'

'You had an … er, accident.'

Ruth looked down at her foot and tried to wiggle her toes again. 'What's wrong with my legs?' She could feel a real terror take hold as she stared down at the lifeless mounds under the blanket that sat unmoving.

'Injury.' Paul was direct.

'Why can't I feel them?'

'It will take a bit of time. You had an accident. You were in hospital for a while.'

'How long ago?'

'A couple of months,' Paul mumbled.

Ruth shook her head. She didn't remember anything.

'What's the last thing you remember?' Paul could see her confusion.

'I … I don't know.' She closed her eyes and felt her head begin to thump again. 'I can't remember …'

'You remembered your parents?'

Ruth tried to shake the growing haze behind her eyelids and felt the tears begin to spill. Paul picked up her hand and stroked it. She let him. His hands felt soft, warm.

'You didn't remember your parents the last time you woke up.'

Ruth hiccupped and opened her eyes. 'When was that?'

'Last night. They were here, but you didn't know who they

were.'

'Why am I not at my parents' house?'

'We thought it was best you were in your own home. Maybe you would remember better. The last time you remembered your own house, where everything was, but not your parents or anyone.'

'No one?' Ruth was incredulous.

'Well, there were names, but I don't think you knew who they were.'

Ruth could tell Paul was not telling her everything. 'How long ago was it? The accident. And what accident, what happened? When did you see me last?' She just kept blurting out things that came to her mind.

'Here, have a drink of water while I call your folks and then we can talk.' He handed her a glass and she just held it in front of her. She didn't want water, she wanted answers.

'No. Tell me now.'

'I'll be back in a minute,' Paul said and left the room. Ruth craned her neck to hear what he was saying, but only bits and pieces that didn't make sense came to her. She kept trying to move her legs while she listened to the snippets of conversation. 'She remembers you guys … no, not me … not even Derek. Place was … I don't know. Good time … I think so.'

He came back into the room with a glass of orange juice and handed it to her. 'Are you hungry?'

'Paul, is it?' Ruth was sure that's what he had said. 'How do I know you?'

'I told you before. I'm a good friend.' Paul smiled warmly and Ruth knew he was.

'Well, as a good friend, could you please tell me what the fuck is going on?'

Chapter 23

'I remember Jerry,' said Ruth one evening when Paul set a dinner plate in front of her. He was a marvellous cook and Ruth was enjoying being pampered every evening. 'He came to my head this morning while I was in the shower.' She suddenly blushed. She remembered Jerry and what she had done with him very well.

It had been two weeks since the day she had woken up and remembered her parents, but there were still large gaps. From what Paul had told her, there was a wedding and then she had been run over. She had dashed out of the church and had just run. A car had sped into her at full speed and taken off. No one saw it and Ruth couldn't remember it either. The police had been to talk to her to see if she did as it had come at her from the front. Only a late wedding attendee, her cousin Jess, had seen it dash away, a yellow car. She didn't see much else, as she had rushed to Ruth's side to help.

She remembered Karen and her sister and other people, including Marielle for some strange reason, but why she remembered her, she didn't understand, even though Paul explained the connection. Marielle had hurried over to help Ruth make the connection, but Ruth couldn't put her face to a place or any particular thing. She just knew that this was the stylish woman whom she had known at some stage in her life.

She couldn't recall where she worked yet, but flashes of an office came to her and Paul had immediately taken her there. But even though she remembered some features, like the glass desk and her coffee cup, the one with the purple flowers, she couldn't remember anyone there, not even her boss or assistant. She came home disappointed.

But after a conversation with her father one afternoon when he stopped by to bring her lunch, she started to realise that some of the things that happened before her accident, she preferred not to remember.

'Dad, I know there was something not quite right before the accident. Do you know anything?'

'What can you remember?' said Gary, unwrapping the foil on her kebab and putting it onto her lap.

Ruth, used to the wheelchair by now, swivelled around to grab a glass of water. 'Not a lot. I remember you and Mum, Karen and Patty, a very different Patty, but not much else. Not even Patty's children or even her husband. Strange one, that.'

Gary rolled his eyes. 'Tables have turned there.' Seeing the confusion on Ruth's face, he waved his hand about in dismissal. 'Not important.'

'I was at my wedding. I don't even know that person, Derek.' Ruth had heard the name from all of them a number of times now when they tried to jog her memory. 'Where has he been, if he was my husband?'

'Well, clearly the wedding didn't happen after …' He paused. 'Ruth, forget Derek.'

'But where is he? If I loved him and he loved me, then where is he?'

'It's complicated, love.'

'You must tell me. Everyone skirts around the issue. I need to know what happened to him. Maybe I will remember something.'

So Gary told her. About Derek and about Mike and even about Oliver and Terrence. Paul had not told her any of that and Ruth wondered if he knew. He must have or else how would her father have known? She was appalled at who she'd been and if it hadn't come from her own father she would have thrown him out of her house.

'I don't remember any of them. Are you sure?'

'Really, girl? Why would I tell you a thing like that if it were not true?' He shook his head and raised his eyebrows, exhaling loudly. Ruth could see a tinge of disappointment that he was trying to hide. But she knew her father; they shared the same genes.

She changed the subject. 'So what happened at the wedding?'

'You ran out.'

'But why? Why did I run out? Maybe I wasn't in love with

him?'

'I don't know, Ruth, but you did. Listen, it's time for your therapy. Gina should be here any minute.'

Ruth looked at her absent legs, there but not there. She tried not to get upset about it but she wanted to walk. She hated the therapy, which always ended in tears, but she knew what she had to do. She nodded and munched on her kebab which was now quite cold.

Paul had been there every day since the accident three months earlier and Ruth had grown attached to him and quite dependent in the last couple of weeks. She felt something for him, but in her state, she couldn't allow herself to. She knew by now that they had been together a long time ago and that he had become a good friend, but she wondered if there was anything between them too when she was supposed to be marrying Derek. It was clear she had no understanding of fidelity before her accident. She didn't question him too much about it and wondered if he was seeing anyone. By the amount of time he spent with her, including nights on the sofa, she suspected not. But after what she had heard about herself, she didn't know what to believe anymore.

Now, as he ladled soup into her bowl, she cocked her head to one side. 'So, who's Jerry?' she asked and saw Paul's mouth curl into an amused smile.

'You really want to know?' He almost laughed.

'Well, I already know about the slut I was, I may as well know it all. Nothing to shock me anymore.'

'Well, Jerry is the only one who no one knows about.' He laughed again. 'Except me.'

'Okay, why you?'

'Because I'm your best friend, dummy,' he said and lovingly pushed at her head. 'Jerry is your secret lover.'

'Haha, they were all secret lovers, from what I hear.'

'Yes, but Jerry was your Sydney friend. You met him quite a lot. You were just, pardon the phrase, 'fuck buddies'. He knew nothing about your life; in fact, I think your name is actually Daisy.' He guffawed now.

'Oh my gosh! I remember that! Seriously, did I tell you all this?'

'How else would I know? You kept your, er, men very secret. You did break up with Mike though before the wedding and you promised you were not going to see Jerry again. So if it makes you feel better, you were going straight.' He winked at her and tried to stop another laugh.

'You make me sound like a gangster,' Ruth said, not really surprised by much she heard about herself these days.

'How did we become friends?'

'Well, you did hate me for a long time.'

Paul told her of Anna and when he mentioned the photograph, Ruth's eyes lit up.

'I remember. It was on a wall. A big wall with lots of other photos.'

Paul nodded. 'Do you remember her?'

'No, and from what you've said, I don't want to.'

She ate the rest of her food lost in thought. These were new memories and she clung to them. It was like a massive jigsaw puzzle. But she really wanted to see Derek. Even if he did hate her.

'Do you think I could see him?'

'Who?'

'Derek?'

'I've tried to call him but from what Karen has said, it's a no-go. He seems to have disappeared off the face of the earth.'

Ruth felt her heart plummet. She must have really hurt him. 'So, he knew?'

'From what happened next, yes, I would say he did.'

'What did he do when I was run over?'

'Don't know. He completely disappeared. It's a mystery.'

Ruth put her fingers to her temples as if trying to conjure up memories, but after a few moments, she dropped them, exasperated. 'It will come back. In time it has to.'

Chapter 24

It was a month later when Ruth decided she needed to go back to work. In that time, not a lot had changed. She went to Facebook to try and find Derek, but there was no sign of him having existed on any social media sites. No one at her work knew where he was either.

'Put in his notice on the twenty-fifth of June,' said a man whom Ruth didn't recognise. He had led her to an office. 'I thought you knew.'

He sat behind his desk, while Ruth did some maths in her head. 'That would be a week before the wedding,' she said, not particularly to him.

He nodded. 'He didn't want to make a big deal of it. I assumed you would be giving in your notice next.' He laughed, then stopped, looking at Ruth's legs.

Ruth was used to people looking down at her unworkable limbs. She tried to move them now, as she always did when she remembered they were still attached to her body. She pushed away the fear that usually accompanied it.

'I'm just glad you're okay. We were very worried.' Ruth knew he wanted to say more by the way his eyes crinkled at her. 'Are you, erm … are you …'

'Am I returning?' Ruth said. 'I don't know.'

'We are keeping your position here, you know.' He smiled warmly. 'Unless you don't want us to?'

Of course Ruth thought she may go back to her job, but she was wondering if she knew everything she needed to. They had been on the phone to her every two weeks. 'Can I give you my answer in a couple of weeks?'

'Of course, you were one of our best,' he said and rose, signalling the end of their meeting.

As she wheeled herself through the offices and work spaces, she tried to find something that would click, something she could remember, but again she couldn't, so she went home feeling more lost than ever.

She remembered her childhood friend and Karen had come over often with her little girl, trying to make Ruth recall events from their high school days. Ruth even remembered her high school friend Erica.

'Yes, I don't know how you forgave her,' said Karen, wrinkling her nose.

'Why would I need to forgive her?'

'Remember Marty?' Karen explained Erica's betrayal.

'So when did I forgive her?'

'A couple of years ago, you bumped into her somewhere. You didn't talk about her much, but I think you kept in touch.' Karen leaned forward. 'Hey, maybe she's in your phone. Try to call. If you remember her, maybe it will spark something.'

Ruth pulled out her phone and excitedly dialled Erica's number. She had scrolled through her phone contacts so many times but had never tried anyone because she thought it completely daft to ask a person on the other end of the line if they could tell her who she was. But she remembered Erica and Karen said she had been friends with her, so this would be okay. She listened twice to the phone ring out.

'I'll try tomorrow,' she said, hopeful.

Ruth tried to find out who Mike was, but no one could figure who he was, apart from Paul, who knew very little about the man Ruth spent so much of her time with, except for the fact he lived somewhere past Geelong. She knew she met him at Karen's wedding, but Karen could not fathom who he was or who he came with. At times, Ruth caught images of a place in her mind with a lot of sand, but the rest of the surroundings, wine glasses atop a wooden table, blue curtains, polished decking, they weren't at all familiar to her. She knew it meant something, but she had been to the beach quite often as a child and in her teenage years, so trying to set those glimpses apart from the many other times she had visited the beach was not easy. She knew it had something to do with Mike, Paul had told her that he lived at the beach, but she wouldn't know where to begin. She decided to try anyway.

'Where do you think we should start?' asked Paul, as they drove into Geelong, a beach city, crowded on a spring afternoon.

'Um …' Ruth looked about at the shops and streets, nothing feeling familiar to her. 'I remember the sound of water.'

They parked near the beach and Paul helped her out of the car.

Ruth was suddenly nervous. 'What if I see him?'

'That's what we want,' said Paul.

'Yes, but what if he hates me?'

'Then he hates you, but at least you will know.'

Even after they had lunch on the beach and Paul had wheeled her up and down the walk, nothing was familiar and Ruth drove back feeling more dejected than ever.

'Why are you helping me?' Ruth looked over to Paul on the drive home.

Paul frowned. 'Because I'm your friend.'

He had been a good friend, even though she still couldn't remember who he was before the accident. He had spent many hours of the evenings with her trying to jog her memory. He had been in touch with everyone he could think of, asking them to visit her. Even Terrence had been called to try to help revive some of her lost memories, but Ruth didn't remember him, although she did think he was very dashing. Paul watched in amusement as she straightened her blanket and flirted with what she did have.

'He's a looker, isn't he?' she said when Terrence had left.

'Yeah, a real playboy,' Paul said mirthless. 'You were a mess when you two broke up.'

'Really?' She tried to calculate the time she was with Terrence and how that related to Paul. 'How would you know?'

'You cried on my shoulder. It's what made us close.'

'That was when we worked together?'

Paul nodded. 'We worked really well together too. And then all that happened.'

Ruth somehow felt uncomfortable when Paul mentioned their being together. 'How is work going?' She changed the subject. Paul had told Ruth of his new business venture but didn't speak much of it.

'It's going.' He looked down.

'Not so good?' She had a thought. 'Is it me? Is it because you spend so much time here?'

He shook his head. 'I just need reliable people.' He gritted his teeth. 'I can't pay too well, and you know what they say …'

'What do they say?'

'When you pay peanuts, you get monkeys.' He stood up. 'I have to go tonight. Some paperwork to do.'

'You can't do it from here?'

'No, I left some things I need at home.'

Ruth looked at the time. 'It's late. It's a long drive.'

'I'll be fine.' He leaned across her to pick up his scarf that hung on the back of the sofa, and that's when Ruth smelled it. The scent of musk. That familiar smell.

She leaned forward and inhaled just as Paul leaned back.

'What?' He leaned back and screwed up his face.

'Your cologne. It's familiar.'

'I've been wearing the same one forever. Habit. You probably smell it on me every day.'

'No, wait.' She wheeled herself to her bedroom and Paul followed. She reached under her bed and pulled out a scarf, quite similar to the one Paul had just wrapped around his neck. 'Is this yours?'

Paul took the scarf and appraised it. 'Yeah, I think so. I had one like it a while … Oh.'

'What?'

'I must have left it at your place, your old place.' He looked at her now. 'You didn't throw it out.'

'I found it a couple of weeks ago. Mum was going through some stuff in the top of the wardrobe. She thought it was Derek's and was going to take it away but for some reason I told her I wanted it.' She reached out for it. 'I don't know why.'

'You kept this thing all this time?'

'I guess so.' A fleeting memory crossed her brain and she closed her eyes as she tried to hang on to it.

Ruth could feel him watch her and she opened her eyes. 'Can I keep it for a while?'

'You can have it.' He laughed. 'Snuggle up to it at night if you want.'

Another flash. 'I think I did.'

Paul snickered. 'I really have to go, but at least you solved the mystery.'

He walked to the door and Ruth wheeled herself behind him. She was getting quite adept at handling this cumbersome wheelchair. He opened the door and bent to kiss her head, but Ruth took hold of the scarf that wound round his neck and pulled his face close to hers. She reached up and kissed his lips. Another memory and a flash of heat pulsed through her. She opened her eyes and Paul pulled back.

'It's not a good idea, Ruth. I'm your friend, remember? This can't become complicated.'

'Sorry,' said Ruth, slightly stung, but also understanding what he was trying to say.

Ruth was angry with herself for what she had tried to do. She knew now that Paul lived with his girlfriend, and had met Danni a couple of times, always getting the impression that she resented her. She put herself in Danni's position and understood how the girl would feel, her fella off babysitting his ex-girlfriend almost every evening. Ruth wondered if she would be as understanding as Danni and realised that she was probably the cause of many a rift between Paul and his girlfriend.

Right now, she just felt jealous of her, that Paul was going home to Danni instead of staying here with her. She knew it was selfish and resolved to try not to be the person she had become before the accident happened. She sighed. It was always a before and after. Nothing made sense anymore.

After he was gone, Ruth knew she needed to do something with her life. She could be in this wheelchair and without her memory for who knew how long. Apparently, from what the doctors were saying, it was psychological, all of it, the legs and the memory loss. There was no pain, which was a worry, but it could also mean that there were other things going on in her brain, something she needed to shut out of her consciousness. She couldn't understand what they were saying sometimes, but she was warned that her memories or the use of her legs may not return. She had to do something other than keep her life on hold for when they did, if they did.

She went to bed, a plan forming in her head.

Chapter 25

'How about I work for you?' Ruth announced when Paul came over the next evening.

He stopped in the middle of the doorway, his arms full of food he had picked up on the way over. It was Friday and he had told Ruth he was dropping off a meal that he had cooked earlier that day. He raised his eyebrows in astonishment and walked over to the dining table, placing the bags on it. He proceeded to take out a number of containers and spread them around the table in silence.

'Did you hear me?' Ruth wheeled herself after him.

'I heard.'

'And?'

Paul turned around and leaned his butt on the table. 'Um … I don't know how to tell you this, but I was thinking of packing it in.'

'Why?' Ruth was shocked. He was so passionate about his work and when he talked about it, a light would turn on behind his eyes. Sure, it wasn't going very well, but Ruth thought that perhaps with her help he could get things running properly again.

'To be honest, I need money and I am not making a lot right now.'

Ruth knew it was her fault. 'But that's just it. I can help. You always said I was good at what I did and if I got back to it, I may pick it up easily. Besides, it may help me remember some things …'

'It's not always all about you, Ruth,' he said softly and Ruth flinched.

'Sorry. What is it about?'

'Come on, let's eat,' he said and went to the fridge to get a couple of cans of Coke.

Ruth ate the delicious meal in silence and Paul didn't offer any conversation to break the awkwardness that had befallen them. Ruth helped him put the dishes in the washer and excused herself to the bathroom. She found Paul on the balcony when she came out.

'It's beautiful tonight,' she said, wishing she hadn't mentioned anything.

'Danni is unhappy.' He didn't turn to her and Ruth remained silent. 'In other words, she's jealous.'

'I'm sorry,' said Ruth, not really knowing what else to say.

He turned around now. 'I'm going to ask her to marry me.'

Ruth nodded, looking away from him, and he turned away again. She watched the back of his sweater that seemed to heave and she suddenly realised what a burden she had been.

'Maybe it's time you did ask her. I think it's time you stopped spending so much time here.'

Paul turned around again and sat on the chair beside her. 'But I don't want to.' He took her hand. 'I have actually enjoyed spending time with you, helping you to …'

'No, that's just it. I can do everything I need to on my own. You have helped and I've just taken advantage because I need …' She hesitated. 'I don't know what I need, but I do know that I'm ready to do more than go for walks or go to places that I hope will remind me of something. I want to get back to living, just the way I am. I know how much of a burden I've been.'

Paul smiled. 'Of course you haven't, but I think we both got used to our new roles and got lost in our own world. But I think it's time we do get back to our own lives. Danni …'

'Just ask her.' Ruth could already feel the heat rise in her, that green-eyed monster that attacked whenever he talked of his girlfriend.

Paul leaned over and lifted Ruth's chin in his hand. 'But how can I when I want to do this all the time?' He kissed her.

She closed her eyes and felt like her stomach was jelly. She leaned back and opened her eyes, to see Paul's staring straight into hers. She put her arms around his neck and he fell on his knees, leaning over her, taking her head in his hands. Ruth closed her eyes again as she felt his cool lips on hers.

Ruth suddenly realised what she was doing. 'Paul.' She released him and he straightened, a look of concern in his eyes.

'Sorry, are you okay?' He seemed to also come to his senses. 'Sorry, Ruth, I'm so sorry, I should never have …' He sat back in his chair, his face contorted with anger and shame. He bowed his head and focused on his fidgeting fingers.

'We can't do this,' said Ruth, fighting her every instinct to reach over and cling back to him. 'I … I just …'

'What is it?' It seemed like an effort to look at her again.

'I can't be this person. This woman, this harlot, who has all these men.' She shook her head in disbelief. 'I still can't believe I did all those things and I can't go to this place where I'm able to do it again. I don't even know what made me do it in the first place. I was a one-man woman. From what I remember, I've never cheated on anyone in my life. But I clearly did and now here I am coming between you and the woman you are going to marry.'

'Maybe it's time to keep a safe distance,' he said, his head bowed again.

'I'm really okay.' She looked at him and he looked tired, worn out, sad. 'But I was serious about working with you.'

He laughed cynically. 'After this?'

'We are adults. You have a partner and I have … other things to think about. It will be good for me, for both of us. Maybe your business doesn't have to be dissolved. Maybe we can work at it; you can show me the ropes and from what I've seen, we work well together.'

He laughed. 'Marielle always said we did. I don't know, Ruth.'

'Give it six months. You don't even have to pay me.'

He laughed again. 'You are already close to defaulting on your mortgage payments. Your accident payment is going to run out pretty soon.'

'Then I'll just move back home.'

'And how will you get to work?'

'You will come get me.' She laughed and Paul laughed back.

****

It was working well. Sure, it had only been two weeks, but Ruth couldn't believe how easily it came to her, designing and formatting advertisements for clients, and how she and Paul worked together, with such ease and fun. She did a lot of the work at home, but she tried to go to Paul's little office, a run-down loft in the city, not too far from where she lived, at least once a week. She was happy to get out by herself and at times her father or sister would drop her over.

'You and Paul,' said Patty one morning, as she drove her to work. 'What's going on?'

'Nothing in the way you think,' said Ruth. 'We are just good friends and now colleagues.'

'Uh-huh,' said Patty and tapped her long pink nail on the steering wheel. Patty was a different woman from how Ruth remembered her, but Ruth liked this Patty, a strong woman, who said what she felt and did as much, not the snivelling, whining girl that Ruth used to scorn. 'Uh-huh,' she repeated and squinted her eyes at Ruth.

But Ruth knew that if it went anywhere with Paul that it shouldn't, she would lose him altogether. He was going to ask Danni to marry him this weekend and Ruth tried to be happy for him. She was not going to be the other woman. She just really wanted to know why she ever was.

'How's Oliver?'

'I wouldn't know,' said Patty with a shrug. 'Why?'

'I think that maybe if I see him again …'

'Oh Ruth, you can't just go around trying to see everyone over and over again hoping something will come back to you.'

'I know. I'm just getting really frustrated.' She thought of the sand that kept coming to her head. She wondered if she could just go there again, to wherever that place was. But all other avenues to her memory had ended up dead-end roads, so why would this be any different?

She resigned herself to her life as it was and even began to enjoy who she was now, in a small way, hoping she would never have to find out who she'd become.

****

She was having lunch with Paul one afternoon when she saw him.

Derek.

She immediately recognised the face that registered shock at the sight of her and she felt something stir in her leg. She was so surprised with the sensation that she looked down at her knees but when she looked up again, he was gone.

'What is it?' said Paul who was in the middle of discussing the project they were working on.

'I think I just saw him. It think it was Derek.'

Paul turned around. 'Where?'

'I don't know.' She put her hand on Paul's. 'I think I just felt something in my legs. A twitch. It happened when I saw him.'

Paul's eyes lit up. 'Are you sure?'

'Yes.' She moved her leg about with her hands but again, nothing. She frowned.

'What is it?'

'I need to find him.'

'But no one can find him. He's not even on Facebook. He's not at work and the place Karen took us to is empty.'

'I just need to see him. Someone has to know where he is.' Ruth realised that Derek was the key to her paralysis. She needed to know what happened to her, what she had done. To remember it herself rather than be told about it.

'What about Jerry?' You remember him. Maybe he knows something,' Paul ventured.

'I don't even know if his name is really Jerry.'

'We'll get there, don't worry.' He put his hand on hers and quickly removed it. 'You have your appointment next week. Maybe you can tell the doctor what you felt.'

These months of not knowing had been torture and although Ruth allowed herself to consider that this may be it, that this was how she would be forever, the use of her legs never to return, she was still unwilling to believe that her memory wouldn't come back. She had to know what happened, who she was, who she had turned into. She went to hypnosis but that didn't work, she went to the beach again but that didn't either. She even began to wonder if it really was Derek she saw, but from the photographs that she had stared at for so long, she knew it was him. She didn't know what triggered it, went over and over what she had done that day for it to come to her, but nothing stood out.

It was a week after she had seen Derek that it all came back. One night, in the middle of a dream. She saw his face, Derek's first. Then she saw Mike's and at first, she couldn't quite work out who this handsome man was, but there she was, in his arms, in his house, in his backyard, on the beach.

She woke up sweating and tried to grasp on to the thought, the little remnant that lingered in her brain, wishing it would remain. To her surprise, it did. She realised she was still awake and she could see him in her mind. It was Mike. It had to be. She raised herself up and swung her legs over the bed and stopped in shock. She eased her foot on the floor and as it touched the rug, it all came flooding back.

Derek

The traffic was busy, there always seemed to be roadworks on the freeway and Derek craned his neck to try to see beyond the four-wheel drive that sat in front of him. He looked at the little clock on the dashboard and cursed the time and the traffic. He turned up the music and hummed to it, trying to calm himself.

He had seen her today and it had completely unnerved him. It was more than six months since the wedding, the accident, everything, and he was still not over her. He thought he was, he thought she had forgotten about him, he'd expected her to. When he heard from Sam at Marks and Sons that she had regained her memory last week, he began to panic. What if she knew?

He honked the horn, knowing it wouldn't make a difference to the line of cars ahead of him, but it still made him feel better. The phone on the dashboard began to buzz and he saw Mike's number come up. A flash of anger ran through his body and he threw the phone face down on the seat beside him.

Mike. What was he supposed to do with Mike?

'I wish I never knew,' he said through gritted teeth, knowing he would be in blissful oblivion if he didn't know about what she'd done.

He still remembered the face of Mike at the door of Ruth's apartment. It was etched in his consciousness. Mike's expression was one of surprise, which turned quickly to fury.

'Are you Derek?'

'Yes, and you are?' said Derek, sticking out his hand, which Mike ignored.

'We need to talk,' he replied and without waiting for a response, pushed past Derek.

'Wait a minute,' said Derek, following him.

Mike stopped in the middle of the room and raked his hand through his hair; he seemed unsure of what to do next.

'Who are you? What do you want?' Derek tried to conjure his most authoritative voice.

'Ruth. Where is she?'

'Sydney … wait a minute. Who are you?'

'I told you. Mike.' He sat down heavily on the sofa. 'A … a friend of Ruth's.' Mike spotted a picture of Ruth on the side table and snatched it up. 'It's true then.'

'What?' said Derek, who was becoming irritated and a little anxious.

Mike turned the picture towards him. 'Ruth. She's your girlfriend?'

'Girlfriend? We're going to be married in a couple weeks!'

Suddenly Mike burst into laughter, a howling laughter, and Derek snatched the photo back from him. 'She's been my girl for the last year,' said Mike, who looked slightly delirious, and Derek was afraid.

****

Derek looked in the mirror at the traffic behind him and knew it was going to be a long, long drive. He sighed. He wished he had just chosen to confront her when she returned from Sydney. But no, he had to do one better. For once, the patience he had been so proud of escaped him.

After Mike had left, Derek's phone number safely inserted into his phone, Derek didn't know what to do. He didn't even know whether to believe Mike, but it made sense. It all fitted into place. The weekend disappearances, the strange excuses. He now wondered whether she was really at her conferences in Sydney. But he knew that she was working there. He would know, he worked at the same company she did. But now his mind was in overdrive. He cracked open a beer and just sat down on the sofa until darkness fell, long after he was due to go out. His friend Sam had asked him to join him for a beer, as his own wife was away, and Derek had accepted as it helped pass the time when Ruth was gone.

When his phone rang, Sam's name flickering on the screen, he ignored it. He could deal with him later. He picked it up after it rang out and his fingers hovered over Ruth's name. He wanted to call her, to confront her, to see if it was all true. But he knew that the way he was feeling was not going to be helpful. She would deny it and he wanted to see her face when he confronted her; that would show him the truth.

The next morning, after a fitful sleep, he arose with the sound of his alarm and sat on the edge of the bed. His head was pounding and he knew he couldn't go in to work. He had to see

Ruth. There were still two days before she was to return; he knew he wasn't that patient. He called the office and left a message on the answering machine that he was too ill to go to work. He barely took any time off and knew they would be okay with it. He lay back on the bed and picked up his phone again. She would still be asleep and he considered calling her, but thought better of it.

An idea struck him. He could go to her, to see her in person, to clear up this mess, to give her a chance to explain. He couldn't wait until she returned. He quickly looked up the flights and dialled the airline, but the earliest flight he could get was for four in the afternoon. He booked it.

After a restless morning and afternoon, he drove himself to the airport. By then he had worked himself into another state and knew he was doing the right thing. He had managed to ignore the ringing phone, one call from Ruth and two from Mike, but the thoughts that entered his head were too much to deal with. He would have this straightened out today.

He hadn't even pushed the large glass door of the hotel open when he saw her. His stomach tightened as he watched the beautiful figure of the woman he loved at the counter, waiting for something. He knew he could forgive her if it were true, he just loved her way too much. And from what Mike said, she had dumped him anyway. He would be understanding, he had to be. He would ask her for forgiveness for not being enough for her and would make it right.

He stopped. Maybe he wouldn't ask her about it. Maybe now

that Mike was out of the picture, they would be okay. He tried to feel happy but there was still a sting in his heart. He watched as she nodded to the concierge, who laughed with familiarity with her, and as she walked with a number of envelopes in her hand to the elevator. He pushed open the door and hurried towards her before she could step into the lift.

He froze.

She had walked straight past the elevator into the arms of a man, who enclosed her in his own and kissed her with abandon. Derek's head pounded as he watched with a surreal feeling as Ruth clung to the man's neck while his hands roamed down to her buttocks that were snug in her tight blue skirt. A laugh together and they were getting into the lift, his arm casually slung around her waist. Derek quickly backed out of sight and stood against a pillar.

He wasn't sure of what he just saw. He had to run it through slowly in his mind before he could fully comprehend what just happened. A hotel worker bumped into him and he quickly apologised before dashing out of the hotel. He was to wait at the airport for another three hours before he could book a flight back to Melbourne. And by the time he got back to Ruth's apartment, he knew what he had to do. She had been playing him for a fool all along and now he would make her pay.

He thought about the time she had questioned his affection, his loyalty, the time he had gone to New Zealand, where he had been propositioned by Doreen, the hot blonde, who he dismissed without a second thought. Maybe he should have just gone for it when Sheila, the waitress at the corner café where he sometimes lunched, turned on the charm. There had been many opportunities, but he never felt the urge, the need or even the smallest temptation. It had been Ruth all along. And he had trusted her implicitly, never for a moment felt that she had her eyes elsewhere. The only time he ever felt jealous was when Paul was around. Paul, her old friend, who he knew had a fling with her long before Derek was in the picture.

He now wondered about Paul too. Were they also together? Did Paul know about the others?

Derek wanted to call and ask him, but Paul was loyal to Ruth and he would never admit it if they were secretly involved. Besides, he didn't want to look like a begging fool. He may only have some pride left, but that was still his own.

Derek didn't know what to do. He thought about calling Karen or even Ruth's parents, but knew they were not going to be on his side. Her father was a little wary of him already and Derek never knew what he had done to put the old man offside.

After another restless night and another day off from work, he decided not to confront Ruth. By this time, he was so incensed that all he could think about was revenge. And he knew exactly what he needed to do.

When Ruth got home the day after, Derek pretended as if everything was as it was before, and the wedding plans continued. He watched her every move, waiting for her to say or do something that seemed untoward, not quite sure how he'd react if she did.

'Not going to Erica's this weekend?' he asked as Ruth settled in for a movie on a Friday evening.

'No,' she said indifferently as she removed the popcorn from the microwave.

By the end of the weekend, Derek realised how casual she was. Nothing seemed out of the ordinary and he almost admired the way she behaved, all the while cheating on him. It was more infuriating than ever, and Derek couldn't believe how easy it was for her and how stupid he had been.

With two weeks until the wedding, he knew he had to hold it in. He knew what revenge would be the sweetest and he was quite happy to deliver her up in all her glory. He already made plans. He was going to confront her right there at the altar and leave her alone and he would be gone. Away from her, without any explanation, without even telling her. She could figure it out for herself. He wished he could be there to see her bewilderment. He also just wished she loved him enough to be shattered. He hoped she would.

When Mike called him on that Friday evening, he hung up on him, but when the phone rang incessantly the next day, he had to tell Ruth he was going to the office as he had forgotten something there. He called Mike back.

'Where have you been? Why didn't you answer your phone?' Mike's voice was impatient, demanding.

'Hello, Mike. I couldn't. I wasn't in a position to.'

'Oh, okay. Well? Did you talk to her?'

'No.' Derek knew what he had to say. He couldn't lie or else Mike would probably approach Ruth and Derek knew Mike had to know that it was over between them, especially if Ruth hadn't been in touch with him. 'Have you?'

'No. I have tried to call but she won't answer. Did you tell her about me?'

'No. She hasn't spoken to you, which means she meant it. She is going to marry me in two weeks.' Derek just wanted to get this man off the phone now.

'Are you crazy? You're still going to marry her?' Mike sounded livid and Derek just didn't want to talk to him anymore.

'It's just the way it is.'

'You're an idiot,' said Mike and hung up.

Derek just hoped Mike wouldn't wreck his plan. He considered telling him about it, but he didn't trust Mike. What if he used it as a way to get Ruth back? What if he were to tell her all about it, and then it would be ruined.

He thought about the wedding. How beautiful he knew she would look, but also about the many other people that would be hurt by what he did, but they were collateral damage. It was her fault, not his. He had been the ever-faithful fool for the whole of their relationship. It was his turn to be the bad guy.

Ruth spent the eve of her wedding day at her parents' house and Derek had taken the opportunity to remove all his belongings from her apartment. He had already booked a rental property in Cairns, where his old childhood friend lived, and had reserved a flight for the evening of the wedding. He would be in the air laughing at his antics as he flew to his new future, while Ruth would be wondering what the hell had just happened. He knew she loved him or else she wouldn't have agreed to marry him and the thought of her heart being broken gave him a sick satisfaction.

He never even knew what happened. When she walked towards him, looking so pure, so beautiful, he almost backed out of his plan. Then she had looked towards Paul, and his resolve returned with a vengeance. He strode towards her and she had run. He stopped in the middle of the aisle and looked around at the astonished faces. He bolted through a pew, pushing past the legs of some dumbfounded guests, and darted straight out of the side door and had kept going, straight to the airport, where his luggage had been waiting for him.

But once on the plane, the gratification he had envisioned was not to be felt. He wondered how he was going to explain it all to his father and his sister. He hadn't really thought it through. They would be shocked at this turn of events and Derek had not even considered anything other than exacting his revenge. He thought about Ruth and how it would have been for her after she ran. An ache pierced his heart and Derek turned his thoughts from her; it just wouldn't do to look back and regret what he'd done. It may change his mind. Once he landed, he inserted a new SIM card into his phone and left a message on his father's answering machine. He was not close to his father, who had become a cold man since his mother had passed away when he was just twelve.

No, he didn't have any explaining to do. He was going to start afresh.

And he did. He found work almost immediately at a bar at Trinity Beach and spent his days chatting up women and spending nights with them. He was going to become a player, something he probably should have been all along.

When he met Alice, he thought he could make it work, but thoughts of Ruth nudged at his brain and he found himself thinking about her and missing her. He looked at her Facebook page, but he could only see so much as he had unfriended her and there didn't seem to be anything new from what he could see.

He had envisioned such a great life with her: similar interests, a job they practically shared and they had even talked about kids, which he now wondered about. But he was restless. He wanted to go back to Melbourne and he wondered if it was too soon. It had already been nearly six months and the weather and people in town were wearing thin on him. He missed the hustle and bustle of Melbourne, the place he grew up, the place he called home. He wanted to go back. He felt he had had enough time to have dealt with everything, and bidding a sad goodbye to Alice, he headed home.

He came back to his own flat, which he kept, knowing somewhere in the back of his mind that he would return. It smelled musty and felt lonely and after sleeping for most of the evening, he set about getting it in order. He knew there was much to do, including finding a job, which he had scouted while he was still in

Cairns.

He hadn't even been back for two days when he saw her. Sitting in that café with Paul. He opened the door and the clanging of the bell atop it made her look up. He locked eyes with her for a moment and froze. But then she looked downwards and he just couldn't do it; he bolted away. He walked quickly down the street, wondering what to do. He knew he would probably bump into her at some stage, but this was too soon.

He got into his car and called Mike.

Chapter 26

She stood at the door and fisted her hand to knock, but before she could, the door was opened and Derek almost crashed into her; she could see he was on his way out.

He froze for a moment and his mouth hung open. Ruth, stepping backward, regained her balance and stared at him. 'You,' she said blankly.

Ruth knew everything now. She recalled the wedding, and before the wedding. She remembered Mike, Paul and Derek. She also remembered who she had become and why she had become that way.

The night she regained her memory was a night Ruth wished she could ban from her memory. Her first impulse was to call Paul, but she knew she couldn't lean on him for this. She had to remember everything on her own. So she walked. Her legs were weak, but she got into a track suit and left the house.

The night was so cool, but the moon was high and Ruth kept walking, making use of the legs that had been so still for the last few months. They were shaky, but she kept going, alone in the dark, ignoring the dangers of the night, round and round the park. She was thinking about Derek and the years they had spent together, how she had never trusted him and how maybe she should have. Oliver rushed to her mind then, seeing Oliver in the arms of another woman and she felt the tears, those that had refused to drop for years. Now she let them flow out, weeping for the girl who had her heart broken and sobbing for the woman that girl became.

Terrence's smiling face came to her and she wanted to hit herself for behaving so badly at his hands. She'd lost her pride and herself as she begged for him to stay and she cringed at the thought. How could she have loved a man such as that? *How could anyone have loved me then,* she asked herself. *I turned into the worst kind of person.*

Memories flooded her mind, and when the dam burst, her brain was flooded and it was hard to process all that happened in such a short time. She thought about her sister, about her job, and even about Jerry, but Jerry brought a smile to her face. It wasn't the sex, it was the escape. That was what Jerry was, an escape from the life she had made for herself, which he had no knowledge or part of, and he had never asked for anything more than she could give. She would always remember Jerry with fondness. He was there when she needed just that.

Ruth went home to an empty apartment and made herself a cup of tea. She turned on soft music and sat on the balcony, watching the darkness turn to light.

She thought about Mike, kind, loving Mike, and she

wondered why he had never contacted her. Then she remembered blocking his number and her distress as she left his house. She scrolled through her phone for Mike's number. Yes, there it was, under the name of Michelle. She shook her head at her insanity, but just staring at his number, something caught in her brain, and she couldn't quite put her finger on it.

And through it all, the image of Paul kept returning to her. Paul, her friend, who had taken her out to get her mind off her sadness after her break-ups, Paul who loved her and made her so happy. Paul and Anna—she seethed at the thought that she may not have become what she was had it not been for Anna and her manipulative performance.

Maybe it just had to be that way: she had to face her fears of being betrayed again in her own way. She just couldn't believe it had to be by hurting other people. But Paul had stuck by her throughout her ordeal, had been with her from the moment she opened her eyes after the accident, up to now. And now he was about to start a life of his own which should not include her. She had to let him go, she knew that now. She was selfish by hanging on to him and stopping him from having a life. He couldn't be with her anyway; he would probably never trust her. He knew too much.

Her mind went back to the day of her wedding. She remembered the jitters she had and why she had them. She pictured herself backing out of the church, the look on Derek's face sending shivers down her spine. She was running fast, she could see that, but did she trip over? Ruth sat up suddenly. She remembered the car and her throat went dry.

The day was bright now and people were already moving about, trams already making their familiar sound, and Ruth sat and watched the glorious sight of the city come alive. It was time for her to live too. It was time to make amends.

'Uh, hi, Ruth,' said Derek, and moved aside to let her in.

Ruth entered Derek's flat and stood near the door, surveying the room, which was devoid of furniture, except for a small settee and a middle table. She was nervous and she could see Derek was too, as he moved things from the sofa to the floor beside it.

'Have a seat.'

'I just … I, um, wanted to return this to you,' she said, holding out her hand with his ring in it. 'I couldn't find the box, I'm sorry.'

Derek stared at the ring but made no attempt to take it from her.

She pushed her hand forward again. 'Please, Derek.'

'I don't want it,' he said and turned from her. 'Would you like something to drink? I don't have much, but coffee? I know you liked coffee.' He began to smile and then stopped.

'We don't have to talk,' she said, moving to the table and placing the ring on it.

'I think we probably should. Just wait, I'll get the coffee.'

Ruth sat on the settee and waited, wondering why she didn't feel anything for this man, the man she was going to marry. She expected to feel something, a rush of love or at least something, anything ... She remembered loving him very much.

'I'm sorry,' he said as he placed the cup on the table.

'You're sorry?' Ruth was dumbfounded. 'For what?'

'For leaving you there, at the altar, to face everyone on your own.'

'Oh.' Ruth didn't remember it that way, not after what happened next. 'Well, I think we both know who should be apologising.' She took a sip of the coffee that was terribly bitter. She swallowed it anyway, along with her pride. She put down the cup. 'Anything I say could not even begin to express how I feel about what I did to you.'

'It's okay, Ruth. I got over it.'

Ruth lowered her head. 'How long did you know?'

Derek smirked. 'About which one, Mike or the guy in Sydney?'

Ruth's eyes popped open and Derek laughed without mirth.

'A couple of weeks before the wedding,' he said and sighed deeply.

Ruth's eyes filled with tears and Derek looked at her in alarm. She shook her head and the tears rolled down her cheeks. 'I'm so, so sorry,' she cried.

Derek looked pained. 'It's the past now,' he said and stood up. This was clearly making him more uncomfortable than he had thought it would. 'I have to go, Ruth,' he said.

'Can I ask one question?' Ruth said and Derek nodded

unsurely. 'Where have you been all this time? I searched and searched for you.'

'I had to get away, cut ties with everyone, everything. I went to Cairns, but I knew I couldn't stay away forever. I even met someone, but I had to come back, just to see if you were okay after … I didn't even know what happened to you until I returned.'

'Really?' Ruth had more questions, like if he knew, would he have returned to her, like how Derek found out about the affairs, about his new life, about why he really came back, but she realised this visit was not for herself. Some things would have to go unanswered. She knew her time with him was over.

Derek nodded, but didn't elaborate. He walked Ruth to the door and as she reached in to hug him, he backed away from her. It stung, but she knew she deserved that. At least he had taken the time to speak with her.

Ruth walked back to her apartment deep in thought. She knew she didn't love Derek, and probably never really did. Perhaps she could have loved him, without everything else that was going on in her life.

She hadn't told anyone about the return of movement in her legs or of her restored memories yet. She wanted to surprise them and invited Paul over for dinner the next day. She was meant to work at home for the next couple of days anyway, so he wouldn't even question her not coming into the office, and lately she had begun to cook, enjoying it more than she ever did before. She called her parents to let them know and Gary insisted they come over to take her out to lunch, which they did even though Ruth didn't feel much like celebrating. She knew she was better off remembering what she had done, but that person seemed so far removed from the person that she was.

'It's okay, love,' said Gary, when she told them how she was feeling. 'Maybe it's best this happened. You were not yourself and hadn't been for a long time.'

'You never said anything,' said Ruth, surprised. She thought she hid her feelings from her parents pretty well.

Gary sighed. 'We didn't know anything really. Just that something wasn't right, something was off, you know?'

'We tried to,' said Roberta. 'We knew you had to do things for yourself. You were never one to share your feelings with us. We thought maybe you'd come around in your own time.'

'You know it's your fault,' said Ruth, watching her parents' eyes widen. 'You guys are perfect. All I wanted was someone to love like you do.'

'It's not perfect,' said Gary and put a hand on Roberta's.

Her mother looked at him and smiled. 'But it's perfect for us,' she said and the two of them gave each other a warm smile.

'Arrghh,' said Ruth and rolled her eyes. 'There you go.'

'Besides,' said Gary, a twinkle in his eye. 'You already have someone perfect for you.'

'Don't say it, Dad,' said Ruth, when the face of Paul flashed through her mind.

When she arrived home, Ruth knew she had to face Mike.

But she wasn't ready to drive yet, so she called Karen, who offered to take her to Geelong in the evening.

'I can't believe it,' said Karen, when Ruth walked out of her apartment.

Ruth hugged her friend and didn't want to let her go.

'What is it?' said Karen concerned.

'Thank you,' said Ruth. 'For just being the best friend I've ever had.'

'I'm just driving you to Geelong, geez,' said Karen, embarrassed.

When she arrived at Mike's place, she saw the car, the one that had hit her, and even though she had been expecting it, it still sent a wave of shock through her.

'I won't be long,' she told Karen.

'Want me to come with?'

'Nope. This is all mine.'

Chapter 27

Her nerves were raw by the time she reached the large wooden door and she scrunched up her fists a couple of times when she saw they were shaking. She could hear the waves from the sea and looked up at the sky, glowing pink, yet ominous. She looked back at Karen who sat in her car watching her, an encouraging smile on her face.

Ruth had paced nervously before Karen had arrived to take her there, trying to envision the scene and how it would play out. She had hurt him, yes, but he had tried to kill her. She became distressed at the thought of what that meant.

He had tried to kill her!

And no one had a clue about who he actually was, so he would have just gotten away with it. Who was this man that she had loved, or thought she loved? Because when she thought about it, she didn't want him anymore. If she remembered everything, their relationship, their love, shouldn't she at least have some lingering affection for him? Her nerves were shot by the time Karen arrived;

she had no idea what she was going to say to him. She just needed to see him, to face him and see what she felt, just to feel, what was that word again, closure. She didn't smile at the word this time. This was going to be one of the most difficult things she would have to do.

She ignored the large knocker and thumped the door instead, the blows on her knuckles relieving some of the tension she felt. Ruth could hear the laughing voice of a woman, a familiar voice, and she craned her neck to try to recognise it but she didn't have long to wait. The door was opened by none other than her friend Erica, who dropped her jaw and also the cup of coffee from her fingers when she set eyes on Ruth. Luckily, the shag of the white carpet cushioned the fall and Ruth stepped back to avoid coffee flying all over her boots.

Ruth looked at Erica, dressed in not more than a man's shirt, and Ruth, now with a wry smile on her face, couldn't tell if there was much more under that. 'Some things don't change,' she said. 'Never could stay away from my leftovers.'

'Mike!' Erica called out and dashed away in the direction of the kitchen.

Ruth waited outside the door and now felt a flash of anger. Erica! She probably helped Mike plan it all. Ruth panicked that she had made the wrong decision to come here and she looked back at Karen, who was watching her, worry written all over her face. She gestured to Ruth, her arms thrown up in a 'what's going on' position.

Ruth turned back to the open doorway and stared straight into the eyes of Mike, who was just standing there, his eyes wide and his jaw slack.

'You wanted me dead?' It popped out of her mouth before Ruth knew what she was saying.

'Ruth …' Mike reached out to her and Ruth fell into his embrace. She felt his strong hands encircle her and she knew what she found in them. Comfort, stability. But now nothing else.

'You betrayed me,' he said after he let her go.

'Can I come in? Can we talk?' Ruth asked.

Mike looked behind him just as Erica came towards them, a bucket and sponge in her hand. Mike thrust Ruth gently out of the door and closed it behind them.

'No.' He looked at his car and Ruth followed his gaze.

'I know it was you,' she said, gesturing to the car. 'I saw it before …'

'I'm sorry. I didn't mean to.' He looked like he was going to cry, and she had never seen Mike shed a tear in all their time together.

'Yes, you did,' Ruth replied. She understood now how much he had put into being with her and how he must have felt when he realised she had lied to him for all that time. She remembered the pain of seeing Oliver with Suzanne, the ache for Terrence and the way she felt when she saw Anna kiss Paul. Hers had been a betrayal of the worst kind. 'I forgive you.'

Mike dropped his head in silent relief and he looked again at her, his eyes deeply troubled.

'I'm sorry too.' Ruth looked at his shattered face and knew this was in fact, closure.

'I love you ... I loved you, Ruth. You hurt me.'

'I know,' she said, 'and I hope that one day maybe you can forgive me too.'

'Maybe one day,' he said and leaned forward, grazing her cheek with his lips.

'Bye, Mike,' said Ruth and hurried back to the car. She wanted to warn him about Erica, to ask him about his life, to find out how his children were doing, but she knew that none of it was her business anymore.

'How did it go?' Karen asked as Ruth punched her seatbelt in.

'I'm okay,' Ruth replied, staring out the window, watching Mike's lonely figure as the car reversed down the driveway.

Karen put her hand on her friend's and left it there for the long ride home.

Mike

He gazed at the car driving away, his head filled with anger and confusion, wanting to say so many things to her. He hated her so much for what she had done to him and he knew he would never forgive her. But he also knew he wouldn't stop loving her, not for a long time.

He looked over at the car and walked over to it, sliding his hand along the bonnet, almost wishing it had done the job. Then he shook his head free of such thoughts. He didn't want her dead, not really, but he didn't want her in the arms of another man either. When he learned that she had lost her memory, Mike was tempted to go to see her, to see if she was okay, but he was too scared that seeing him may trigger something in her and she would remember what had happened.

He knew he had been a coward, but he was just so enraged, so absolutely, terribly broken.

When he was about to propose that night, he was sure she would accept, he had no doubt. So when she left him that evening, he was at a loss, cut up and confused. He called Eve, his ex-wife, of all people, who didn't seem very surprised.

'Why not?' he demanded, pacing up and down the hallway, a bourbon in his hand.

'Oh Mike, I saw it a mile away. How could you not?'

'What do you mean?'

'You talked about her all the time when she wasn't around, but didn't you wonder where she was?'

'What do you mean?' Mike was a little confused. 'She is away a lot, travelling for work.'

'Okay, Mike,' Eve said, in a placating voice.

'Don't condescend to me, Eve, be honest. What do you think is going on?'

'I don't know anything, but didn't you wonder why she never asked you to her place?'

'She lived with her parents. It would have been awkward.' Mike's mind was searching now for any invitations from Ruth that he may have dismissed.

'Okay, fair enough, but in all that time, did you ever even meet them, meet anyone on her side? Friends? Family?'

'She didn't like her family, I told you that. And I did meet Erica.'

'I don't know Mike. I know you don't like to be reminded of my … my betrayal, but I just felt something was off,' said Eve.

'But you said you liked her.'

'Oh, I did. I love how she was with the kids, and honestly, I think I just wanted you to be happy after what I did. And I didn't want to think she would hurt you.'

'You should have said something about how you felt,' Mike sulked, leaning his pounding head on the front door, of which Ruth had just walked out.

'It wasn't my place and I don't think you would have listened.'

'But I love her and I know she loved me too.'

'Then find her, demand an explanation,' said Eve. 'I have to go.'

'Thanks, Eve,' said Mike and hung up.

He had a drink and kept going late into the evening. He tried to think of some hint, something that suggested that Ruth would do this to him and he couldn't come up with anything. But he did think about what Eve had said. How could he not have wondered where she was all the time she wasn't with him? Maybe it was because he had been busy too and it just hadn't occurred to him. Well, it was his M.O. He had lost Eve that way. But what was the real story? Did she just have too much on her plate, just worked too much?

He thought of the nights when she wasn't with him, so many nights, when he wished she were. Now, his blood became warm at the thought. Where had she been?

He remembered the evening he met her. At her friend Karen's wedding. He hadn't even known anyone at the wedding. He had just come as a guest of his work friend, whose date had let him down at the last minute. And that was it for him, he knew it was meant to be. How could it not be?

'Erica!' Mike scrolled through his phone but realised he didn't have her number. He knew Erica would know something. She was Ruth's friend, so she must.

Erica did know, not a lot, but she did know where Ruth lived. Mike had wandered the town for the next two days hoping to bump into her, and as predictable as she was flirty, Mike found her sitting on the dock with a man, licking on an ice-cream.

'Mike!' Erica jumped off and hugged him warmly.

'I want to know everything,' he said, and Erica's expression became worried. 'About Ruth.'

Mike looked at the man standing by, who gave him a

questioning look.

'What is it, Mike?' Erica waved the other man away and entwined her arm in Mike's, strolling with him along the pier.

And when he left Ruth's place after seeing Derek, he saw red. She would pay, and dearly. He didn't want it to be true, but he knew it had to be this way. She had fooled both of them; that poor sod had no inkling either. And he had nearly proposed to her, to someone who was already engaged. How could she have lied so beautifully? He never suspected anything, not even once!

Well, she would pay. And if Derek wasn't going to help him, he would do it himself. But he was not going to let her drive off into the sunset with another man, happily, with no idea of the damage she had done. He drove home in a fury, making plans on how to avenge himself, but nothing was going to be bad enough for how he was feeling right now. She wasn't even in town! He got out of the car and slammed the door so hard, the car shook. Mike stopped and contemplated his pride and joy. He knew what he was going to do.

Derek had wanted no part of it, but that was fine, he was up for the job himself.

She would never do this to anyone else.

Except now Derek was back and he had some explaining to do. But after seeing him that evening, just a couple of days ago, he knew he was in the clear; Ruth didn't remember anything. He hoped it would stay that way.

****

'Hey, Mike, are you okay?' Erica was at the door and Mike turned around. He wished he knew Ruth well enough to believe her forgiveness.

'I think so,' he said, and putting his arm around her, he walked inside the house and closed the door behind him.

Chapter 28

When Paul arrived the next evening, Ruth was ready. She had cooked a complicated meal that consisted of prawns and honey and a dessert that was pure chocolate. This was going to be a wonderful evening.

He knocked once and let himself in as he usually did.

'Ruth,' he called out and she prepared herself, her excitement growing. She had done so many things in the last two days, and she knew Paul was the last of it. Soft music was already playing and her mood was high. She took a deep breath and opened the door of her bedroom, walking in with two glasses of champagne in her hands.

'Surprise!'

Paul's eyes nearly fell out of his head when he saw her and he dropped his briefcase on the floor, striding over to her, picking her up in his arms and twirling her around, while she laughed and tried to balance the glasses so they wouldn't fall.

'Oh my gosh! Ruth. You're walking!' He let her go and took

a glass from her. 'What? When?'

Ruth led him to the kitchen, where the meal was ready to be served. 'I will tell all with this magnificent meal I made just for you.'

And she did. She watched his mouth drop a hundred times through her story of the last couple of days. Ruth felt like she was on air, it was such a relief to be completely free.

'Could you serve up dessert? I have to—freshen up.'

'I don't think I could fit anything more in,' said Paul, getting up, but when he saw the mousse in the fridge, he sighed. 'Nope, have to make room for that. Go on.'

Ruth closed the bathroom door behind her, a feeling familiar to her. She loved Paul, she knew that. She was on fire just sitting across the table from him; so many times, she wanted to reach out and pull him to her. She knew he cared for her, he showed it in that moment on the balcony. Only thing was, Ruth didn't want to be the other woman. Now she wouldn't be. Paul would choose her, she knew that. And she was being honest about everything else in her life, so it was time he knew this truth too. Another memory popped into her head. The night when Paul told her he loved her and she couldn't say it back. How stupid she had been, so insecure and untrusting. She should have lunged at his love with open arms. Now she had the chance.

The mousse was already set out when Ruth returned to the table, a nervous tension in her belly. She looked at Paul who was slurping at his spoon, a look of pleasure on his face.

'I love you,' Ruth blurted.

Paul's eyes caught hers and in that moment, Ruth knew he loved her.

'I think we both know we should be together,' she continued quickly as his jaw began to fall. 'I know you love me,' said Ruth, worried at his non-reaction.

The silence that fell for how long Ruth didn't know was deafening.

'I'm going to be married in twenty-eight days.' Paul looked like a wooden puppet. 'I don't love you.'

'But …'

'This is so unfair, Ruth.' He put down his spoon, wiped his mouth with his napkin and stood up. 'You know how to ruin everything.'

'Paul,' said Ruth, her heart pumping hard in her chest. 'I'm sorry. Forget I said anything. I'm sorry.'

'I have to go,' Paul said, grabbing his briefcase. 'Thanks for dinner.'

And he was gone.

And she let him go.

Allowing him to leave, Ruth realised, was actually one of the most difficult things she'd ever done. Everything else in the last couple of days blurred to obscurity. She cleared the table, washed the dishes, dried them and put them away, her head in a daze. She didn't understand what had just happened. It was all beginning to work out so well for her and now this. 'Idiot!' she shouted to herself. 'A stupid little fool.'

Ruth went to bed that night with Paul's scarf in her bed; thoughts of his face, his words, 'I don't love you' kept returning to her. She smiled cynically. She got hers.

As the clock ticked over three thirty, Ruth got out of bed and took the scarf, which was now wet with her tears, and went outside. In the freezing night, feeling like a burglar, she threw it in the dumpster behind her block of apartments. She knew it would be gone by morning. She went back to bed and cried for her mistakes.

In the morning, she sent Paul an email. She was leaving him; she was sorry to let him down. There was no reply.

She searched for work, preparing her resume again and practising her interview skills. She was not going back to Marks and Sons, it would just be too weird, too many memories and too many reminders of who she used to be. She didn't mind waiting a little to find the right place, as long as it didn't take too long. Her mortgage payments were catching up with her.

But in the meantime, the time she had was what she needed. She visited her parents, Karen and even Patty, who seemed to be making it work with Mark. She had gained so much respect for her sister, how she had stood up for herself, how she became an independent woman; it was a shame that it had to take what she had been through to lead her there.

Ruth sighed. It had taken just as much to get her to where she was right now. 'Everyone has their journey,' she said aloud to herself as she sent out another email. Then she laughed, again realising how much like her mother she sounded. She smiled; it wasn't such a bad thing.

It was two weeks later when Ruth received a call from none other than Marielle, who had contacted her and invited her to the warehouse, somehow knowing she was looking for work.

'Interesting how things come full circle,' said Marielle. 'But I'm getting you back, even better than before.' She led Ruth to her new office and showed her around. 'You want to know how I knew you were looking for a job?'

'I know,' said Ruth and Marielle laughed.

'You two need to get your shit together,' she said, with a sigh. 'Don't let him get away again.'

'It's done. I don't think he wants to see me ever again.'

'Don't be so stupid.' Marielle clicked her tongue. 'You can be so dumb for someone so smart.'

But Ruth knew it was true. She knew Paul well enough now.

'Get me that portfolio, the one Paul had of yours. He showed it to me.'

'Ah, well, can you just get it from him?' Ruth did not want to face Paul.

'Just get it for me, please.' Marielle could be so demanding, but Ruth usually loved her for it. She knew what to expect from her. She also knew that folio was not at the office and Ruth dreaded going to his home. She had only been there a couple of times after her accident but had never gone in, they had just stopped to pick something or other up. Ruth really didn't want to see Danni either; she felt sick about what she'd done and said.

She decided it would be better to do it now, while Paul would still be at work. It was better to face Danni than Paul. She drove to his place, a sick feeling settling in the pit of her stomach, and it turned to jelly when she saw his car parked in his driveway. She tried to calm her nerves by shaking her hands out, but she knew there was nothing that could be done. 'Let's get this over with,' she said as she stepped out of the car.

She knocked on the door, trying to work out how to do this really quickly, but when the door opened, she just stared at his surprised face.

'I've come for the folio. Marielle said …'

'Yep, I need to find it. Come in.' Curt, clipped.

Ruth walked into the little townhouse, looking at the photographs on the walls, some of people she knew, others of random subjects, and she remembered another time she looked at another wall. She wished she had never set eyes on that picture. She wandered further in and found Paul with his head buried in a large drawer.

'It's in here,' he said.

'I can wait, it's fine,' said Ruth, still looking around.

There it was. A picture of her, Ruth. A large, framed photograph, taking pride of place on the mantel. It was one of those he took when they had spent the whole day together in bed. Ruth was trying to hide her face with a pillow, and the happiness she had felt was easy to see. She picked it up and looked closely at the embarrassed laugh, the natural way she had been with Paul, so happy, so free. That was one of the best days of her life and here it was, sitting in the middle of the room, where there was no escape from it.

'That's my favourite photo,' Paul said behind her, and Ruth jumped. 'Of all time.'

'Danni must love this right here.' Ruth raised her brows.

'Danni's, erm, gone.'

Ruth's heart soared but she kept her feelings in check. 'Got that folio?'

Paul handed it to her, and Ruth walked to the door, the frame still in her hand.

'You want to give me my picture back?'

Ruth smiled. 'No. But you can have the real thing anytime you want.' She opened the door and turned back to Paul, who was running his hand through his hair, a smile on his face. 'See you … soon.'

She walked out and closed the door behind her.

This was definitely not closure.

Ruth laughed aloud.

The End.

Acknowledgements

Thank you to John, my biggest fan, Emerald, Alexis and Dean, my superfans, and of course, Mum, my forever fan. Your continued support and encouragement spurs me on.

A big thanks to Natalie and Maria, my friends, who read my work in its infancy and give me critical feedback and to Anita, my editor, who is just amazing.

A special thank you to Sophia, who pretends it's fun to design my covers and is just a fabulous human.

A shout-out to Karen, who planted the seed of this novel in my brain.

And as always, thank you, dear reader.

Rita H Rowe.

About the Author

Hailing from India and growing up in Melbourne, Rita has a passion for words, encouraged by a mother who spent most of her spare time with her head buried in a book. Of course she was going to become dazzled by the words of Enid Blyton, Louisa May Alcott and later on, the likes of the Brontë sisters, Dickens and even Sidney Sheldon.

It was finding her own style that was problematic. Trying to recreate stories in the same vein as her gurus was not fulfilling in the least and in 2019, she embarked on a Master's in Writing. Finding her passion, she established her style; so keen was she to get going, that by the end of the year, she had completed, edited and published her first novel, *Never The Moon*, a gritty romance. The second, *She Remembered*, a traumatic story of love and loss, came soon after. *The Bad Seed* came next, starting out as a short series which delves into the machinations of small town hypocrisy. Becoming Ruthless is her fourth novel.

Rita teaches English and art at a high school in Melbourne's west.

Find out more about Rita H Rowe

Website: https://www.ritahrowe.com/

Facebook: https://www.facebook.com/ritahrowe/

Instagram: https://www.instagram.com/ritahrowe_writes/

Other Novels by Rita H Rowe

Never The Moon

Passion and betrayal. Two men who couldn't be more different. One woman caught between them.

Jennifer lost the love of her life. David married another woman, and that was it. Over. Finished.

Fleeing to New York for a fresh start and a new chance at life, Jennifer meets Jack—rugged and handsome. He's everything she thought she could never have.

But things are never as easy as they should be and Jennifer's whole world is plunged into chaos and violence once more. An abusive husband, a loveless marriage—and no way out.

When David comes barrelling back into Jennifer's life, she's torn between the men once again, but the stakes couldn't be higher.

Never the Moon interweaves the lives of Jennifer, David and Jack, revealing the power of love and the destruction it can leave in its wake.

She Remembered

Her beauty is a curse. Her memories a void.

Elena cannot remember. All she has are fragments of a past life that feel foreign to her, only glimpsed in fleeting moments through violent nightmares.

Struggling to put her life together and find acceptance, she takes comfort in Luke, a charming boy who seems to like her as much as she likes him. But nothing has ever come easily to Elena—and when she wakes up between blood-soaked sheets next to the body of a man recently stabbed, what little stability she had comes crashing down around her.

With no one to help her and nowhere to go, Elena has to salvage the broken pieces of her life all on her own. If only she could remember …

The Bad Seed

Love, betrayal and murder.

He's the new kid in town, complete with a sordid past and a tarnished family name, doomed to fail even before he begins. Jenna is the only person who sees beyond Joey's past and they fall deeply in love.

But there are already forces determined to separate the pair by any means necessary. Tommy, the thug, who is hell-bent on breaking Joey by brute force, Jenna's mother, whose connection with Joey cannot be ignored, and Joey's own past, the strongest weapon against them.

Only Tim, the local police officer, shows any compassion to the plight of Joey and Jenna, but is Tim all he seems? And what role will he play in their fate?

Can young love survive in a town filled with discrimination?

Can Joey and Jenna get out before they fall apart, or is it already too late?